"I want to see you in a bad mood."

That didn't come out the way Jem meant it to...

"What? Why?"

The look Lacey was giving him could have made him feel awkward. Except that it seemed warm. Maybe he needed to slow down on the wine.

"They say you don't truly know someone until you've seen them at their worst. I want to really know you." Now, that had come out right.

"So...you show me your worst and I'll show you mine."

He grinned. "I don't think I can find it right now."

"Me, either."

Leaning forward, he reached for her. Pulled her toward him. She stood. And so did he. And they were just standing there, looking at each other.

"You are the most beautiful thing I've ever seen," he said.

She shook her head. "You've seen..."

With a finger to her lips he tried to silence her.

"But it's true, Jem," she continued softly, her gaze imploring him to understand. "Life's hard enough without hiding from the truth."

Dear Reader,

This book is...not ordinary. I think it's powerful. And emotionally compelling. And I hope so much you give it a chance. I can tell you why I think this, and hope this. I can describe Jem to you. He's the hero of my heart. But I'm afraid if I say too much, you'll move on without giving him a chance.

Jem's a construction worker. Okay, yeah, he owns the business, and wears a shirt and tie to work every day. But he wears them with jeans. And he learned the business with his hands before he ever considered being the brains behind it all.

He's alpha all the way. And he's a single dad to a four-year-old I wish I could hug. He's a good dad. Involved. Aware. And firm, too, when he needs to be.

And...Jem is...well... I hope you'll give him a chance. I can't imagine a romance reader not being glad they did.

Then there's Lacey. Sometimes I wanted to just do her hair and makeup, force her into an attention-getting outfit and push her out the door. But she has Kacey for that. My job was to be patient. To listen. And tell her story. Her story touched me deeply. So here it is...

I love to hear from readers! You can find me on Facebook at Facebook.com/tarataylorquinn and on Twitter, @tarataylorquinn. Or join my Friendship board, Pinterest.com/tarataylorquinn/friendship.

All the best,

Tara

www.TaraTaylorQuinn.com

USA TODAY Bestselling Author

TARA TAYLOR QUINN

His First Choice

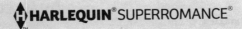

HARLEQUIN®SUPERROMANCE®

Recycling programs
for this product may
not exist in your area.

ISBN-13: 978-0-373-60958-1

His First Choice

Copyright © 2016 by Tara Taylor Quinn

This edition published by arrangement with Harlequin Books S.A.

For questions and comments about the quality of this book,
please contact us at CustomerService@Harlequin.com.

Printed in U.S.A.

An author of more than seventy novels, **Tara Taylor Quinn** is a *USA TODAY* bestselling author with more than seven million copies sold. She is known for delivering emotional and psychologically astute novels of suspense and romance. Tara is a past president of Romance Writers of America. She has won a Readers' Choice Award and is a five-time finalist for an RWA RITA® Award, a finalist for a Reviewer's Choice Award and a Booksellers' Best Award. She has also appeared on TV across the country, including *CBS Sunday Morning*. She supports the National Domestic Violence Hotline. If you or someone you know might be a victim of domestic violence in the United States, please contact 1-800-799-7233.

Books by Tara Taylor Quinn

HARLEQUIN SUPERROMANCE

Where Secrets are Safe

Wife by Design
Once a Family
Husband by Choice
Child by Chance
Mother by Fate
The Good Father
Love by Association

Shelter Valley Stories

Sophie's Secret
Full Contact
It's Never Too Late
Second Time's the Charm
The Moment of Truth

It Happened in Comfort Cove

A Son's Tale
A Daughter's Story
The Truth About Comfort Cove

HARLEQUIN HEARTWARMING

The Historic Arapahoe

Once Upon a Friendship
Once Upon a Marriage

MIRA BOOKS

The Second Lie
The Third Secret
The Fourth Victim
The Friendship Pact

Visit the Author Profile page at Harlequin.com for more titles.

This book is dedicated to Tim Barney,
who is Jem to me in so many ways...

CHAPTER ONE

"Ms. HAMILTON? THIS is Mara Noble calling from Busy Little Minds preschool…"

"Yes, Mara." As a social worker employed by California Social Services in the child welfare department, Lacey Hamilton had familiarized herself with the reputations and locations of all of the child care facilities and schools in her district of Santa Raquel. Busy Little Minds was one of the best rated for both intellectual and emotional development. "What can I do for you?" While there was kindness in her words, there was no smile attached. If Busy Little Minds was calling her, chances were a serious issue was at hand.

With her phone on speaker behind the closed door of her private office, she opened a new document on her word-processing program.

"I have a little boy," Mara said. "He's four, and I suspect abuse…"

The woman knew her stuff. Issuing silent points to Little Minds for employee training, Lacey asked, "Is he there with you now?"

"Yes, ma'am."

"Is he in need of medical attention?"

"No. He's already had medical attention. His father took him to the emergency room at the Santa Raquel Children's Hospital over the weekend."

Call the hospital. And Ella. Ella Ackerman was the hospital's representative to the High Risk Team, a group comprised of professionals from various fields that fought to prevent domestic violence deaths. Lacey was the team's child protective services member.

"So right now he's not in any immediate danger." She went back to the checklist she knew by heart. *Determine the immediate safety and medical condition of the child first.*

"Not at the moment."

Could the child be in imminent danger?

"Do you suspect the abuse took place in or outside the home?"

"It's not here," Mara said, her voice solemn and low, as though making sure she wasn't overheard. "And as far as I can tell, he doesn't have babysitters and is not in any other activities outside of ours."

Parents? Lacey typed onto the blank page. Many of her colleagues still took notes by hand. She always took them electronically, even if she had only her smartphone with her at the time. As if engaging with technology gave her a tiny bit of the distance she had to maintain to be emotionally capable of doing her job.

"What about siblings?" she asked. "Are you aware of anyone in the home other than his parents?"

She had to assess the situation to determine which course of action to take: an immediate trip to Little Minds to secure the child within her care while she investigated, or the more preferred, less harsh approach of a call to his parents.

"No. He's an only child. And…his parents are divorced."

She wrote that word with a capital *D*. Sadly it showed up in more than 50 percent of her reports.

"Who has custody?"

"Our records indicate that they have shared parenting. Dad is the one who always drops him off and picks him up."

She typed *Father controlling?* and then a few notes to herself, to be used later when she made an official report.

Now for the hardest part.

"Why do you suspect abuse?" Thousands of kids went to emergency rooms every day, because kids were naturally inquisitive, adventurous, without the wherewithal to calculate danger, making them prone to accidents.

"This morning he showed up with a cast on his arm. He says he fell, but he mumbles and looks down when he says it. We asked him what he was doing when he fell. He shrugged. No matter what we ask, he shrugs."

"What did his father have to say when he dropped him off?"

"That he fell down."

"That's all?"

"That's it. Mr. Bridges isn't the chatty sort."

More typing, ending with *Father evasive?*

Still, kids and broken arms went hand in hand. This one could have fallen off a bike, or from a tree. Not that many four-year-olds were climbing trees or riding bikes. But some did. And some fell from bunk beds, too.

"Anything else?" she asked, wanting to know why the woman thought this broken arm was different from the norm. A kid not talking about the incident wasn't all that unusual. He very likely could have been into some kind of mischief and knew he was in trouble. If he'd climbed on a cupboard to sneak a cookie, for instance, or...

"Yes, Ms. Hamilton, I'm sorry. This is very difficult for me. It's the first time I've ever had to make a call like this and..."

"I understand," Lacey filled in, softening her tone, when the woman paused. Abused children were her business. Sometimes she lost sight of the world outside of her small circle, where coming face-to-face with the monstrous fact that heinous people abused children was an anomaly.

"We've had Levi since he was three months old. He started out in day care and then moved to preschool when he was two, which is a year earlier than we usually move them. He's a precocious little guy. What I'm trying to say is that we know him. And in the past six months, he's changed. A lot."

She needed to know if there were other signs of physical abuse. But listened patiently. She didn't want to lead her caller into saying something she might not have mentioned, giving it more weight than it deserved.

Lacey had been at this awhile. Going on ten years. She knew her business. And had given up hoping it would ever get any easier.

"He's withdrawn, to the point of not playing well with others. He cries easily, rarely smiles. I can't remember the last time I heard him laugh. He seems fearful. And...a couple of other times, he's had bruises. Once on his torso. It had fingertip marks on it."

She was pounding the keys hard, her lips pressed together. It could be nothing. Kids went through phases...

"Do you know if there's been any changes at home? You said his parents are divorced. Do you know for how long?"

She'd ask the question again—and more—of the mother and father. Separately. She already knew, just from the little she'd heard, that she was going to have to interview them.

"Levi was one when his folks split. I remember

because we had his first birthday party here with both parents present, at the request of his mother."

"So you *have* met her?"

"Of course. I know her. She's just never been the one to drop him off or pick him up on a regular basis. And I haven't seen or heard from her in at least six months. I could check our sign-in records to tell you the last time she dropped off or picked up."

"I would appreciate that." Lacey typed as she talked. *Was Mom isolated from the boy? Had she been threatened? Was she afraid to get help?*

She'd seen it enough to expect such an outcome, but had certainly had many, many calls that, upon investigation, had turned out to be false reports.

"Where do Mr. and Mrs. Bridges work?" She needed as much information as she could gather, as quickly as she could gather it.

"He owns a contracting company. It's a small one, but they build houses. Last I knew she was working at an investment firm, but I don't think she's doing that anymore."

"Why not?"

"A while back Levi made a comment about his mother being the boss of a money place. I meant to ask Mr. Bridges about it, but I'm not always out front when parents pick up. I guess I just forgot."

"Don't you need work numbers of all of your parents?"

"Yes, but Mr. and Mrs. Bridges...they both asked that we always call him. They said because she dealt with money and couldn't always take calls, but being the boss, he could get away for a few if he had to. We have a cell number for her in case of emergency when we can't reach him."

Control. Control. Control. She typed on.

"Is there anything else you'd like me to know?" she asked, her fingers pausing over the keyboard.

"It's just... I notice a pattern. Levi isn't an accident-prone kind of kid. He used to be boisterous, like a miniature version of one of those guys who's confident and goes through life getting it right, you know? He almost had a swagger about him. He'd try anything, usually master it, assuming it was age appropriate, but with a certain kind of...grace. He focuses more than most kids his age. But every couple of weeks or so now, he shows up with skinned knees, or a scab on his chin. All explained by play. But... why doesn't he ever fall down here? And why is it only every couple of weeks?"

Lacey's fingers pounded. If she'd been playing the piano she'd grown up mastering, she'd have been bellowing out a crescendo.

"Do you know his shared parenting schedule?" she asked, careful to keep her tone neutral. With a lifetime of hiding hurt feelings, it was a part of the job that came naturally to her.

"No."

Did Dad pick the boy up and take him to his mother? And then pick him up from her, as well? Had he threatened to take her to court for full custody if she balked at his rules?

She wondered. Maybe even suspected. But she didn't know.

Which meant there was room for another explanation. A better scenario.

"There's another thing," the woman said. "His schoolwork is faltering. He did better last year, as the baby of the class, than he's doing this year..." She talked about numbers and letters, pre-reading and easy reading. Following directions. Shapes and colors that had been mastered the year before seemed to be giving Levi some difficulty now.

"I guess maybe I'm overreacting," Mara Noble said next. "But in all my years working in child care, I've never had the feeling I get about Levi. There's something odd about that broken arm of his. He can't tell me any details. He's a smart kid, Ms. Hamilton. He'd know what he was doing when he broke his arm."

"Sometimes trauma can wipe out immediate memory," she said slowly. She typed *Smart little boy, suspicious break.*

"So you think I'm overreacting?"

"I think you did exactly as you are supposed to do. You suspect, you report. It's the law." There could be no doubt about that. Second-guessing could cost a child's life. "You don't have to be right, Mara," she said, softening her tone more. "You just need to have reasonable suspicion, which you do. You did the right thing here. Thank you."

"So…what happens next? Is Mr. Bridges going to know that I called? Because if he is…"

"Does he frighten you?"

"He never has before."

"And now?"

"Now I'm just… I love this kid, you know? We aren't supposed to have favorites, and I care for all my kids. I don't play favorites. But this little guy stole my heart the first day he was here."

Lacey couldn't afford to love her kids that way. Couldn't let emotion cloud her judgment. Though to do her job she did have to care. Be aware. And sensitive…

"In answer to your question—no, Mr. Bridges will not know, at least not immediately, where the report came from. It could just as easily have come from the hospital."

Which was the first call she was going to make, to find out why a report hadn't been made and if there'd been any other trips to the ER for little Levi.

"So when he comes to pick up his son, I'm just to give him to him like usual?"

"Yes. If anything different needs to happen, you won't be the one to police it. You just do your job and leave the rest up to me."

"Will I hear from you again? I mean, if this turns out to be nothing, will you let me know?"

"Absolutely." And the fact that the woman was asking told Lacey that Mara was on the up-and-up. Someone making a false report generally didn't give consideration to the fact that it might be found to be false. Or want to be told if it was.

But she had to ask, "Other than seeing them through day-care-related activities, have you ever associated with either Mr. or Mrs. Bridges?"

"No, ma'am." Straightforward sincerity—Lacey liked that.

"And will you have a problem handing Levi over to his father?"

"Not if you tell me it's okay to do so."

The buck stopped with her. She hadn't understood, when she'd signed on to this career, that one wrong decision on her part could get a child killed. And still, there wasn't any other job, any other life, she'd rather have.

"It's okay," she said now. But only because she knew she had enough time to intervene, to get to the day care and put other plans in motion, if upon further investigation she decided differently. The day was young yet.

And obviously, since he'd dropped his son off on schedule as usual, Bridges wasn't currently posing a flight risk. She wanted time to do some searching before he was onto her. "Just one more thing," she added. "For now, just until I tell you differently, please don't say anything to anyone, other than possibly a coworker where appropriate, about your conversation with me."

"Of course not. I don't want anyone to know it was me."

Lacey understood. And hung up filled with mother-bear determination, doing her best to ignore the heavy sadness lurking within her.

Chasing down abusive parents, stopping them, was her life.

And she was good at it.

CHAPTER TWO

JEM WASN'T IN a great mood. Levi's cast was putting them a bit off their game, and while he was certainly up to the challenge, his son had not yet mastered the art of dealing with frustration. Or disappointment, either. May in Santa Raquel meant T-ball, and since they'd started a new five-game program for four-year-olds, Levi had been determined to play. Tryouts were happening that very night and his little boy was sitting at the table with a partial plate of spaghetti, wearing it and a frown.

"I wanna go," Levi said, the sound that curious mixture of baby voice and male determination giving Jem's heart a bite every time he heard it. Had he ever been that bent on anything when he'd been young? That unwavering? Or that damned cute? Sure didn't feel like it.

But then his upbringing had been different from Levi's. He'd been spoiled rotten, loved to distraction by both his parents and raised at home. Not at day care. He'd never had to fight for anything.

Not that Levi didn't have everything he needed,

as far as physical wants went. Difference between him and his son was the constancy of a mother's love, and growing up at home. Tressa loved Levi every bit as much as Jem's mother had loved him. She just wasn't the constant type.

Still, none of that had to do with playing ball.

"You want to go watch other boys play when you know you can't?" he asked, feeling cruel. But better say the words and stop the train before it crashed. Because taking that young man to a T-ball field and expecting him not to throw a tantrum when he was told he couldn't play with a cast on his arm—something Jem had been telling him repeatedly since the night before when it had dawned on Levi that there were worse things than the pain in his arm—was definitely a train wreck in the making.

"I can try," Levi said, his tongue still struggling over his *r* a little bit. The tiny bit of baby left in him. Jem would miss it when it left, but knew, too, that it had to do so.

"No, you can't, son," he said now, taking his son's pint-size fork and turning it in the spaghetti left on Levi's plate. If he'd had his way, the pasta would be cut in little pieces, like he'd been doing since he'd first introduced the boy to table food. But part of Levi's new insistence that he wasn't a baby anymore and could do everything like Daddy did was an adamant refusal to eat spaghetti cut up in little pieces. Hence the food on his clothes. "You know the rules. You can't play because your cast puts other kids in danger. You could accidently hit one of them in the head with it."

Not to mention the fact that he could trip over his feet and fall on his way to first base and do further damage to a very tiny arm that was already broken in two places below the elbow.

Handing the filled fork to his son, Jem clamped down on his own negative emotions where the whole thing was concerned. His weren't as easy to deal with as his son's were. Not in his shoes, at any rate. Anger didn't sit well with him. He'd grown up in a home where talk was the way to resolve issues. Where an open forum of understanding took the stage when there were difficulties. Or time-outs did.

Aggression was for hard work. For athletics where appropriate. For protecting those you loved.

Not for circumstances beyond your control. Or the control of others. It wasn't Tressa's fault that Levi had climbed up her bookcase trying to get a video he wanted to watch, or that as she'd grabbed his arm to help him down, he'd slipped and she'd lost her grip.

Just because he'd expect a mother to know that you grabbed a child around his middle, not by the arm, to steady him didn't meant that Tressa would automatically think to do so.

Taking the fork, Levi ate, but the sustenance didn't relieve his frown any.

"I thought we'd go for ice cream for dessert," Jem said, winging it now. "Like we were going to do after tryouts. You can still eat ice cream with a cast, can't you, buddy?"

Levi shrugged.

"And as soon as the cast comes off, we'll set up our own tee in the backyard and play every night if you want to."

He'd been planning the tee and batting net as a present for Levi's fifth birthday, if his son loved the sport as much as he'd thought he was going to after playing a few games.

"I don't want to." The succulent tone took away any validity Jem would have given to those words.

"You want to help me with the boat?" He was, very slowly now that he was a single dad, building a boat out in the second car portion of his garage. Nothing big or fancy. But one that would be seaworthy. If he ever got it done. "We can work on sanding the wood for the bow together."

Normally he saved boat building for the times when Levi was with his mother. It could be dangerous business, depending on what he was doing. And it helped him pass the time that the boy was away, without pacing a path in his carpet.

"I don't want to."

Levi attempted to wrap spaghetti—clearly a work in progress—and raised the fork backward to his mouth, balancing a lone noodle until it nearly reached its goal before sliding off the fork onto his lap—leaving a bit of red sauce on the table as it bounced by.

The boy wrapped again, lowered his head to his plate and slurped up the pasta on his fork, creating a ring of red around his lips.

"Good job, sport," Jem said, raising his hand in the air for the high five that Levi generally landed with a meaty slap when he accomplished a task. "That was a whole bite!"

The boy shrugged. He didn't high five. He didn't even look up.

Sliding from his seat to crouch on the floor by his son's chair, Jem moved his head until he could look directly into his son's downcast gaze. "You mad at me, son?"

Levi shook his head.

"You sure seem mad."

Another shake of the head, and then those big blue eyes—so like his mother's—filled with tears. "I wanna play T-balllllll," he wailed and, throwing himself at Jem, started to sob. "You said I could and we been waiting and I wanna play balllll," he said again, smearing red sauce all over both of them as he clutched Jem with his dinner-caked pudgy little hands, cast slung around the back of Jem's neck.

"I know you do, son," Jem said, standing with his son clutched to his chest, wishing he could make the world right for the little boy, and hating the fact that he couldn't.

And knew that particular pang was probably only just beginning to be a force in his life. One that was going to follow him to the grave, no doubt.

There was a hurricane storm of tears, and then they dried up.

"Is it time for ice cream yet?" the boy asked, pulling away to play with the top button of the now-stained white dress shirt Jem had worn with his jeans to work that day—along with the tie he'd discarded the second he'd climbed into his truck afterward.

"Let's see how much of this spaghetti you can eat first," he said, setting the boy gently back in his booster seat and scooting him up to the table. "The more we eat, the less we have to put away for later."

Levi twirled, slurped and chewed, wiping his dripping chin with the back of his hand as often as with the napkin Jem kept reminding him of.

When Jem burped, Levi laughed, mocked the sound deep in his chest and laughed again. T-ball tryouts, and the Great Disappointment, apparently a thing of the past.

Jem went with the flow. Oh, to be young again. Able to cry away the hurt in a blast of snot and tears, and then move on.

He'd do well to take a lesson from his son. Minus the snot and tears, of course.

ONE OF THE things that suited Lacey was that her lifestyle complemented her job. No family waiting for her to come home to, expecting dinner on the table and numerous other things. No, she was free to work the hours required of her—hours that also included time when most people weren't at work, as that was when she could observe them at home—without taking flack for it like some of her coworkers had to do.

Ella Ackerman had officially stepped down from her position as Santa Raquel Children's Hospital's representative to the High Risk Team when she'd found out she was pregnant, but still two months away from delivery, she was filling in for her temporary replacement while the other woman was on vacation. She fully intended to take up the position again when she was back to work full-time after the baby's birth.

A neonatal charge nurse, Ella, like Lacey, was another one who couldn't walk away from the little ones who weren't fortunate enough to be born to the safe and healthy life most assumed to be a given. Ella's cause was more encompassing than the children, though. Married to the founder of the Lemonade Stand, a unique domestic violence shelter hidden within Santa Raquel boundaries, Ella seemed to live and breathe the fight against abuse. She and her husband, Brett, the Stand's founder, dedicated much of their spare time to the women and children who'd been displaced from their homes due to the violence enacted upon them by family members.

She was always ready to help and never seemed to run out of energy or hope.

Yet even Ella had sounded a bit downhearted when she'd called back that afternoon to let Lacey know that Levi Bridges had been in the emergency room a total of six times in four years. He hadn't been flagged as a potential victim of abuse because none of the incidents looked at individually had appeared as anything more than accidents that might befall a young child.

His parents were educated, employed and, from chart notes, were appropriately attentive, concerned, aware and loving with the little boy. There'd never been any noted substance abuse or smell of alcohol on anyone's breath when the boy had been brought in.

The first time was for a cut on his head when he'd been six months old. He had scooted himself off his blanket on the floor and over to a wall, where he'd pulled on a cord plugged into a socket. He'd yanked a lamp off the table and down on himself, where the base had cut his forehead, leaving a wound that had required six stitches.

The second time he'd had a pea up his nose. Third had been a serious laceration to his foot.

It hadn't required stitches, but the father, who—
it had been charted—was visibly distraught, had
also requested an X-ray, wanting to make certain that the foot wasn't broken. He'd had his
son strapped into a seat on the back of his bike
and the little boy's foot had come loose and had
been caught in the spokes. The fourth time he'd
stepped on a hot coal that had fallen out of a backyard pig-roasting pit. And fifth had been for a
high fever for which they'd never found an explanation. His temperature had come down quickly
after medication; lab work showed a healthy toddler and a follow-up doctor's appointment had
been a well-child visit.

Possible scenarios of misconduct ran through
Lacey's mind as she turned her midclass black
sedan into the neighborhood of the address she
had for Jeremiah Bridges—Levi's father.

Six hospital visits, followed by a call of suspected abuse. A home visit was going to happen.
Immediately.

And would have whether she'd had a family to
go home to or not.

THANKING THE FATES that had seen to it to deliver
such a great kid to him, Jem lingered over dinner,
giving Levi all the time he wanted to invest in
mastering the art of spaghetti rolling. While tear
streaks still showed in the tomato sauce smeared

on the little guy's cheeks, you'd never know that they'd just come through a major crisis.

Chances were it wouldn't come up again, either. Levi didn't generally revisit a storm that had passed. One of his better qualities, Jem thought. One that would serve him well into adulthood.

So would his lack of vanity where his looks were concerned. Jem didn't expect that one to last much past kindergarten. He himself hadn't started to care about his appearance until at least junior high, but kids grew up a lot quicker these days...

The peal of their doorbell stopped him in his thoughts. Not pleasantly. Dread hit the pit of his stomach, as it did anytime something unexpected happened. Would the sensation never dissipate? Fade away like Levi's mourning of his T-ball season?

"Stay put, buddy," he said with a serious look at his son.

"Okay." The little boy's answer was one Jem trusted implicitly. Levi had his less than stellar moments, but Jem had learned to discern when he could count on the boy to do as he was told. Which, thankfully, so far was most of the time.

If it was Tressa at the door—and who else would it be at dinnertime on a Monday night?— she was probably upset about something. Or pissed at someone. Neither of which were moods their son needed to see. She'd want Jem to take care of whatever or whoever it was. And if he could, he would. Tressa, for all her waywardness, was a good mother. And she adored her son.

Pulling open the door with what he hoped was an expression that would calm down his drama-ridden ex-wife, he was shocked to see a slender blonde standing on his front porch. Obviously she had the wrong house, but…he suddenly didn't mind. She was a looker. More than a looker. That body… Those drab pants and shapeless jacket were hopefully hiding some sexy lingerie…

"Mr. Bridges?"

He blinked. *What the hell?*

Had he just been fantasizing about a stranger on his porch? In broad daylight? With his son just feet behind him?

Clearly time for him to get a little…in an appropriate place at an appropriate time. As soon as possible.

Tressa was generally accommodating… He just usually lost all desire anytime he thought about her in that way these days.

"Jeremiah Bridges?" The woman spoke for a second time. Her hair was pulled back tight in a twist thing on the back of her neck. He actually thought about reaching back there and pulling out the hairpins. He had to know how long it was.

"Yes," he blurted, embarrassed that he was still standing there like an imbecile, thinking about sex. "I'm Jem Bridges. What can I do for you?"

Was one of his men in trouble? He didn't know all their wives, but he'd met most of them at one time or another. And couldn't remember any looking like this.

So maybe she was a girlfriend…attempting to catch someone out in a lie… He gave himself a mental shake. Most of the world was not like Tressa.

"I'm Lacey Hamilton, Mr. Bridges." She handed him a card. "I'm from child protective services."

Jem's chin dropped. His gut knotted over the spaghetti he'd had for dinner.

Not a wife. Or a girlfriend. She was an agent from child protective services. And there could be only one reason she'd come to his house.

Only one child there. Only one child in his life. One child he knew well enough to answer for to any child agency.

With a mother who, on occasion, tried to make Jem's life hell.

Which meant only one thing to him. The beautiful woman standing on his doorstep wasn't there to feed his sexual fantasies. She was there to implode his life.

CHAPTER THREE

THE FIRST THING Lacey noticed from her spot on the front porch looking in was a clean home—at least what she could see of it. The father, not so much. He was clean-cut enough, but the red stains on the front of his white button-down shirt were a bit off-putting. His open blue gaze kind of captivated her—until she blinked, and broke the contact, and remembered that the man's lean, cowboy-type good looks had nothing to do with her reason for being there.

Other than giving her a sign that she wasn't dealing with someone currently drunk or obviously down on his luck.

Well-to-do, well-dressed, gorgeous fathers abused their kids. And cowboys with stained shirts could, too.

"May I come in?" she asked. If he refused, she'd get a warrant. Then there'd be a strike against him in her estimation.

"Of course." He stepped back.

Once she was inside, she could see the living room and what looked like a smaller living area with books and a piano off to her right. The home was one of the older, antebellum-type houses that dotted the town of Santa Raquel. But where the big mansions on the beach, and across from the beach, carried seven-figure price tags, Bridges's home was farther inland. And not quite as large.

"What can I do for you?"

The contractor stood directly in front of her. Arms crossed. Defensive and possibly aggressive posture. Daring her to come in any farther?

She'd followed protocol, had logged her intent to make the home visit and had her phone's GPS location on. Her whereabouts could be traced. If he tried anything untoward, he'd get caught.

Still, she could have waited for another agent to accompany her. If she'd been so inclined. If she'd have been able to sleep without assuring herself that little Levi wasn't in immediate danger.

She could also have called the police—they often partnered on child protective services cases that involved anything of a criminal nature.

Looking around, taking her time to answer the man still standing guard over his home, Lacey assimilated as she'd been trained to do.

She didn't have definitive proof of illegal activity. But Mara had noticed finger-shaped bruising weeks ago.

A broken arm could indicate escalating injury. She wasn't frightened, just cautious by nature.

"My office received a phone call," she started

slowly, softly, as she heard sounds coming from a room in the back of the house. A utensil dropping on a table or counter?

"Is your son here?"

"Of course he's here. He lives here."

"May I see him?"

Frowning, the man studied her. "I need to see some picture identification. Anyone can have cards printed up."

Reaching into her black strapped leather satchel, she pulled out her badge and handed it to him.

Apparently he was cautious by nature, too.

Or stalling while he tried to figure out what to do?

Nodding, he handed the card back to her. "You said you had a phone call."

Someone was tapping a rhythm—*thump, thump, thump.*

She nodded, taking a step toward the sound. "May I see your son?"

"Of course you can. But I'd like to know why first."

"Clap along...nah nah nah nah das what you wanna do..." The faint sound of the childish voice interrupted them from the distance and Lacey stared in the direction her feet wanted her to go.

"Pharrell Williams," she said. The song "Happy" was one she played full blast in her car on those days when her job seemed heavier than she was.

The tapping continued, not at all in rhythm with the words. The tune wasn't bad, though.

"He's a little off beat," Jeremiah Bridges said. "And he's supposed to be eating, so I need to get back to him before I have spaghetti sauce splattered on the walls in line with those beats."

The sounds continued. And Lacey's suspicious mind wondered if Mr. Bridges had somehow triggered his son's impromptu performance for her benefit. Except that he'd have had no way to do so. He hadn't known she was coming. No one outside the logbook in the office had.

Of course, the boy could be programmed to begin the performance anytime the doorbell rang...

A far-fetched thought even for her.

"Don't let me stop you from getting back to him," Lacey said. "I'm here to check on his well-being."

"His being will be well until I return to him," the man said with a confidence that could have been endearing if it didn't make her wonder just what made a grown man so certain that a little boy would stay at the table. "It's the walls I'm worried about."

"He's confined, then?" she asked. Strapped in a booster? Or...heaven forbid, did the man keep a four-year-old in a high chair?

She'd seen it before. A mother who'd lost a toddler, not letting her second baby grow up. One of the saddest situations she'd had to oversee. Because in the end, she'd had to take the woman's second baby from her, too.

"No."

"Then how do you know he'll be okay?" She was being difficult. She knew it even before she said the words. But the man was...bothering her.

"Because he gave me his word he wouldn't get down from the table."

Impressive? Or oppressive?

"Now." Mr. Bridges's arms were crossed again. "I want to know why child protective services is in my home checking up on my son. What's this phone call you mentioned?"

"Someone is concerned about Levi's welfare."

"Nuh nuh nuh..." came from the distance.

"Someone."

"Yes."

"Who?"

"I'm not at liberty to tell you that, Mr. Bridges."

"I'm his father. I have a right to know if someone thinks that another person is hurting my son."

"Not while the investigation is ongoing."

"The investigation..." His eyes narrowed and then widened. "Wait a minute. You think *I* hurt my son? I'm the one being investigated?" He sounded as shocked as any parent she'd ever heard.

And she'd heard some doozies—from the innocent and the guilty.

"Everyone in Levi's life is being investigated,"

Lacey said, softening her tone in spite of how much the man was knocking her off her mark.

It was as though she'd known him before...in another life, or something as absurd.

"Well, I can tell you right now, no one is hurting my son. I'm with him every day. I'd know if he was being mistreated. Wouldn't I?"

The catch in the deep voice struck her as he uttered those last two words, lodging someplace in her chest.

"It's still my duty to check." Her visit wasn't personal. Had nothing to do with her at all—other than as an agent for the state.

"By all means." He stepped back. And then, when she made to move forward, stood in her way again. "If someone is hurting him, I want them stopped," he said, his gaze flint sharp.

Swallowing the lump in her throat, Lacey nodded.

"That's what I'm here for," she told him.

And hoped to God the call was a false alarm.

HE WANTED TO grab his son out of his chair with both arms, shield him against his chest and run. But instead Jem led the drably dressed woman slowly down a hall to the old kitchen he'd remodeled himself in his spare time when Tressa had been pregnant with Levi.

He couldn't panic. Not yet.

Not if someone was hurting his boy. Possible

suspects ran through his mind. The only people he knew who had access to Levi besides himself were preschool workers and his mother. No one who would hurt him.

And who'd called?

Tressa sprang to mind again. But would she really go that far? She'd pulled some questionable shit a time or two, but only to lash out at him.

As far as he knew, she didn't have any reason to be pissed with him right then. Things had been good. Better than they'd been in years…

And then something else dawned on him. Social services, child protective services, could take his son away from him if they felt the choice was warranted.

Surely Ms. Hamilton wasn't there with that thought in mind. Levi was his son. His life. No one was going to take better care of the boy than he did.

Or love him like he did.

She had to have some kind of real proof…

Didn't she?

Ready to grab the woman back, to haul her ass through his house and put her firmly but kindly outside his front door and then lock it behind her, Jem could only stand and watch as she rounded the corner, went through the archway to the kitchen and approached the table.

"Hi, Levi, I heard about you, and your dad said it was okay if I came to meet you."

He'd heard of a devil in sheep's clothing. Had quite possibly grown up with one, in the form of his older sister.

And hoped to hell he hadn't just let one into his son's world.

CHAPTER FOUR

"WHAT'S YOUR NAME?" Levi asked.

Lacey understood, the first second she heard that little voice, what Mara had been telling her about Levi's precociousness. In a perfectly serious tone, he sounded as self-assured as his father had done. All mixed in with soft *r*'s and a spaghetti-sauce-smeared face.

It took her two seconds to put that sauce together with the stains on the front of Mr. Bridges's shirt. Had there been some kind of physical tussle with the boy? Was that how Bridges could be so certain his son wouldn't move out of his chair?

"I'm Lacey," she said, taking a seat at the big butcher-block table with the little boy. His father's place, empty dirty plate with silverware sitting neatly in the middle of it, was within easy reach of Levi. "Lacey Hamilton."

The boy stared at her. "You have blond hair."

She said, "Yep," and smiled. She was good with kids. Always had been. Which was part of the reason she'd chosen to go into social work.

"I have a broken arm," he said, holding up his cast as he pursed his lips.

He'd been crying. She could see the streaks left by his tears. And had to wonder...

As if just noticing the telltale streak marks himself, Jeremiah appeared from over by the sink. "Let's get your face wiped up, buddy." He had a wet paper towel in hand.

"I can do it." Levi took it from his father, lifted his chin and scrubbed at his face. He then handed the cloth back to his father and held his hand up to him.

Jeremiah wiped each finger. "You through eating?" he asked. The plate in front of the boy was scattered with stray strands of spaghetti, but mostly empty.

"Is that enough bascetti for ice cream?"

"Yep." The man didn't miss a beat as he took the cloth, the plate, and moved back to the sink, which was on the boy's side of the table.

Lacey had to give him points for letting her sit alone at the table with the boy, as though giving his consent to his son to be friendly with her and letting Levi know that she was friend, not threat.

But he'd been crying. Violently enough to leave stains down his face. Mara, who'd known him since he was three months old, who'd been caring for him all day most days ever since, said there'd been a drastic behavioral change in him.

An alarming change...

"How'd you break your arm?" Lacey asked. He'd brought it up, so it made the question natural enough.

The boy looked down. "I fell." The words were barely discernible in the mumble that came out.

She leaned forward, wishing she could take that little body into her arms, lay his head on her shoulder and promise him that no one would ever hurt him again.

It was a reaction she hadn't had since her first years on the job. At least not often. It wasn't that she didn't care about each and every child who crossed her path. She did. Enough to keep the distance mandatory for her to do her job and make the hard decisions that would keep them safe.

"Fell how?" she asked when Levi's chin finally lifted off from his chest.

"Did the hospital call you?" Jeremiah Bridges, wiping his hands on a dish towel, came toward the table.

With a glance at the boy, back at him and then back to Levi, she ignored the question.

"How did you fall, Levi?"

"I dunno. I just fell," Levi said, then looked to his dad. "Can I go play now?"

With a glance in Lacey's direction, Jeremiah left the decision up to her. She nodded.

The boy was well kept—was obviously used to washing up after meals, too—and well fed, at least that night. And every day, as well, judging by the lean strength in his four-year-old body as Jeremiah turned the chair and assisted as Levi hopped down from his booster seat.

"No video games," he said as the boy walked slowly toward the archway. "And don't forget, no Batman or Superman for another day or two."

"I know…" The boy's head hung again. But as Levi passed his dad, Jeremiah held his hand up for a high five and Levi gave him one.

Not the actions of a frightened child.

"Aren't you forgetting something?" Jeremiah asked the boy. And then, with a nod of his head in her direction, he gave the boy a questioning look.

"Oh, yeah," Levi said and turned to her. "It was nice to meet you, Lacey," he said. He looked at his dad again. "Did I do it right?"

"Yes, sport, you did it just fine," Jeremiah said, grinning at Levi. "Now go play for a few minutes."

The little body was almost at the archway when Levi turned back. "Just until time for ice cream, right?"

"Right."

Jeremiah's grin was all for his son, but Lacey caught the tail end of it as he turned back to her. She started to respond before she caught herself.

He was looking at her full on by then. And he'd sobered completely. So had she.

"Tell me about that broken arm." She kept her tone quiet. She itched for the tablet in her purse. She needed to type about the arm. And when they were done with that, about the cause of those tears.

Kids cried, sometimes daily. Most particularly the little ones. It was a part of life. The testing of boundaries, and the impromptu bursts of emotions that learning right from wrong elicited. Tears were no reason to suspect wrongdoing here.

Still, a vision of those particular streaks on those particular cheeks had burned itself in her mind.

"What's to tell?" Bridges asked, leaning against the counter with his arms crossed in front of him again. "He fell. And if that's what this is about, if someone is trying to make something out of the fact that a kid fell and broke his arm, I'd suggest they take a look at…well…" He shrugged. "Even I broke my arm when I was a kid. Boys do that. It's not a crime."

The way his eyebrows were drawn—as if he was confused, lost—sent a mixed message, combined with the defensiveness of the rest of his posture.

His dark hair wasn't overly long. Or short, either. He reminded her of a citified cowboy, one who wore work boots instead of cowboy ones. He was a contractor, she knew, and owned his own business, which had rave reviews online: a Better Business Bureau endorsement, and a stellar record with the Registrar of Contractors.

She'd had a busy afternoon.

"Are you with me?" he asked now, switching from left foot crossed over right to the opposite, drawing her eyes to the jeans that fit those legs well enough to star in a commercial for... anything manly.

"I am," she said. "I'm listening. Not just to what you're saying, but for what you aren't. It's my job to be observant." She was going to stop there, but for some reason added, "And to make sure that I take enough time that I don't jump to conclusions." The last was true. On every job. Just not something she generally shared with a parent under investigation.

"Do you fear you're doing that here?" he asked, his glance changing from lost to piercing. "Because I can save you some time. I have not, ever, even had a split-second urge to lash out at my son. Not in any way that could be considered abusive. I've gotten impatient. Spoken more sharply than I'd have liked. I've raised my voice to him. But I have never, ever lifted a hand to him or in any way trampled his spirit."

It was one of the better "I'd never do that" speeches she'd heard. Maybe that was why she so badly wanted to believe him. But she had to have more than a statement of innocence. A four-year-old child's life could be at stake.

"How'd you break your arm?"

He blinked, stood up straight and uncrossed

his arms. "What?" Then crossed his arms again in an arrogant expression of nonchalance.

She didn't blame him his defensiveness. Nor could she let it keep her from finding out what she had to know.

"I fell off my bike," he said.

"See, now, that's a lie." She probably shouldn't have said the words aloud. But she'd known instantly that he was lying. For the first time since she'd entered his home, he avoided her glance.

Or he was a master manipulator who was playing with her.

"No, I did," he said, meeting her gaze now. "I was eight years old. Racing my older sister. Went up a curb and flew over the handlebars. I landed on my arm."

She believed him. And where did that leave her? She'd been so certain a second ago that he was lying.

"Boys break their arms," he said softly, almost as though he felt sorry for her. A heat wave passed through her, leaving her unsure for the time it took her to draw one deep breath.

She wasn't being paid to feel. Or sense. Or even "believe." Certainly not at that stage. She was there to gather facts. As many as she could get. To look for inconsistencies along the way. And then to assimilate.

She was getting ahead of herself.

"You want to know what's bothering me?" She

looked up at him, needing to stand and face him head-on. His entire demeanor seemed to dare her to do so. But she stayed in her seat to show him—and maybe herself—that he couldn't intimidate her.

"Yeah," he said, surprising her as he suddenly pulled out a chair and sat with her. "If you want to know the truth, I really do want to know what's bothering you. I'm sitting here having dinner with my son, helping him deal with the grave disappointment he's experiencing for missing out on something he's been looking forward to for six months, and suddenly here you are, disrupting our lives in a very unpleasant way. I think I deserve to know why."

Wow. The man sure knew how to deliver his punches. Funny thing was, she didn't feel like she'd been hit. At least not by anything that smacked of evil, or even foul play.

Stick to your known purpose. Don't let him pull you off course. The words of a mentor from her early days in social services surfaced in her mind.

"What's bothering me is that neither you nor your son have told me how he came to fall. When I asked you how you broke your arm, you didn't just say you fell. You said you fell off your bike. And then when I challenged you, you provided detail that was aimed at convincing me you were telling me the truth."

He was assessing her. But she had no idea what he was thinking.

"I can't tell you the details about my son's broken arm."

Aha. Now they were getting somewhere. "Why not?" Because they would incriminate him? Half expecting to hear him say that he needed to call his lawyer, she waited.

"Because I don't know them."

Disappointed, not because there'd been no lawyering up, but because she'd thought he was being honest with her, Lacey figured she was wasting her time there. If she'd had her tablet on, she'd have shut it off.

"Levi was with his mother when it happened."

No. Don't lie to me. You're going to force me to take a harsher stance if you lie...

"The emergency room report said that you were the one who brought him in."

"She called me. I went and picked him up. She's not good with medical stuff."

"And neither one of them told you what happened?" Did he really expect her to believe this?

"I know my ex-wife's version. And frankly, I didn't explain more completely because I didn't want you finding fault with her. She's a good person and doesn't react well to being hassled. She's a bit of a drama queen. But she loves Levi and would never do anything to harm him."

Lacey sat up straighter and clutched the strap

of her bag. Ex-spouses throwing each other under the bus was a classic. Common.

And here she was, disappointed in him for playing the card. For being on a potential abusive parent investigation, she had far too high an expectation of this guy.

He'd soon be telling her that his ex-wife lashes out. That she responds physically to anger and then regrets her actions. Or some version thereof. She knew the ropes.

"Can you be more specific?" She led him down his trail, thinking only of Levi now, of what resources would best help the boy. Family counseling? A caseworker—her—stopping by on a regular basis?

The state of California was pretty firm on its stance to remove kids from their homes only as a last resort.

In rare circumstances, an in-home advocate could be placed on a temporary basis...

"Levi was climbing up her bookcase to get a video he wanted to watch. I've suggested to her that she keep his videos on the lower shelves where he can reach them, but she says that that makes them too accessible to him and he'd be watching them all the time."

She waited, listening in between the lines. Clearly Bridges was experiencing a gap in parenting philosophy with his ex-wife, which could create stress and confusion for a child. But the gap alone didn't break arms. Or bruise little bodies.

"When she saw him up there, she got scared that he might fall and grabbed him to help him down."

Then what, she dropped him? The story was almost believable. Lacey waited for the fall.

"Unfortunately, instead of grabbing him around his middle, Tressa just grabbed his arm..." His voice fell off, as if that explained it all.

"You're trying to tell me that your ex-wife's grasp was so strong she broke your son's arm in two places?"

"No. She didn't have a firm enough grip to support his weight, and he fell off the shelf. It was an accident. Believe me, if Tressa had been rough with him, if I thought that she would in any way hurt him, I'd be in court to sue for full custody yesterday."

It was hard not to believe him. But...

"So why won't Levi talk about it?"

"Because he knew he wasn't supposed to be climbing up on the shelves. He's already been firmly spoken to about misbehaving and knows that he's living with the consequences of having done so. I think at this point he just wants the whole thing to go away. He doesn't want anyone else reading him the riot act. Levi's usually a great kid. He takes it personally when he screws up."

So maybe it was a great cover-up story. Maybe Bridges was a think-quick-on-the-fly kind of guy. She couldn't afford not to consider the possibility.

But even if it was true, he'd failed to tell it the first and second times she'd asked him about what had happened. Because he'd thought the story could get someone in trouble?

It made her wonder what else he was covering up.

Or would cover up in the future.

"Are you aware that your son had finger-shaped bruises on his upper torso?"

"He absolutely does not." Bridges stood. "We can prove that one right here, right now." He made as if to move toward that archway through which his son had passed.

"I don't mean now," she said, keeping an even tone. He sank back to his seat, shaking his head.

"You're telling me that someone reported bruises on him in the past? Why haven't I heard about this before now?"

"What you heard isn't important here, Mr. Bridges. What matters is the truth of the allegations. Are you, or have you ever been, aware of bruises on your son's skin that were distinctly caused by fingertips?"

"No! Of course not!"

Lacey wished she'd brought a colleague with her. She needed another read on this guy.

"Who's telling you this shit?"

She wouldn't have chosen to swear at the social services worker at that moment, but it wasn't a crime.

"I'm going to need to speak with Levi privately," she told him. "Can you bring him to my office tomorrow?"

There wasn't substantiated proof, nor any need as far as she could see, to remove the boy from his home that night. He'd exhibited no signs of fear of his father. There was nothing in the home to indicate anything other than loving care. Right down to the child-safe electrical plugs in all of the wall sockets. Even the one above the countertop in the kitchen.

"Of course I'll bring him," Bridges said. "I just…" His voice broke off.

She stood. "I'd like to see his room before I go," she said, satchel back up on her shoulder. She wanted to see the father's room, too, but didn't ask to do so. Which bothered her, too. She didn't normally have a problem making whole house assessments.

"It's right this way."

With a sure stride Bridges led her back the way they'd come, down a hall and into what was obviously a playroom. Levi, who was busy on the floor making "varoom" noises with a car he was pushing on a toy track, sat up as they entered. He stood, abandoned his cars, took her hand in his good one and proceeded to introduce her to every nook and cranny of a childhood dream. First his playroom, then the bathroom with a net of toys hanging from a decorative fish hook above a tub outfitted with colorful fish-shaped slip-free adhesive on the bottom. She saw no soap scum or dirt anywhere—with the exception of a glob of toothpaste in the sink.

Finally they ended up in the room adjoining the other side of the bathroom. A sleeping room with scenes beneath the ocean painted on the walls.

Dresser drawers were closed. There were no clothes or other clutter on the floor. The bed was made.

She could have suspected that Bridges had planned the whole thing. Cleaned up because he'd known she was coming. Except that he hadn't known. No one had. Her colleagues also had no way of knowing—except by the log they'd read when they needed to.

Neither had he given any indication that there'd been any change in his son's behavior in the past months.

Because he hadn't noticed?

Because he was hiding something?

Or because, this time, she'd received a false report?

CHAPTER FIVE

JEM DIDN'T SLEEP. Not a wink. He'd start to doze off and every single time he'd jerk awake—his heart pounding with dread.

How could he prove that he wouldn't hurt his son? Not ever? No matter what?

Who was saying that he had?

Or had that even been said? At three in the morning he made his third trip—he was allowing himself only one an hour, as if that small bit of self-control was going to prove something to someone—to his son's room to look in on the sleeping boy.

Levi had always been a back sleeper. Open to the world had always been Jem's estimation of his son's slumber habit. And there he was, sprawled with abandon, arms and legs spread, covers tangled around his lower torso, giving his all to sleep just as he gave that same zest for life in whatever he approached while awake.

The thick white plaster on that tiny arm gave Jem pause. As it had every single time he'd laid eyes on it since the doctor had put it there. He wanted to take Levi's pain, to slay every dragon that attempted to enter his son's life.

He couldn't even prevent a broken bone. The helplessness that came with that realization wasn't welcome. Or to be tolerated.

Just as he'd told the Hamilton beauty, boys broke bones. Most by accident—the boy's or someone else's.

As a vision of the woman came to mind, her blue eyes beneath that tightly pulled-back blond hair, Jem quietly left his son's room.

Taking thoughts of Lacey Hamilton with him. They'd been his constant companion since she'd left a short half hour after she'd arrived so unexpectedly on his doorstep.

He had his rights. He knew that now. Knew, too, after the reading he'd done as soon as Levi had been down for the night, that the state of California was pretty stringent about removing kids from homes. It was done as a last resort. Period. There were a lot of options between a home visit and removal—unless, of course, abuse was obvious at the outset.

And in that case, Jem would be the staunchest of supporters for removal.

Still, one caseworker had a lot of power. Even ones who made you feel like you wanted to make dinner for them every night. Especially those ones.

He thought about calling Tressa. He wanted

the support of their bonding together as they protected their son. But didn't want it to look like he was tipping her off. From what he'd read, they'd be visiting her, too.

Unless, of course, she'd been the one to file the complaint.

As much as he wanted to, he still wasn't completely ruling out that option.

With the child monitor he kept with him whenever he was out of earshot of his son's room, Jem popped the top on a beer and, opening the back patio door, sat outside by the stone fireplace he'd built next to the outdoor counter and grill. The sink and miniature refrigerator were flanked by a waterfall feature that lit up at night to show off the goldfish that Levi had picked out. Jem barely noticed any of it.

They hadn't shown Lacey Hamilton the goldfish.

Still, he'd had a feeling that she'd softened a bit before she left. That she'd maybe even started to believe him.

He would not hurt his son. And would also not stand idly by if someone else did.

LACEY HAD ALREADY worked on nine other cases by the time Jeremiah Bridges showed up with Levi just before ten the next morning. He'd said he'd take his son with him on his morning rounds, which started at seven, and then bring him in to see her before dropping him at preschool for the afternoon.

Levi had his own hard hat, he'd proudly boasted.

"He's never around a construction site while there's dangerous work going on," his father had quickly asserted. He'd started to explain the safety procedures he'd enacted before ever bringing the little boy to a work site.

At which time Levi had interrupted with "I can't leave the trailer unless all the machines is off."

"There's a job secretary in the office trailer at all times," his father had added.

If Lacey had had her tablet out, she'd have typed something about those striking blue eyes—both pairs—looking at her so solemnly.

She'd wanted to trust them.

She still felt that way as she led the duo back to her office, Levi's strides as long as his little legs could make them, attempting to synchronize with his father's.

"You want to see my playroom?" she asked the little boy just before they reached her office.

With a glance at his father, who nodded, Levi said, "Sure!" She held out her hand. He took it.

"You can wait in my office," she told his father, pointing toward the door. All case files, including his, were locked in her file drawer. Her computer was off and couldn't be accessed without her password, anyway. But there were magazines for him to read.

"We won't be long." Why she felt the need to reassure him, she didn't know. Her concern was Levi. And the possibility that someone was abusing him.

At the moment, nothing else could matter to her.

JEM PLAYED A trivia game on his phone while he waited. It was either that or think about his insides eating him up. He probably should have had some breakfast. Levi had offered to share the scrambled eggs and toast he'd had waiting for him when he'd shown up in the kitchen, sleepy-eyed and hair tussled, early that morning.

Jem was a fix-it kind of guy.

Kind of hard to fix what you didn't know was broken.

He had six trivia games going—all with guys on his crews. He generally won, but now answered six questions wrong in a row. When he missed one about the pitcher for the Los Angeles Dodgers, he closed the game. Having been on the farm team when the pitcher in question had been pitching, having had beers with him and some of the other guys during a road trip, he knew the guy's name.

But he just wasn't in the game, so no point in wasting turns.

Hands in his pockets, he walked around the small office. It was as neat as a pin. No personal pictures on the desk.

But he took note of a message scrawled on a little sheet stuck to the side of the computer monitor. *She needed a hero and so she became one.*

Something about that note eased his tension and made him feel kind of sorry for the social worker who'd interrupted his life so abruptly.

Reminding him, as it did, that everyone was human.

And no one's life was perfect.

"Do I scare you, Levi?" The minute the little boy had realized that she was going to stay with him in the playroom—and that his father wasn't going to be there—Levi had begun to shrink in on himself.

There was no other way for her to describe the reaction. His shoulders hunched slightly as he kept his cast close to his stomach. "No. 'Course not," the little boy said, that softened *r* grabbing at her.

It was okay for her to care about the children. They could never have too much love. Or so she'd told herself on those times when the professional boundaries she had to keep didn't quite diminish those occasional heart tugs.

"You want to put this together with me?" The twenty-five-piece teddy bear puzzle was probably too easy for him, judging not only by what Mara, his preschool teacher, had relayed about him, but by the activities she'd observed in his room the night before.

She sat on the floor with him while he worked silently on the puzzle by himself, putting each piece in place without hesitation.

When he'd finished, she handed him another equally easy puzzle. She wanted his concentration.

"I need the box," he said.

"What box?"

"For the other puzzle." That *r* again. He was pointing to the teddy bear puzzle he'd just completed. She'd expected him to leave that and do the second one. Instead, he cleaned up the first one before moving to the next. "Miss Mara says you have to pick up one before you can bring out a other," he told her.

"You do a lot of puzzles at school?"

"Uh-uh." He shook his head, not looking up from his task.

"Where'd you learn to do them so well, then?"

"Daddy and I got lots of 'em."

"What about your mommy—does she do puzzles with you, too?"

"Uh-uh."

Lacey had stopped to see Tressa Bridges on her way to work that morning, but there'd been no answer at the door. Such was sometimes the case when you made unannounced house calls.

He was turning a piece around the wrong way. She wanted to help him, but got the distinct feeling that he didn't want her to.

"Where were you when you fell and broke your arm?"

"I don't know."

"Of course you know, silly," she teased. "You were there at the time, weren't you?"

She was grinning at him. And earned herself a confused frown as well as a quick glance from those striking blue eyes. Then a shrug.

"Well, your arm didn't run away from your body, did it?" she asked, her tone playful.

"Noooo." He giggled and put the piece he'd been struggling with in place.

"So why don't you tell me what happened. You aren't going to be in any trouble. I just want to know."

"I fell." Another piece slid into place. His upper torso was bent completely over the puzzle.

"From where?"

"Mommy's bookshelf."

Relief flooded her so thickly Lacey sat back. She grinned for real. Then it occurred to her that his father could have told him to say that, could even have rehearsed it with him this morning on their way to see her.

"Was she in the room?"

He shrugged again, and she realized her question could be confusing. In the room when he first misbehaved by climbing where he'd been told not to go? Or when he fell?

"Before you started to climb, I meant."

He shrugged again. And rather than upset him, she let the matter drop.

Levi finished the puzzle. At her invitation he wandered around the room, touching things. A plastic tic-tac-toe board. A car track with little cars—not as elaborate as the one he had in his room at home, but still worth a little boy's notice.

Lacey put the puzzles back on their shelf, washed her hands in the sink and sat at a pint-size plastic picnic table. "You want a snack?" she asked, holding out a shortbread cookie she'd just taken from the cupboard.

He looked at the cookie, shrugged and pushed a car on the track.

"What kind of ice cream did you get last night?" His father had told him that they'd have some.

"Chocolate. I get chocolate. Daddy gets 'nilla."

Leaving the cookie on the table, she sat down on the floor with him. "In a cone or a bowl?"

He shrugged again.

"Do you ever eat so much it hurts your stomach?"

Another shrug.

There were games she could play with him, activities designed to give her insights into his psyche. She had hoped she wouldn't have to re-sort to something that formal. But...

"Let's play a little game," she said, leaning back against the wall. He seemed happier when she gave him his space.

He didn't seem to have heard her.

"Levi, will you play a game with me?"

"Then can I go back to my daddy?" Those blue eyes were wide and sad as he looked at her.

"Yes." It was the only answer she could give him. Her purpose was not to make him unhappy. Or to make him dislike her, either. They needed to work together, Levi and she, to make certain that he was safe. Even if he didn't know that.

"Okay."

"So this is a talking game," she started. "You can still play with your cars while we do it."

Picking up another car, he had one in each hand and circled one around the track.

"So in this game, I tell you one of the best things that ever happened to me, one of my happiest times, and then you tell me yours. Okay?"

He nodded.

"So, one of my happiest times was when..." She'd been ready to give him the rote—the memory she'd chosen long ago for this exercise, the same one she used every time.

And then she stopped. He wasn't exhibiting any need to confide in her, didn't seem to need an excuse to open up, and he certainly wasn't going to care about her and her identical twin sister playing a trick on their fourth-grade teacher.

Not at that moment, at any rate.

"When I was little, my twin sister and I were picked to do some television commercials," she told him. "The best one was when we got to ride on the hood of a sports car for a little bit, right on the track."

He looked at her then. "Did you go fast?"

"No. We were on the hood. But when we were done, my sister got to ride in it."

"All the way around?"

"Yes."

He pushed the car around the track again.

"It's your turn now. What's the best time you ever had?"

She waited.

"My fish."

"Your fish is the best time?"

"Uh-huh."

"What did you do with your fish?"

"Daddy and me goed fishing on a boat and I got to pick out goldfish for my pond we builded."

"You have a pond?" She'd missed that the night before.

He nodded and pushed the car in his left hand for the first time.

"Where?"

"With the stuff outside."

"What stuff?"

"Chairs and cooking and stuff."

Lacey would have picked up a little car, too, if she'd felt herself welcome. Instead, she watched the adorable little boy pushing his miniature vehicles with such precision while she leaned back against the wall.

"And you went fishing for goldfish?"

"No!" His giggle slipped inside her, lightening the weight she carried. "You buy them in the store, where they dunk that thing in for 'em."

She smiled then, liking this child—a lot—and knowing that, regardless of what she found out, he was going to be one of those she never forgot.

CHAPTER SIX

THRUMMING HIS FINGERS on the arm of the chair, Jem stared at the magazines on the table beside him. He stared at his phone, too, scrolling through his favorite news site, but seeing nothing. He reholstered his phone.

What in the hell was taking so long?

Was it possible that someone really was hurting his son?

Impossible.

He'd know.

But one thing he'd learned since Levi had come into the world, turning his life upside down—kids had incredible imaginations.

They were apt to say anything that came into their heads. Fabrication or not. To a kid Levi's age, everything seemed real. From cartoons, dreams he'd had and stories he'd imagined.

Jem had always encouraged his son's free thinking. And when Levi came up with outlandish stories, he'd asked questions to play along. Because to Levi, in those moments, they were real.

He'd also taught his son never to lie. He could

imagine. He could make up. But he could not change facts that he knew to be true.

But Lacey Hamilton, her crew at social services, whatever other professionals she might have involved in their lives—none of them knew that.

Shooting up out of the scarred wooden chair, he strode to the door, opened it and caught a woman's questioning look as she passed by the room on her way down the hall. She probably knew who he was. Why he was there.

Obviously she'd know in whose office he'd been waiting.

Back inside, he closed the door and sat down. What was taking them so long?

Pulling his phone back off the holster at his waist, Jem started making calls to his site bosses. He fielded problems and offered solutions, helping those who worked for him to do their best work.

All the while trying to ignore the fact that he'd never felt so helpless in his life.

"So THE NEXT part of this game is, I tell you my worst memory." Lacey felt like a creep as she sat there in the small playroom with a little boy who had no good reason to trust her. Pumping him for information that could make a drastic change in his life. *If* his life needed a drastic change.

Fully knowing that for most kids, even when

the change was needed, it wasn't welcome. The devil you knew was much better than facing the fear of the unknown. And being ripped away from those you loved—even if they weren't good to you—was the worst.

"It was when I was little and had to be in the hospital and I was really scared."

She had to make it bad enough that he wouldn't feel intimidated talking about his, no matter how bad it was.

And yet not so bad as to give him nightmares.

It also had to be true. Her rule. The kids in her life generally had major trust issues. She was not going to add to them by lying.

He looked up at her. "Were you sick?"

"I had to stay overnight," she said. "I thought I'd done something really bad and that I was being punished."

Levi shifted, sitting on one foot, with his chin resting on his upraised knee. He grabbed a new car—a pickup truck—and ran it around the track, crashing it into the smaller white car he'd left there.

"What's your worst memory?" she asked, knowing full well that a child his age would most likely access only the past couple of weeks.

"I dunno."

Not an atypical response, even from a well-adjusted, happy four-year-old.

"Levi, I'm going to ask you something. And

I need you to be completely honest with me. Do you understand?"

He backed the truck up.

"Levi? Look at me a second."

Without lifting his chin, he glanced in her direction.

"Will you be honest with me and answer my question?"

"I don't tell lies."

A prevarication. At four. She almost smiled.

"Has anyone ever told you not to tell something?" A leading question if ever there was one.

She was counting on the fact that he wouldn't be savvy enough, at four, even four going on forty, to see that.

He didn't answer. His hand stilled on the truck, but he didn't let go of it.

"You don't lie, remember?" she said.

He sat there.

"Has someone told you that?"

The next time he glanced up, there were tears in his eyes. She had her answer.

"Levi…"

"Do I gotta tell?" His lower lip trembled.

"Yeah." She nodded. "But you don't have to tell me what you can't tell. Just who told you not to."

He didn't say anything more. So she tried to make it easier on him.

"Was it your daddy?"

Chin on his knee, he shook his head.

"Was it Mara at school?"

Another shake of his head.

"Someone else at school?"

He shook his head again.

She thought about that broken arm. About where he'd been when it had happened. About a mother who never dropped her son off or picked him up from school.

"Was it your mommy?"

He didn't respond. Not even a shake of the head.

Lacey had her answer.

THERE WERE SOME days a guy just needed a burger. The biggest, juiciest patty of beef he could find. And when a guy had a pint-size sidekick, it had to be at a place that served pint-size versions of the same.

Instead of taking Levi straight to preschool after their meeting at social services, Jem turned their truck in the opposite direction and drove until they landed at the beach. At Uncle Bob's— one of his and Levi's favorite spots.

Lacey Hamilton had told him basically nothing when she'd come into her office alone less than twenty minutes before. He'd been about to say a whole lot, until she'd explained that Levi was with a coworker of hers, looking at her goldfish, and would be along in a second.

"Can I play in the sand?" the boy asked as he unhooked his seat belt.

"Yep."

Levi climbed out of his car seat in the back and made his way to the front of the truck to get out with Jem.

Jem had been thinking about making the little guy wait until he opened the back door to get him out, but figured Levi would be opening doors on his own—exiting them without wanting his father close—soon enough. He swung the boy up on his hip and carried him toward the entrance.

It was a testimony to their dual state of mind when Levi put his arms around Jem's neck and rode the whole way in. Most days he'd have been pushing his feet against Jem's thighs, eager to be down and on his own.

"I don't have school today, do I?" Levi asked as they waited to be shown to their table. He'd requested one by the big sandbox play area. Tuesday before noon and the place was already crowded.

"Yeah, you do," he said. He wouldn't have if Jem wasn't feeling overly paranoid about having his every move watched. He didn't want someone thinking that he was suddenly changing his schedule, afraid to take his son to day care, for fear of what someone might report.

Not that he thought, for one second, that Mara or any of the ladies at the day care would report him for abuse. No, he'd pretty much figured out it was either the hospital, because they had to report frequent hospital visits, as he'd learned last night during his reading—Levi had been to the emergency room six times—or Tressa.

She'd wanted to have sex the previous weekend. He hadn't been interested enough to pull off the pretense, but had thought he'd made a pretty good excuse. She'd seemed to roll with it at the time.

But his ex-wife had a tendency to be vindictive where he was concerned. Someone had to take the blame for the things that hadn't gone right in her life. Might as well be him.

LEVI CHATTERED ABOUT building a sand castle while they waited for the burgers and fries Jem had ordered. Not only were they by the big sandbox, the hostess had seated them at a table with a view of the beach.

Jem would have loved to spend the day out there. Playing in the sand with his son. Building castles. Or surfing the waves like he used to do. Before he'd met Tressa, become a husband—and then a father.

"What's a twin?" Levi's foot, swinging beneath the table, caught Jem on the knee. The boy's chin barely reached the top of the table, but he'd been pretty particular about not wanting a booster seat.

He was a big boy and not a baby, at least that day.

"A twin?" he asked, giving his son his full focus.

"Mmm-hmm." Levi's chin lifted. "Lacey said she has a twin. What's a twin?"

An immediate vision sprang to mind. Not one but two of the beautiful blondes, hair down, of course...

What in the hell was it with him? He was bordering on disrespectful the way he kept picturing the woman.

The next second he was shrugging off his propensity for doing so. He was a guy. It was what guys did.

Not that he could remember the last time he'd mentally undressed a woman he'd just met...

"A twin is someone who has a brother or sister who was born at the same time they were," he said.

"With a different mommy and daddy?" the boy asked, screwing up his nose like he did when he wasn't understanding something.

"Nope. With the same mommy and daddy."

"You said I came out of Mommy's tummy." Technically, he hadn't offered up that technical tidbit to a four-year-old child. Tressa had, one night when she'd been explaining to Levi why he was hers and why he should want to spend more time with her. Jem had been left to explain, as best he could, what she'd meant.

"That's right," he said now.

"Does everyone come out of a mommy's tummy?"

Obviously his lesson had lacked some pertinent details. "Yes." He waited. The last time they'd dealt with this topic, he'd answered Levi's questions and left the rest for when the boy wanted to know more.

Thanks to Lacey Hamilton needing to tell his son about her birth situation, now was apparently the time for more. As if the day wasn't already challenging enough.

Both little feet beneath the table were swinging now and softly kicking him. Jem thought about reaching down to stop them, but chose to take the blows instead. If Levi didn't expunge his energy one way, he'd find another.

Levi's gaze followed a waiter with a tray full of ice cream sundaes and Jem was pretty sure they were done with the topic. He was ready to ask his son if he wanted a sundae for dessert, in spite of the fact that they didn't do dessert at lunchtime, when Levi turned back to him.

"Lacey's mom had two babies in her tummy at one time?"

"Yep."

"How come my mommy didn't have two babies at one time?"

Levi had talked a time or two about having a baby brother or sister. So far Jem had avoided the hows and why that couldn't happen, saying only that mommies and daddies had to be married to have babies. A weak excuse if ever there was one.

"Because you took up so much room, silly," he said now and grinned for real when he saw their waitress heading toward them with two burgers. One big and one small.

As expected, Levi moved on from the whole twin thing as he ate. Talking about playing in the sand again. And about cars. He wanted a blue one with turbo twin spoilers like the one he'd played with that morning.

"It was really cool, Dad."

Jem promised him the car. Knowing that on any other day he'd have given Levi some task to complete to earn the toy that he wanted.

Levi seemed to have shaken any of the trepidation he'd had after his encounter in Lacey's playroom.

But Jem couldn't shake his awareness of Lacey Hamilton from his mind quite as easily.

And wondered what it had been like for her, growing up with a built-in best friend. Wondered if her twin was a brother or a sister.

Wondered, too, why he gave a damn.

CHAPTER SEVEN

LACEY'S LIFE WAS her work. She didn't try to hide the fact or apologize for it. She'd made choices and was at peace with them. She liked her life.

She hadn't grown up thinking she'd be a career woman. She'd gone to college more because it was expected of her than because she had career goals to pursue. But time, experience, clarified things.

As she drove through the streets of Santa Raquel on Tuesday, mingling with rush-hour traffic, Lacey followed the instructions from her GPS.

She hadn't known, until the summer before her sophomore year in college, when she'd had to declare a major, that she was even going into social work. She'd always had a way with children. And her aptitude test had scored measurably higher for a career that involved working primarily with children. Science and math weren't her thing, so that had ruled out anything in medicine.

"In zero point two miles you will be arriving at your destination. On the right." The slightly accented female voice came through her sound system.

When she'd been little, Lacey had assumed she'd just grow up and be a mom someday. That thought had never really changed. It, like so much in her life, had just slowly drifted apart from her. There'd been nothing that stood out as a conscious realization of what her life would be. She'd just become what she was.

A woman married to her career.

One who was fulfilled, satisfied. One who contributed to society in a positive way.

And who was financially secure, too.

Really, if one had a choice, who wouldn't want to be her?

Pulling up in front of the little cottage that would have looked more in place on the beach than on the nondescript street in an older neighborhood on the outskirts of town, Lacey picked up her tablet, turned it on and opened the file she'd created the day before. And then opened the document that was, as of yet, mostly blank.

The next half hour would be critical. She couldn't afford to make any mistakes as she met the woman who quite possibly was abusing Levi Bridges.

"SOMEONE'S HERE, JEM, I gotta go."

Heart trying to thump blood through a gut of rock, Jem stood at his kitchen window, looking out over the backyard, listening to the fountain through the window he'd opened when he'd come in to prepare the vegetables he'd be grilling with chicken for dinner that night.

"At least I think they're here. Someone just pulled up in front of my house. Hold on, let me look. I don't recognize the car, but..."

Tressa's voice sounded expectant. Which was better than mistrustful. This was good, considering the drama-ridden world in which his ex-wife lived. And he, thankfully, did not.

Chewing on his lower lip, he waited, deliberating over his options. He'd called to see if she'd tell him anything. Give him any clue as to whether or not she was behind the call to social services. To the fact that his world had once again been turned completely upside down.

It had been why he'd left her. Or rather, taken her up on one of her oft-repeated "offers" to leave him. He couldn't have his son growing up with the drama-based tension that Tressa brought into every room she occupied.

If she stayed there long enough, that was.

"Who is it?" he asked now, trepidation knotting his insides to the point of decimating his appetite. A feeling he'd grown used to during his years with the woman who'd captivated him and then slowly instilled pity within him. Heart-wrenching pity. For her.

She'd given no indication, in the five minutes

they'd been talking, that she'd had a visit from social services. Or any indication that anything was wrong, either.

Other than her job, but that was another story...

"I don't know. No one's getting out. But I can see her there. It's a woman. Her hair's in a twist."

Lacey. But if she'd been there to report back to Tressa, as in, his ex-wife being the one who'd called to report him, Tressa would surely have recognized her and made a quick excuse to ditch him. Unless she had concerns...

"She's blonde. Looks about our age..." There was curiosity in Tressa's tone now. But the tone was still soft. Still the calm and therefore quite likable side of the woman he'd married. "She's wearing some kind of jacket, sky blue. Who wears sky blue jackets anymore?"

So Tressa.

And also, so Lacey. He knew exactly what the outdated jacket looked like. She'd had it on that morning when she'd escorted his son down the hall and away from him. To play with cars, according to Levi.

Jem reached for a beer. If Tressa had not called social services, this was not going to be good.

Lacey hadn't said a word about visiting Levi's mother that evening when she'd called just as he was basting the chicken that was already on the grill.

She'd called to check on Levi, she'd said.

Like a storm chaser, he could predict what was coming. He also knew that he wasn't going to say anything to Tressa about it—a decision made right that second. After all the years he'd spent defending his wife's actions, her words when she went off inappropriately, so many years of smoothing feathers she hadn't meant to ruffle, he didn't want anyone associating him with her anymore.

Not in a partner sense.

And most particularly not when a decision maker from social services was involved.

"She's getting out now," Tressa was saying. "Probably just selling something. I hope it's not clothes." His ex-wife chuckled, still at ease.

Jem gripped the back of his neck.

"If it's jewelry, I'll buy some. Poor thing, having to go door-to-door to make a living. I can always give it for Christmas presents. Nice car she's driving. I wonder if she just lost her job. Or maybe her ex dumped her for someone a little more fashion conscious..."

Sounding truly compassionate now, Tressa's voice was fading.

"I'll talk to you later," Jem said, reminding her that he was still there.

"Yeah, fine, Jem. Call me."

She'd disconnected before he heard the doorbell ring. *Call me.* That was Tressa. *I only want people in my life who prove they want to be there.*

It was always about meeting her expectations. As long as you could do that...

Jem looked down at the bundle resting on the counter beside him. He'd been about to carry it out to the grill, but had decided to check in with Tressa first—right after Lacey had called him, butting into his evening, bothering him all over again...

He picked up the bundle—broccoli and corn with a little bit of butter, wrapped in foil. Weird way to prepare them, maybe, but Levi liked them that way.

And only broccoli and corn. Not carrots. Not beets. And certainly not the Brussels sprouts Jem tried on him one time.

He'd eat raw cucumbers, too. But only if they were peeled...

Not once, in the entire five minutes they'd been on the phone, had Tressa asked him how Levi was doing with his cast. She'd asked about his day in school, asked if he'd missed her. But not a word about the broken arm their son was carrying around, learning how to adjust to. Not a word about the T-ball he'd missed.

In that aspect, she was a bit like their son—able to let go of regrets. Except Levi's disruptions were truly gone once he let them go. Tressa just swept hers under the rug.

Lacey Hamilton didn't seem like the type of woman you swept away.

HAVING TAKEN A moment to prepare herself, to erase her morning with Levi and focus only on the woman she was about to meet, Lacey felt ready as she climbed the step up to the small, neat porch.

She liked the wicker bench and table, the red geraniums blooming in a pot in the corner. Geraniums took care to maintain, she knew.

The only way to help Levi was to open her mind up to whatever facts might present themselves. No matter how hard or bad they could turn out to be.

The flowers were a nice touch. And based on the pale pink discoloration of the white picket rail behind them, the blooms had been there awhile.

She knocked, expecting to wait a minute while the resident checked her out through the peephole. Or the nearby window, she revised, as she saw the curtain move.

Would the woman answer the door? Or slip out the back?

Pretend she wasn't home?

She'd once had a parent climb out of a second-story window with the endangered child in her arms.

There was no second story here. And she knew for a fact that the child wasn't in residence. She'd called Jeremiah Bridges before she'd left her office to see how Levi was doing after his meeting with her that morning. She'd wanted to know if he had any questions that needed answering. She'd told him that he was to refer all such questions to her. According to him, there hadn't been any.

Could be true. Considering the fact that Levi was only four. It could also be that his father was very calmly and politely telling her to go to hell.

The front door opened.

"Hi. Can I help you?" The first thing Lacey noticed, besides the warm and welcoming tone, was the woman's smile. Had she not been working, it might have put her immediately at ease.

"My name is Lacey Hamilton. I'm from social services. May I come in?"

The model-beautiful blonde frowned. "Social services? Is there a problem? Someone in trouble?"

The questions came faster than she could answer them. The woman's bewilderment seemed completely genuine.

"Is it my brother? I told him not to come to me if he got himself into trouble again. I just can't help him. I promised Jem... Sorry." The woman shook her head. "That's my husband...ex-husband, really...but if you're here about Kenton, you probably already know that."

Wow. Could someone put on an act that good if they were really feeling tense inside?

Records showed that Tressa Bridges was working as a manager of a small local branch of a major bank. She'd had the job for a little over a year. Before that she'd been an account manager for a well-respected investment firm. People who worked with large amounts of money had to first pass rigorous background and character checks.

People who did poorly in one financial institution, or left under negative terms, were not generally hired by another. Not in the same town, nor in a close time frame.

Tressa had paused long enough to ask her in. "I'll tell you anything you need to know about Kenton. I'll do anything I can to help him. But he needs to know he has to stay completely away from Jem. I mean, he's lucky Jem didn't press charges. And he can't live with me, and I can't give him any money."

Wow, again. Lacey followed the vivacious woman to a small but meticulous living room with a camel-colored sectional that perfectly complemented the one camel-colored wall. The other walls were a peaceful cream color.

Lacey's eye went straight to the built-in bookshelves on either side of the mounted flat-screen television set. In addition to books and DVDs, there were some trinkets. And a lot of photos of Levi.

Scanning the movies, she did indeed notice preschool titles on a higher shelf.

Wondering if the trunk-size wicker basket that served as a side table contained the preschooler's toys, Lacey said, "I'm not here about your brother."

"Oh." The woman blinked and sat down. "I'm

so sorry," she said, "going on about my personal stuff like that. Jem says that I need to watch that. I tell him I will, and then off I go again, not even realizing. So, forgive me." She stood up. "I was about to have some tea. I've just come in from work. Can I get you a glass?"

"I'd like that," Lacey answered, more because she wanted to be able to follow the woman to the kitchen, to get as much of a look at the house as she could, to see how Levi's mother lived when she wasn't expecting company, than because she actually wanted a drink.

Tressa didn't ask why she *was* there. Contrary to her previous behavior, she didn't say anything at all, just pulled a couple of glasses out of the cupboard and filled them with ice. "Sweet or un-sweetened?"

"Sweet." She didn't allow herself the indulgence often.

"Me, too." Tressa crinkled her nose and then grinned. "I manage to make myself drink it un-sweetened about half the time."

Lacey was up to about three-quarters of the time. Most weeks.

Maybe not this one.

Walking around to the other side of the break-fast nook off the kitchen, Tressa pulled out one of four white wooden chairs at a block table similar to the one Lacey had seen at Jem's house. "We might as well sit out here," she said, indicating the chair directly across from her. Lacey sat.

The table had professionally embroidered, flowered linen placements. Bright and colorful. A matching print on the wall behind Tressa caught Lacey's eye as she sat down.

"I love this room," Lacey said, glancing out the sliding glass door to a small walled court-yard lined with flowers and a little birdbath-type above-the-ground fountain.

"Me, too," Tressa told her. "I work at a bank, and while I love the challenge of making money work for you, some days I can't wait to get home to my little oasis."

What about her son? What did she think about not getting home to him every night? And on days when Levi was there, did he disturb the oasis?

Lacey looked from the woman, who was sitting perpendicular to her, to the wall Tressa was facing. She also had a view of the kitchen. For the first time she saw the side of the refrigerator facing the breakfast nook.

All available space was covered. Magnets held up drawings, scribblings, photographs. All done by, or taken of, Levi. It was a shrine to the boy. Which his mother faced every single time she sat down at the table.

Maybe Levi Bridges was just accident prone

and was exhibiting changed behavior because of a developmental stage he was going through.

Maybe she had to be looking more closely at the day care.

"I'm afraid to ask why you're here." Tressa smiled. A tremulous, timid smile. No hint of defensiveness. Or authority, either.

Lacey smiled back, offering all she could offer at that moment—compassion.

If Tressa was hurting her son, she needed help. It would be Lacey's job to connect her with resources...

If she was hurting her son.

Lacey liked the woman's home.

And hated the case.

CHAPTER EIGHT

"Whatcha' doin'?"

Jem glanced down at the little boy staring so solemnly up at him. And swore to himself, then and there, that he'd take the boy and run if need be, to protect him. He knew he wasn't hurting Levi. And he'd be damned if some stranger thought she could come into his life and proclaim that he was…

"Getting ready to put the veggies on the grill," he said, picking up the foiled bundle that had been sitting on the counter for far longer than he'd originally intended.

He'd been waiting for Tressa to call him back. He'd wanted to deal with whatever drama was coming his way before he started cooking dinner, because once the food was cooked, he intended to sit outside with his son and enjoy the meal. Sans drama.

"That was before Whyatt." Levi's stare was no less piercing for his youth. When he'd headed to the kitchen to start dinner, Jem had told Levi that he could watch one episode of *Super Why!* Which meant he'd been in the kitchen a full twenty-five minutes. It took ten, at the most, to prepare veggies for the grill.

"Well, sometimes these things take a little longer," Jem said, off his mark for having to be less than straight up with the boy.

"You was just standing here looking…"

"Were," he corrected, and with veggies in one hand, he scooped Levi up with the other. "What do you say we go look over the boat while dinner's cooking?" He swung Levi high and then landed him on his hip.

Parenting books said to distract as a form of behavior management.

"Can I help?" Levi was fascinated with the old schooner that took up most of their garage. Jem couldn't wait until the day his son would be old enough to really participate.

And hoped that by then he'd still want to.

"I painted this weekend while you were at your mom's. You can help me sand." No tools. Nothing dangerous. Just in case they had a surprise visitor. Not because he didn't trust himself to take perfectly good care of his son.

Purposely leaving his cell phone on the kitchen counter, Jem headed outdoors.

"I'M HERE TO ask you some questions about your son." Lacey hated this part of her job, where she tried to instill confidence so she could determine whether or not she had to become the person's worst nightmare.

In order to help. Always in order to help. Unfortunately, most parents in need of help didn't see her as someone to turn to.

That night, for whatever reason, she wished she could just be having a glass of wine with the woman across from her, finding out what besides decorating styles, blond hair and a penchant for iced tea they had in common.

"You want to know about Levi? Social services wants to know?" Tressa sat up straight, mouth open and brow furrowed. "Something's happened to him? That can't be. I was just talking to Jem. He'd have told me if anything was wrong. As infuriating as that man can be, he's great with Levi. That's the only reason I can bear to be without my baby. Because I know that Jem's such a great dad."

"And you don't think you're a great mom?"

"Of course I do," Tressa said. And then added, "Well, mostly. I'm not as goofy with Levi as Jem is. I don't make him laugh as much. Those two, from the very beginning, they had this rapport. Everyone noticed it. I had a baby and it was like I became a third wheel. But I'm a good mom. I've been reading to Levi since he was born and I taught him to read. He's only four, you know."

Tressa took a sip of tea, as though confident that everything was going to be just fine.

Jeremiah's energy had been more like that of a caged lion.

"My office received a report that someone's been abusing him."

Those big blue eyes opened wide in shock, and alarm. Lacey read no subterfuge there. Noticed no dropped glance or prevarication. Tressa was staring her straight in the eye.

"That's a lie," the woman said. "I just had him this weekend and he was perfectly fine. He's always fine. Every single time I see him. He may not live with me full-time, but I'm his mother. He's my only child. I'd have noticed if he wasn't okay."

Not an atypical response. Either way—if she was an abuser or if she wasn't.

"So you don't think your husband could be hurting him?"

"Jem? Are you nuts? He's the most gentle man I know. Except maybe when people screw up at work, and only then because construction is a dangerous business and people could get hurt. He's really protective of his crews. It's not like anyone would think they could walk all over him or anything. But he'd never hurt Levi. Not ever."

Curious, that an ex-wife defended the man so much.

"And what about you? Has there ever been a time when, not meaning to, you grabbed him too tightly?" Unless Mara Noble had lied, *someone* had left finger-shaped bruises on that little boy's body. And someone besides a day care worker would have to have seen them.

"Of course I haven't." There was no indignation in Tressa's voice. Because the woman found the idea so far-fetched it wasn't even an issue? That was how it seemed to Lacey. But she'd been lied to by the best, and she knew better than to take the interview at face value.

Losing some of her conversational passiveness, she leaned forward. "How did Levi break his arm?"

Tressa's lips pushed out as she held them together. Her chin dimpled. She blinked away a sudden flood of tears. "Is that what this is about?" she asked. "Did he tell you I hurt him?"

"No. He won't tell anyone anything."

Tressa's expression didn't clear—no sign of relief at finding out that she had not been accused of wrongdoing.

"He was climbing on the bookcase," she said. "He'd asked if he could watch Whyatt, and I said yes, and then the phone rang. It was Amelia, and I was talking to her, and so he decided to help himself to his video. He knows he isn't allowed to climb on that bookcase. He could…" She stopped. "Well, we all know what could happen, because it did."

"You're saying he fell?"

She shook her head. "He probably wouldn't

have if I hadn't panicked. I rushed over to save him from disaster, but I didn't have a secure enough grasp on him…" Tears filled her eyes and she shook her head. "It's just like Jem used to say, I overreact."

"He blamed you, then?"

Tressa blinked. "What? Jem? For Levi's arm? No." She shook her head softly. "He said it was an accident. It *was* an accident. But I still feel horrible about it."

Lacey believed her. About all of it. The story was the same, with minute differences, like the fact that she'd given her son permission to watch his video and then taken a phone call…

It didn't sound rehearsed, and it explained Levi's shame.

She didn't like that Jem always told Tressa she overreacted. Though if it was true, if Tressa had out-of-control emotions, that could be a concern.

And if it wasn't true, it pointed to an unhealthy behavior by the ex-husband—demeaning and be-littling the mother of his child.

"Have you ever noticed bruising on Levi?" She was back to the bruises Mara had reported on Levi's torso.

"No. But all little boys get bruises now and then. It's not like I would have found it unusual or of particular concern. I might not have com-mitted one to memory. Also, Jem has him most of the time. I just have him on weekends. And only every other one."

"Why is that?"

Tressa shrugged. "I have a tendency to make issues where there are none. My whole family was that way. And probably why my brother got into drinking and drugs at such a young age. We're drama queens, or king in Kenton's case. Every one of us. And while it's something I'm used to, Jem isn't. I don't want Levi ending up like my brother. Kenton was really sweet before he started drinking and taking drugs—to be able to survive under one roof with my mom and dad, he said."

So it was true. Which meant the ex-husband wasn't belittling the mother of his child. She made note.

"Can you give me an example of what you're talking about?" Lacey hadn't touched her tea.

"With Levi and Jem, or with my brother?"

"Let's start with Levi."

Nodding, Tressa continued to hold Lacey's gaze openly. "Levi would get a runny nose and I'd be wanting to keep him home, just in case. I'd be listening to his chest and worrying about pneumonia. I take things to extremes in my mind. Maybe it's so that I'm always prepared."

She paused. Lacey nodded and waited.

"So...say someone looks at us in the park. I'm

immediately carrying on like he might mug us or shoot us."

The woman was so genuine Lacey couldn't help but like her and want to help her. It's what she did. Attempt to help families live healthy lives together.

"So if you know you have a tendency to do that, are you able to reel yourself in?"

"Yeah, but I'm still emotional, you know? I cry at commercials. Or when I see someone hurting an animal. I still worry about everything even when I know it's not likely to happen."

"And you think that was a result of growing up in a turbulent house."

Tressa nodded. "It wasn't good for my marriage, I can tell you that. And it's not good for Levi to live like that all the time, either."

"Jem told you that?" She used the shortened version of his name on purpose, to keep Tressa at ease.

The other woman shook her head. "No, I saw it. He's happy, carefree and funny when Jem's around. When it's just me and Levi, he gets quiet, reserved."

Exactly the behavior Mara had described.

"I make him nervous. Like he never knows if something he does is going to make me upset."

"Did someone tell you that?"

"No. But only because I didn't bother going back to counseling."

"Back?"

"I grew up in a dysfunctional family," Tressa reminded her, as if that explained everything. "And that's an understatement." She looked at Lacey. Her shoulders relaxed and she gave a little smile.

"I'm guessing anything I tell you isn't going to shock someone like you," she said. "In your job, I mean."

Lacey sipped tea, having to work harder than normal to keep her professional distance. First the father and now the mother pushing at her boundaries, making her feel…personal. More than a decade on the job, and it had never happened before. Not like this.

And then there was Levi. The little guy was an anomaly. One who had somehow touched her differently—just like Mara had said he'd done with her. There was something special about him with his little-boy lisp, cocky swagger and intelligent, curious, guarded gaze.

"I've seen and heard a lot of unimaginable things," she said now. "Why don't you tell me a little bit about your family."

Half an hour later Lacey was still sitting there, listening to Tressa talk about a mother who'd tell her, on a regular basis, that she wished Tressa had never been born, that Tressa had ruined her life, that she was the devil—and then, in another breath, when Tressa was agreeing with her or taking her side, hug her and call her a princess. A mother who would withhold affection to get what she wanted. Whose love was clearly conditional.

About a father who'd ask her mother if she knew how many times a day he thought about killing her, and then would hold her hand every time they went out. Who would take a typical childhood misbehavior and broadcast it to perfect strangers in an attempt to shame Tressa and Kenton into never doing it again.

And about the brother who'd fly off anytime anyone tried to tell him something he didn't want to hear. The louder the yelling got, his or anyone else's, the more he turned to drinking and drugs in order to cope.

The more out of control anyone got, the more everyone in her family hurled horrible insults at each other.

And the more they all clung to one another, as well. Clearly Tressa had loved them.

Her parents had been killed in a car accident shortly after she'd met Jeremiah Bridges.

"He was my rock," Tressa said now, an almost dreamy smile on her face. "In some ways he still is."

"Whose idea was it for the two of you to divorce?"

"Mine. As good as he is to me, Jem just doesn't get my intensity. I can't really be myself with him, you know? I had to continuously clamp down on every reaction—from loving a song on the radio to issues on an election ballot. I bring equal passion to everything." She paused, then grinned. "I've done a lot of work on myself. Faced my issues. And…I met someone. Another woman, actually, though our relationship isn't sexual. We hang out most every night. She gets me. And when I started putting her first, over Jem, I knew that wasn't fair to him."

"Did you discuss this other woman with him?"

"Of course. That's the one thing about me. I don't keep anything to myself."

Lacey was beginning to see that. She smiled and then quickly sobered. "So when you get upset, and you're drama ridden, do you ever lash out like your parents did?"

"Absolutely not. I might say what's on my mind, but I'm not cruel like they were. I threw a stick once. It flew through the air and hit my friend on the arm. I felt sick about it. She wasn't hurt, but the look in her eyes, when she looked at her arm and then at me… It's the last time I ever threw anything."

"How old were you when that happened?"

"Thirteen. I was on my period and I'm always more dramatic then."

"And your friend…did you remain in contact after that?"

Sometimes the best way to see the full picture

of a person was to see how others treated them. How others judged them.

Not always.

Because victims treated poorly by abusers tended to invite those into their lives who would repeat the treatment. It was the pattern of abuse. Insidious hell.

She knew it well now.

Being treated poorly didn't mean you were bad. But it could.

"Yeah, we were in contact. It wasn't like I meant to hit her. She knew that. We were, like, best friends all through school. We've lost touch, but we're friends on Facebook."

"You work in finance, right?" Lacey asked.

"Yeah."

"So you have a degree?"

"Yeah, I went to Cal State. That's where I met Jem, actually."

"He went to college?"

"Are you kidding? He has a master's in business administration."

He owned a construction company, had a hard hat hanging in his truck behind the driver's seat. She'd figured he'd worked his way up.

Not that there was a damned thing wrong with that if he had. It just wasn't her job to assume, one way or another.

With the heat of shame working on her from

the inside out, Lacey admonished herself for stereotyping.

It was so not like her. She'd discovered several gems cloaked in mud during her years with social services, people with integrity who'd been dealt blows and were struggling so hard to keep air in their lungs they couldn't worry about the mud on their skin.

A phone rang and Tressa pulled out the phone that had been sticking out of the back pocket of her skinny jeans. "It's Amelia," she said, letting it ring. "We're hooking up for dinner. I'm supposed to be at her place. If this is going to take a while, I need to let her know I can't make it."

Lacey had no real reason to stay. Levi wasn't in residence, and his mother had already denied hurting him or knowing anything about anyone else hurting him.

"Do you mind if I see Levi's room before I go?" she asked.

"Of course not." After sending off a quick text, Tressa stood. "It's this way," she said, heading back toward the living room before veering off down a hallway with fresh-looking camel-colored paint. "I made it like a racetrack," she said. "He loves it."

She stepped into an opened door halfway down the hall, and Lacey stopped. "Wow," she said, smiling again. The floor was a series of carpets painted with roadways. The walls matched, so there was no break in the road. There were stop signs, speed limit signs, stoplights. There was a park, and a store with parking lot spaces out front.

"He can run his cars to the store, the park…" Even a firehouse.

"Yeah. He loves it," she said again. "It was Amelia's idea. I'm the artist, though. I offered to do one for Jem so that Levi would have this at home, too, but he said it was good to keep it special for here so that Levi associated it with me."

She was dealing with a model couple for healthy divorced parenting. Levi had aware, concerned, loving parents who clearly doted on him.

The only problem was, no one could explain bruises on the little boy's body. No one was even admitting to seeing them.

Except a day care worker.

Who could have been wrong.

CHAPTER NINE

ON A WEDNESDAY morning in mid-May Jem received a call from social services, from Lacey Hamilton, telling him that while Levi's file would remain open for a required period, she had written a report clearing Jem of any suspicion. If there was any other report of concern, or hospital activity, that could change, she warned. But she'd found no evidence that Levi was being abused and saw no reason to continue an active investigation.

She did suggest that he and his ex-wife consider going back to counseling to maybe give Tressa ways to manage her emotions so that she could be around her son more often.

And she gave no indication who'd called her to make the mistaken report in the first place. It had to have been the hospital. A protocol thing due to the number of visits.

Before she'd hung up, Lacey had told him it had been a pleasure getting to know him and his family.

He wished he could say the same about her.

Yet...over the next couple of weeks, he thought

of her more than he might have expected, considering how relieved he was to have her out of his life.

As he grilled hot dogs for his son, he wondered what Lacey did when she was off work. Was she close to her twin? Did she have a big family—one that was all together and perfect and never at risk of having someone over your shoulder, trying to implode everything you'd worked so hard to build?

Not that he made a habit of feeling sorry for himself.

Of course, it didn't help that Tressa was in needy mode with an out-of-control job situation.

Or that his parents, who were solidly settled in Georgia, where Jem had grown up, had told him his older sister was going to be in LA sometime that summer and they thought it would be nice if he offered her a place to stay. It didn't matter to them that Santa Raquel was an hour north of the city.

Or that Jem and his only sibling had never been close.

Family was everything to them. As evidenced by the fact that both his maternal and paternal grandparents lived within five miles of his mom and dad. They all went to the same church, the one Jem had been raised in.

He supposed family was everything to him, too, in spite of the fact that he hadn't been able to wait to get out of Georgia and, as soon as he'd graduated high school, had packed up for the college as far from his hometown as he could get and still be in warm weather.

He called his sister and invited her to stay with him, and prayed that Lacey Hamilton didn't get another bug in her ear while JoAnne was in town. His sister made him nervous.

Family being everything to him was the only explanation he had to give himself for agreeing to spend four hours out on the golf course one Friday toward the end of May.

Jem was a baseball man, but when he'd thrown out his rotator cuff after making it as far as the farm team of a major league California baseball team, he'd had to face the fact that even though he'd healed well enough to have a normal range of activity, he'd never be able to throw a baseball the same. He then became a water-sport man.

"Listen, Mick, I know Tressa comes on strong sometimes, but you know as well as I do that she's gifted when it comes to knowing when, where and how to move money around." He shot wide and pretended to care.

"She told him to fuck himself."

He cringed. Closed his eyes and pictured himself and Levi sailing the ocean on a finished schooner that looked amazingly like the half-built one in his garage.

"She went that far?" he asked as the bank's

regional director, in from LA, made a perfect shot to the green and picked up his bag. With his own bag on his shoulder, he followed along, letting the older man set their pace.

"She didn't tell you?" The gray-haired man gave him a sideways glance. Mick Hunter, in his late sixties, had a gaze that was as sharp as any Jem had ever seen. Wrinkled skin and slowed pace aside, the man was as strong-willed as ever.

"Only that she'd been understandably upset and had said more than you thought appropriate."

Nodding, Mick walked in the direction of Jem's misplaced ball. He'd do better to get the game right so that he didn't wear out the man he was there to appease—on his ex-wife's behalf.

"She needs this job, Mick." He couldn't believe even Tressa had lost her composure to that extent. Not at work.

And wished he couldn't believe that she'd let him come into this meeting ill-prepared.

"I can't have the head office getting calls from wealthy investors because one of my managers doesn't have the ability to reel herself in."

"He called her a thief."

"He's a bit senile, Jem, and he wasn't understanding his most recent investment statement. All she had to do was listen to his concerns and explain things to him. And then, when he saw how upset she was by his accusation, he apologized. In person and in writing."

"Didn't he offer to pay her off for her trouble?" Jem said, dropping his bag as they reached his ball. Pulling a nine iron out of his bag, he lined up a shot for the tee. If he focused, he'd make it. "That's bribery." If he gave a rat's ass about the game, he'd probably be good at it. "Usually when a man offers a bribe, he has something to hide." Jem played his best card.

"He doesn't want his kids to know that he forgot about moving money from one fund to another. And he only offered her money after her response to his apology was...so inflammatory."

Straightening, Jem looked over at the other man. Mick's hat shaded his forehead, but not the serious light in his eyes, or the frown beneath that grayed mustache. That afternoon was the first he'd heard that the man had apologized at all, let alone in writing. Tressa said he'd tried to "pat her on the head" afterward.

"She mouthed off when he accused her," he clarified. She'd specifically said she'd been a bit tactless when the elderly investor had first accused her. Tressa wasn't one to admit to wrongdoing. So when she did, he knew she was telling him the truth.

"That's when she called him an asshole."

Obviously the "tactless" reference. *Oh, hell. Tressa, will you ever learn to hold your damned tongue inside your mouth?*

She wasn't anything like her parents; he'd give

her that. And couldn't imagine what it had been like growing up with them constantly berating her, withholding love on a regular basis.

But how much did she have to lose before she realized that people did not tolerate the verbal lashes that seemed perfectly normal to her?

Lord knew he'd tried to tell her. She thought he was the one who didn't get it. Until she was in trouble. Then she came running to him.

And so he came out to play golf. Or find some other way to chew on her crow.

"Okay, look, Mick, she made a mistake. She was pretty shaken up, a banker being accused of theft. She said the conversation took place where other customers could have heard him."

Tressa thought she had a case for slander. Jem didn't agree. He just needed her to be able to keep her job. He made good money, but he wasn't going to support Tressa forever. They were divorced. She had to learn to take care of herself.

But still, she was the mother of his child, and a woman with a good heart.

"And other than this one incident, she's been good for the bank," he continued. "She tells me your accounts have grown a third in the year and a half she's been there."

"She's good at helping people see how to get their money to work for them."

"Right." At least she had given that to him straight. "They benefit and so do you. Everyone wins. Which is a hell of a lot better than having a salesperson who can convince people to do anything, but then later have it not be good for them."

That kind of thinking backfired eventually, as Mick knew—and knew that Jem knew, too. Tressa had come into a branch that was on the verge of closure due, in part, to the previous manager's smooth tongue and inability to deliver the low interest rates and other terms he'd promised in order to close loans. After homes and cars had been purchased, sometimes even after a client was driving a new car, he'd call the client back with the bad news. If they wanted to keep the car, or have the house actually close, they'd have to agree to higher terms. Most often they did. But the bank had acquired enough of a clan of unhappy customers to do it measurable harm.

"Look, I appreciate what you did, Jem, delivering Tressa up to me at a time when I had no ready answer of my own. You hooking me up with her, that was decent. But I can't..."

"Let me talk to her," Jem interrupted before the man said something that would be difficult for him to take back. Mick had hired Tressa on Jem's word because Jem's company had built the half-million-dollar addition to the man's Beverly Hills home. He had to hope that his word would be good enough a second time. "I'll have her apologize, in writing, to the customer. And I'll make sure she understands that the customer comes first and she has to treat every one of them with respect. Even when they're rude."

The man looked at him, his eyebrows drawn together against the bright sun. "You sure you aren't making promises you can't keep?"

Tressa might be unhappy at work, but she wasn't stupid. Her alimony was up in the next month. And deep down, Tressa knew she didn't have a slander case. She'd have to actually prove that someone else had overheard what the elderly customer had said, and then prove that the statement had somehow damaged her or the bank. She didn't have a case.

As Amelia, her soul mate, and also a lawyer, had no doubt already told her.

"I'm sure. Just let me talk to her. You'll have something in writing before Monday."

Jem shot and made it to the green.

Not saying a word, Mick made the par three in two, watched while Jem made it in four and led the way to the next tee.

He never did actually agree to keep Tressa on, but Jem knew he'd won his ex-wife another chance. He just wished Tressa didn't put him in positions where he had to hang his own reputation on her. Most particularly when it came to people he liked and respected.

He'd stuck his neck out for her, getting her this

bank job after she'd walked out on the investment firm because an account she'd believed should have been hers had been given to someone else. The least she could do was see that his head didn't get cut off.

LACEY WENT HOME to San Diego for the Memorial Day holiday. She'd had fantasies about getting out of the traditional family barbecue at the beach cottage her parents had purchased when the twins were little. But in the end she'd gone. As she always did.

As she'd also known would be, Kacey's latest handsome guy was there, doting on her—as her sister certainly deserved. Kacey was beautiful, inside and out. *More* inside than out—which, looking at her, was hard to believe.

The guy this time, Dean Bates, didn't deserve Kacey, though. They never did. Kacey was so sweet and had such a selection lined up out her door, that she never had a chance to find a real guy. One who'd love her even if she wasn't Kacey Hamilton. *The* Kacey Hamilton. Of *The Rich and Loyal*.

Not that Kacey resembled her on-air heiress soap-opera character, Doria Endlin, all that much without the short blond wig and stage makeup.

Scrubbing at dishes they'd all left in the sink when they'd come in from a bonfire on the beach the night before, Lacey worried about her twin. Kacey was getting a little hard around the edges—with some brittleness seeping into her laugh.

"I was planning to help with that." Recognizing the voice almost as though it had come from inside her own head, Lacey glanced over her shoulder to see the subject of her thoughts grabbing a dish towel off the oven door handle and coming toward her.

"I was awake," Lacey said. "I've got to get back up north. I've got an appointment this afternoon." Truth be known, she'd planned to leave the night before, but when her sister had asked her to stay for the bonfire, she'd had a beer and sealed her fate for the night.

"Can't you just take one more day?" Kacey asked. If she'd been pouty, or whiny, Lacey wouldn't have had as hard a time answering.

She shook her head. She could make a phone call. Her only appointment that day, the Tuesday after Memorial Day, was with a potential new service to clean the rented office used by Santa Raquel social services. They'd been given the governmental all clear to switch services, and Lacey had been elected spokesperson for the department on the project.

"We've hardly had a chance to talk all weekend."

She finished with the small sauce dishes she'd washed first because they fit in the bottom of the drain board and she could stack other dishes on top of them. "What about Dean?" He'd been glued to her sister's side and was mainly the reason they'd had no time to talk.

"He left last night," Kacey said. "After everyone went to bed."

Lacey didn't just hear the things her sister wasn't saying. She felt them. Physically. In her gut.

Picking up a dish to dry before Lacey could put another on top of it, Kacey rubbed thoroughly.

Their father, a truck driver who'd had his own fleet of trucks by the time the girls were ten, had never put a dishwasher in at the cottage.

She might not have liked Dean, but... "I'm sorry." Because she knew Kacey was.

"Can't you stay, Lacey? Just one more day? We can go up to my place and you'd already be partway home."

Kacey owned a condo in Beverly Hills, the kind with a doorman and a half-acre all-adult pool with mountain views.

Lacey washed the watermelon bowl and the pot with baked beans caked on. Thank goodness they'd used paper plates.

"Even half a day," Kacey said, keeping right up with her drying duties. "We could leave within the hour and be at my place in time for a mimosa on the balcony."

Mention of alcohol on a Tuesday morning

bothered her a bit. But then, Kacey was still in holiday mode.

Looking at her sister, who was wearing no makeup and whose long blond hair was falling straight and loose, Lacey could have been looking at herself in the mirror. The experience would have been disconcerting if she hadn't had it her entire life.

"I'll make some calls," she said against her selfish wishes. She just needed to get home, back to her own space and the life she'd made for herself. The life she was happy with.

But when she felt Kacey's smile as well as saw it, when she sensed how much peace her capitulation brought her sister, who'd have done the same for her, she was glad she'd made the choice she'd made.

THEY HAD TEA instead of champagne and orange juice—partially because Kacey didn't have any champagne—leaving Lacey to wonder if her sister was drinking so much she'd forgotten that she'd finished off what she had, or wasn't drinking enough to know that at some point she'd opened the bottle she'd thought she'd saved.

As she put ice in their tea glasses, she didn't ask. Because she didn't want to know the answer.

But as soon as they were settled, bare feet up on the wrought-iron bars around Kacey's spacious covered sixteenth-floor patio, Lacey said, "I'm worried about you."

"I'm fine."

She wasn't.

"You drank twice as much this weekend as you normally do."

"I was thirsty."

Didn't assuage her concerns at all.

She could tell by the way Kacey watched the hills in the distance that her sister was avoiding her unspoken question and her heart sank. Because she also knew that Kacey wouldn't have asked her to stay if she didn't need her help.

"Is it a problem, Kace? Or are we still just at the warning stage?"

They'd talked about this before. Once. Right after Kacey's third broken engagement. Her sister had it all. Got it all. And sometimes all just wasn't enough. Because it wasn't what mattered.

Kacey's shrug out and out scared her.

"You drinking every night?"

"Maybe."

"A lot?"

"Not always."

"For how long?"

Kacey turned to her then, her blue eyes filled with pain. "Not long, Lace, I swear. I just... I love my job, but my character, she's not real. I know that. I don't even want her to be. I'd hate to live like she does. But everyone I know, everyone I meet, they all think I'm her and…"

Lacey had been thrilled when the offer had come in for Kacey to join *The Rich and Loyal* cast the year before. Until then she'd been making a very healthy living as a print and commercial model. But if she was smart with her money, the move to daytime television could secure her future for the rest of her life.

But she'd also been worried when the offer had come in. Because at heart, Kacey wasn't all that different from Lacey.

Other than that, where Lacey just filled the space her body took up, Kacey exuded all over every room she walked into.

"How much longer does your break last?" she asked now. *The R and L* cast was on summer break. She'd known that, but had just figured Kacey would be doing promos during the time off as she'd planned. She hadn't known until this weekend that her sister had turned down offers so she could spend her summer traveling with Dean, who'd yet to produce even a glimpse of the private jet he'd told her he owned. And, she was guessing, wasn't going to be around at all after the previous night's hasty departure.

"Another month."

"You want to come to Santa Raquel?" She didn't usually ask. Actually, she never did, as was evidenced by Kacey's open mouth as she turned to look at her.

"You're serious."

She nodded.

"But…"

Lacey had made a big deal about needing her own space. A *big* deal.

"You're the world to me, Kace." She'd rather live every moment of the rest of her life in Kacey's shadow if it meant keeping her sister healthy. And alive.

"I promise not to look at or talk to anyone," Kacey said.

She was serious, and Lacey felt sick. Physically, like she had a ball of warm, mushy clay in her stomach.

"I made a mistake, Kace." She prayed her sister was emotionally open enough to read her. "Those things I said, I was blowing off steam…"

"You were right."

"But it's not your fault. You don't *do* anything to attract people. They just gravitate to you."

"I'd give anything to send them your way. Well, not the Deans. But the good ones…"

For some bizarre reason a vision of Jem Bridges popped into her mind. "It's really okay," she said. "I've been on my own for more than a year." Since she'd moved out of the condo she was sitting in and transferred to the Santa Raquel branch of California state social services. "And I'm over all that." At least in any way that mattered.

"You aren't just saying this? You really want me to come up?"

How could her sister have been hurting this much over the talk they'd had when Lacey had told her she was moving out, and Lacey hadn't known?

"Look me in the eye," Lacey said now. And when Kacey's gaze was glued to hers, she leaned in closer. "Feel me, Kace."

Kacey nodded.

"Now you tell me. Do I want you to come up and stay with me?"

The tears that filled Kacey's eyes hurt Lacey's heart. And she was ashamed of herself for having caused her sister so much pain.

CHAPTER TEN

JEM HATED HOW much Lacey Hamilton's brief intrusion into their lives had affected them. If the vulnerable look on Tressa's face when he'd picked Levi up from Amelia's little beach house on Monday afternoon hadn't been enough, the fist clenching his own gut as he dropped Levi off at day care on Tuesday would have done it. But he'd already been disturbed by Lacey's effect on him.

Fantasies of the woman had followed him all over his boat as he'd spent the weekend alone in his garage, building his dream, with a couple of jaunts out to celebrate the holiday.

Dillon, his most trusted foreman and college buddy who'd dropped out to marry his pregnant girlfriend, had had him over on Saturday night for a barbecue with him and his family. On Monday he'd met a group of the guys at a local bar for a couple of brews.

Still, if it hadn't been for the social worker hanging around in the back of his mind all the time, he wouldn't have worried at all when he had to leave his son in safekeeping so he could get to work on time Tuesday.

Levi had been a little weepier than usual.

Weepy. A girlie term. Which didn't describe his son at all. But the little guy hadn't been whiny, and he really hadn't cried all that much, either.

He'd just almost cried over things that normally didn't bother him. Like being told that he had to go to day care when he'd wanted to spend the day with Jem.

And finding out that they were out of peanut butter and he'd have to have his toast with just jelly that morning.

The woman had said their file was still open, but with no active investigation. But what if she heard that Levi showed up at school out of sorts?

He knew why Levi was upset. And he kind of blamed Lacey Hamilton for that, too. When he was feeling particularly sour. Mostly he knew the woman had just been doing her job. That she'd invaded their lives out of true concern for Levi. And that she'd done exactly as he'd have wanted her to do, as he'd have done, if Levi were really in any kind of danger.

But didn't she see that her descending on them as she had had affected all of them?

Levi had had a nightmare Sunday night. According to Tressa, he'd been screaming for Jem. Because he'd dreamed that someone had come and taken him away from his father.

Which didn't totally make sense. He'd never given Levi even a hint about why Ms. Hamilton had been so briefly in their lives.

Unless... Had she?

"Tell me again about your dream...car," he said as they pulled into the day care. He'd promised himself he wouldn't bring up the nightmare unless Levi did. He didn't want to make it more than it was. The four-year-old had slept just fine the previous night at home in his own bed.

Jem knew because he hadn't slept much. And when he had, it had been with the nursery monitor on the pillow beside him.

"It's that one with spoilers on it that I already told you about." Levi sounded more sad than cantankerous.

Jem preferred cantankerous. That he knew how to deal with.

"You going to be okay at school today?" he asked.

"I wanna go to work with you."

"I know, but you can't. I'm on-site all day today, a smaller job without a trailer for you to stay in." Electric had been laid at a million-dollar house he'd been commissioned to build and the inspectors were coming out. "So you going to be okay in here?" He'd yet to shut off the car.

Looking from Jem to the school, Levi unfastened the belt on his car seat. "Can we be at the beach tonight?"

"Yep." *And have chocolate for dinner, too, if it will bring the smile back to your face.*

"Okay." It was a disgruntled sound, but Jem took it. He hoped that they were on their way past this most recent crisis.

When Tressa had called him, panicked, in the middle of the night because Levi had been flailing around in his bed and screaming and she'd been unable to wake him, Jem had thought his ex-wife was overreacting. Again. He'd told her to calm down, to rub Levi's back and talk to him and see if that woke him up. And then to call him back in five minutes.

She'd called him in ten. Levi had been having a chocolate cream cookie and a glass of milk.

The crisis had passed, he'd thought.

Once again he was back to wait-and-see.

He hated that place.

KACEY HAD BEEN with her almost a week and Lacey was getting spoiled. The little house she'd purchased a couple of blocks from the beach was spotless and she hadn't lifted a finger. Dinner was waiting for her no matter how late she got home each night. Her laundry was not only done, but hung in order exactly as she liked it.

And neither Lacey nor Kacey had had a single sip of alcohol.

"It's like you said," Kacey was saying as they

strolled along the beach the Saturday after Memorial Day. "I didn't need it, I just wanted it."

Lacey had hoped the words were true; she believed them to be true. Still, it was good to know for sure...

"If you kept your mind blurred, you didn't have to face what was really going on."

In denim shorts that showed off her long, tanned legs almost up to her butt, and a cropped white shirt, Kacey looked like every guy's dream—at least in Lacey's estimation—but for the frown on her face. It matched the vibe Lacey was getting.

"Talk to me," she said.

At Kacey's urging, Lacey had left her hair down that day. It hung even longer than Kacey's and had the same loose natural curls, giving it body. But where Kacey's hair glistened and hung sexily around her face, Lacey's looked dull and hung in her eyes. She didn't have to look in a mirror to know that.

It didn't matter if they both went to the same stylist, used the exact same product and washed their hair at exactly the same time... Kacey's hair had more glow.

Kacey kicked up sand with her bare toes and then turned to the water, standing and facing the horizon as her toes sank into the sand.

Waiting for a middle-aged couple who were holding hands to pass, Lacey joined her at the water's edge. She'd worn shorts, too. The six-inch ones she always wore. Black, that day. And a sleeveless, button-up white blouse with a little lace collar.

"I love my job," Kacey was saying. "I just don't like my life."

Kacey loved the condo she'd bought when they'd both received a healthy royalty check for a year's worth of commercials they'd done their last year of high school. Lacey had used the money to pay for college.

"You don't like the men in your life." Lacey homed in on the real problem, the one most difficult for her to talk about with her sister.

If ever there was a sore spot between the two of them, men would be it. Which was why Lacey usually kept her mouth shut on the subject.

With a sideways glance at Lacey, Kacey made a face. "You're right, I don't. But it's more than that. Being here…with you…it's making it all so much more clear to me."

"Being with me? Why?" Lacey frowned at her sister. Truly perplexed. Yeah, they shared a bond that was stronger than life. But they didn't have to be together to have it. It just was. Like their identical features.

"Just being here," Kacey said, shrugging.

A pair of twentysomething guys passed by. Closely. As though they'd made the trek down the beach specifically to get close to them. To Kacey. Neither one of them tried to meet Lacey's gaze, which was fine with her. She'd learned a long time before that life was about a lot more than looks.

"You've got a great life, Lace. Full, like you don't get home until after dark, and when you do, you're tired, but it's a good tired. Like you spent your day doing things that make you feel worthy. They fill you up. And...your house—it's like a real home. You have your own yard, a driveway."

"You can more than afford a house in Beverly Hills, Kacey. Or anywhere else, for that matter."

"I know."

The guys passed by a second time, making eye contact with Kacey. She turned back to the water.

"It's just...your house, your life...it feels like... substance, you know?"

"I live alone," she pointed out. "It's you being here that's giving my house all that substance and life you're talking about. Picture me coming home every night, to an empty house with no lights on, unless I failed to turn one off in the morning, with no dinner cooking and laundry to do. You'll be liking your life a whole lot better. At least you have hall lights and a doorman to greet you every night. You have people at the pool who greet you when you go down. Same for the gym on the third floor."

Lacey would still pick her house in Santa Raquel, but that was beside the point.

"Are you going to tell me about him?"

"About who?"

"Whatever guy's finally managed to snag your interest."

Lacey moved her foot in the sand sinking beneath her feet and almost lost her balance. "There's no guy in my life," she said quite clearly. "I haven't been on a date in over a year."

And then it had been a date Kacey had set her up on. Not that she was going to admit that to her.

Knowing the truth about the differences between her and her identical twin was one thing, looking pathetic because of them was another.

"I could date if I wanted to," she added, a tad bit defensively. She'd been asked out. She just hadn't wanted to go.

"Of course you could—you're gorgeous." Kacey was looking at her and then turned her head just a fraction. Lacey didn't need to turn around to know the two men had returned.

Her sister smiled, but then turned back around. "It's not a matter of you being capable of finding a date, Lace. It's a matter of you being open to finding a date."

She didn't want to talk about it.

"And something tells me that you've met someone."

She hadn't said a word. And just because one particular face kept showing up in her thoughts didn't mean that anything had changed in her life.

"You're imagining things," she said now, waiting for Kacey to turn back around and put the guys out of their misery. Hoping at this point that she would. And was uncomfortable when she didn't.

"You watched that aftershave commercial last night like you were memorizing every detail," Kacey said.

The guy in the commercial had been a construction worker. She'd taken a little side trip, trying to remember if the only other construction worker she knew personally, Jeremiah Bridges, wore cologne.

"That's ridiculous," she said now, wondering how long they were going to stand there staring at the horizon with the ocean lapping at their feet. Until the tide came in? The tips of her shorts would get wet and she hated driving with the wet, soppy feeling at the back of her knees.

"You had a pretty good study of the men's underwear section at the department store the other evening."

It was the whole "boxers or briefs" thing. Yeah, Jeremiah's face—and, well, other imagined parts of him—had come to mind, but that only meant the guy was memorable.

He was a reprobate. And prickly, too. The fact that he stood out in her mind was hardly her fault.

"You're wearing your hair down." Kacey broke into Lacey's silence.

"You told me to!" No hiding the accusation in that tone.

"I always tell you to. You never listen."

"I do, too." Pretty much every time her sister nagged her, she'd leave her hair in a ponytail rather than putting it up in the twist she preferred.

"I want what you have, Lace," Kacey said.

"I don't have anything."

"You have a chance."

"Right. Like you don't?"

"You think I'm going to meet some nice normal guy who'd like to make a real home with me?" Kacey's pain cut through Lacey's defenses.

"You will," she said, grabbing her sister's hands and turning her to face her. "Just stop spending all of your time in the clubs and Hollywood hangouts."

"I go to the library one night a week," Kacey told her. "I actually joined a book club. Not a single normal guy has even talked to me."

Because she effervesced sex and power and money, which intimidated "normal" guys. Even when they'd been little with parents who'd had a middle-class income, Kacey had fit right in with the celebrities they'd encountered at the studios, as though she'd been born to be a star.

Lacey had liked the work, liked a lot of the places they got to go; she'd just been more reserved. It had been a lot easier to let Kacey charm all of the strangers with whom they'd come in contact. She was a natural at it.

Lacey had no idea what to tell her. Except...

"Well, one thing you can do is stop going out with guys who clearly aren't what you're looking for."

Nodding, Kacey dropped one of her hands, kept hold of the other and started walking again.

"So...you aren't going to tell me who he is?"

"There is no one."

"I understand, you know?"

"Understand what?"

"Why you won't tell me."

"There's nothing to tell."

Kids ran and played in the sand. Some darted in and out of the chilly Pacific waters. Men, women, teenagers lounged in the sand. It was Santa Raquel in the summertime and Lacey loved it.

"It's okay, Lace."

"What is?"

"That you don't want me to meet him."

Oh, God.

Stopping in her tracks, she pulled her sister to an abrupt stop, as well. A girl jogging on the beach veered around them and gave them a dirty look.

"It's not that," she said, looking Kacey in the eye. "I swear, Kacey." Though, if truth be told, if there really was a guy, then...maybe...

"I just want you to know that I understand. I don't blame you if..."

"He's a client, Kace," she said, words pouring out of her without forethought. "Or rather, was a client. Very briefly. He doesn't even like me. I swear, I'm not seeing anyone. I just…think about him. No clue why. And I'm going to make sure I stop."

"He wasn't hurting a kid, was he?" Kacey knew what she did for a living, in every detail Lacey was at liberty to give.

"Of course not." Jeremiah Bridges doted on Levi, who obviously not only adored his dad, but felt secure with him, too. It hadn't taken Lacey long to assess that one.

"So…he's…"

"Nothing." Lacey started walking again back the way they'd come, toward the car. They could go shopping again, or something. "He's nothing. So nothing he wasn't worth mentioning except that I couldn't have you thinking I don't trust you."

"It's not a matter of trusting me," Kacey said. "You know I'd never date a guy you even thought you liked."

Yeah, she did know that. Kacey was right. She wasn't the problem.

Guys were.

CHAPTER ELEVEN

JEM COULDN'T BELIEVE his eyes when he pulled into Uncle Bob's on Saturday, glanced toward the beach and saw Lacey Hamilton in double. In both forms his fantasies had taken. One was drably overdressed, and the other rather undressed. He skipped over the version with long, tanned legs exposed, and stared at the one with loose black cotton shorts that hung to her knees.

He much preferred taking his time to unwrap his own package, not have it arrive out of the wrapping. He'd always been weird that way.

But her hair... It was the first time he'd seen those blond locks down in real life. It fell almost to her waist and he...

"Come on, Dad!" Levi's little feet kicked the back of his seat and he heard his son unfasten the belt in his car seat. "We haveta eat."

They were a little late for lunch. He'd taken Levi to work with him as he always did on Saturday morning and had been occupied much longer than planned getting through the list of problems his foremen had handed him during their weekly meeting. Nothing he couldn't handle, though. A straight driveway that was now going to be curved. Some wiring that had blown when a drywall screw had missed a stud. Windows that didn't fit. And roof tiles that had been delivered in black rather than the rust brown the customer had ordered.

Keys in hand he got out of the truck, opened the backseat door to help Levi down and watched as the two women made their way slowly toward the beach parking lot that was adjacent to Uncle Bob's.

He wasn't going to call out to her. He didn't ever want to see her again.

"It's her and her twin, Dad! See?" Levi said, loudly enough for anyone in the parking lot to hear. Uncle Bob's parking lot, not the adjacent one.

So much for thinking that the woman had given his son nightmares.

"Yeah, I see." Jem, giving a small tug on Levi's hand, turned toward the restaurant. "And her name is Lacey."

"Lacey!" Levi called out immediately. Not at all what he'd intended. Should have kept his mouth shut...

He thought about telling his son they absolutely did not want to see the other woman. Telling him that for their own safety they had to stay away from her. But he couldn't figure out how to do so when Levi had been told she was a friend.

He'd let her take Levi alone to a playroom. He'd let her in their home, to see Levi's room and most prized possessions.

The women were almost at the first row of cars. He didn't see the one that had been parked outside his home on one of the worst nights of his life.

"La-a-a-a-a-ceeeeey!" Levi called again, turning around to watch her as Jem pulled him toward Uncle Bob's.

"She stopped!" Levi said, digging his feet into the graveled pavement. Deciding that dragging his son in front of his ex–social worker wouldn't be a smart move—he'd never drag him, period— Jem stopped, too.

"Come on, Dad! She sees us!" Levi was pulling him now, away from Uncle Bob's front door.

Coming up with no other options, Jem looked toward his son's goal. "I want to see a twin." Levi's voice was not getting any softer.

"You've seen twins before," he told the boy. If he'd been able to remember when, he'd have pointed the instance out to him. There weren't any in preschool, that he could think of. None of Jem's buddies had twins... Surely...

"Hi, Lacey!" Levi called as they got close to the women. Short-shorts was coming toward them now. Jem knew an uncanny disappointment that the big, welcoming smile on the unknown woman's face didn't also appear on the identical face next to hers.

Clearly Lacey was no happier about this meeting than he was.

Or than he wanted to be.

But, damn, she looked good.

"You still got my car?" Levi asked as they all met at the guardrail separating the two lots. "The green one with the turbos?"

Lacey's grin lit up the sunshiny day as she knelt down. "Why, yes, I do, Levi. I just saw it when I was in the playroom yesterday and I thought of you."

She'd had another child in that room. Someone else she was investigating. Possibly ripping from his or her home.

A child in danger whom she could be saving from serious harm.

Her job couldn't be easy.

"I wanted to see a twin," Levi told her, his hands on the guardrail that came up almost to his chin.

"Hi, I'm Kacey." Jem saw the perfectly manicured fingers reaching toward him, noticed the shiny polish and looked into eyes that weren't Lacey's. Instead of seeing a sunset, he was blinded by the light.

"I'm Jem," he said, taking the hand, shaking it. He was curious, but not moved at all. Which was crazy, since he couldn't get Lacey Hamilton out of his mind and the only difference between the two was the fact that Lacey had threatened to take his son away from him.

Sort of.

"Dad, Lacey says that her sister's visiting her. We're having a sister visit, too, huh?"

Levi had overheard his phone conversation with his sister. It had been brief. *Mom and Dad said you were coming. You're welcome to stay with us.* She accepted the invitation. Told him she'd let him know the exact date of her arrival—sometime in August. And they'd hung up.

"Yes, we are," he said now, embarrassed as hell as he looked at the two identically gorgeous women. He thanked God they couldn't read his mind as he tried to wipe it clean of every fantasy he'd ever had. About them, or anyone else.

"We're going at Uncle Bob's," Levi said next. "Do you like Uncle Bob's?" The question was directed at Kacey.

"I've never been there," Lacey's look-alike said, kneeling down as Lacey rose. "I'm visiting, remember?"

"Does Aunt JoAnne know Uncle Bob's?" Levi was frowning as he peered up at Jem.

"No, son." JoAnne had been at his home only once, and hamburgers at the beach weren't her thing. At least not if Jem thought it was a good idea. Maybe if Levi made the suggestion...

"Well, you should bring her here if you like

them so much," Kacey was saying while Jem stared at Lacey. With her hair down she looked more...approachable.

He smiled at her.

And then grinned like an idiot when she smiled back.

"We could bring you, couldn't we, Dad?" Levi turned to look at Jem, who felt like he'd been caught with his pants down.

"Well..."

"No, we were just heading home," Lacey said. "We've got..."

"I'd love to have an Uncle Bob's sandwich," Kacey blurted just a little too loud. "I'm starving. We haven't had lunch yet, either."

"We had a late breakfast," Lacey said, looking at her sister.

"I'm starving," Kacey said again.

And then the strangest thing happened. Lacey Hamilton stared at her sister. Her shoulders straightened. And she agreed to have lunch with them.

If they weren't intruding, of course.

Of course he had to say they weren't.

And tried not to feel like he should be adding a fifty-thousand-dollar deposit to his son's college account.

SHE'D HAVE TO have lunch. Kacey had figured out that Jeremiah Bridges was the client Lacey had mentioned. She knew it the second she'd met her twin's gaze. Probably based on some unconscious reaction Lacey had made. She never had been able to hide anything from Kacey.

Which was both good and bad.

"I apologize," Jem, as he'd told Kacey to call him, said as he walked behind Kacey, who was being led by Levi, and next to Lacey toward a table out on the patio that overlooked the beach. "If you had plans…"

"We really didn't," Lacey told him. The only way she was going to prove to her sister that Jem Bridges meant nothing to her was to make it so.

Clearly she wasn't going to be able to hide.

"Your sister seems nice."

"She is. She's my best friend."

They were through the restaurant and almost outside. Another few feet and she could grab a chair next to Kacey and across from…

"I want to sit next to Lacey and you can sit there," Levi said to Kacey, pointing to the seat directly across from him. "We can play the peg game."

There was a triangular board with holes in it that held golf tees, and the object was to jump tees until there was only one left. It was harder than it looked.

"Have you ever been here before?" Jem asked as he took the seat across from Lacey.

"No."

"Lacey's only been here a year and a half and she works all the time," Kacey said. Lacey would have kicked her under the table if she hadn't been afraid of catching Jem's ankle in the process.

Pulling her hair back, she took the elastic she'd slipped around her wrist as they'd headed out and used it to secure a ponytail. There. At least she could be somewhat business-minded.

"Where did you live before you came here?" Jem asked, looking like he might grin again as he watched her secure her hair.

"With me," Kacey piped in. And then, with a pointed look at Lacey, proceeded to become absorbed by the golf tees Levi was putting in and out of holes with no rule following whatsoever.

"You lived with your sister?"

"While I was in college," Lacey said. "And then I just stayed."

"I'd rather see my sister...never," Jem told her with an unapologetic air that she kind of liked. "A phone call every few years would do me fine."

She looked over at her sister, sure that Jem really just wanted to hear about her. And knowing she could comply.

Knowing, too, that the surest way for her to convince Kacey that she had no interest in Jem Bridges was to see him go gaga over her sister. It worked every time. If her goal was to never have a boyfriend.

Which, this time, it was.

"Kacey really is my best friend," she said now. "I don't know what I'd do without her."

"Where is she visiting from?"

"She owns a condo in Beverly Hills."

That was a sure head turner.

"Really." Jem nodded, glancing at Levi and then back at Lacey. "I like the city, but I'd never want to live there."

"You've never been to Kacey's place. The pool alone is on half an acre of paradise."

"So why didn't you stay there?"

"I wanted…"

To be out from underneath my sister's shadow.

"A home." *Lame, Lacey. Really lame.* "A house, I mean."

"So you have a house here in town?"

"A couple of blocks over."

"You walked here?"

"I do most nights. Even in the winter. It's one of the reasons I bought the house. It was close to the beach."

He wondered where *she* lived. He wanted to know about Kacey—that internal reminder put a stop to her wondering.

"Kacey's a movie star, Dad! On TV like Whyatt Beanstalk!" Levi's voice boomed over several tables as he named the star of *Super Why!*, one of his current favorite videos.

"Inside voice, son," Jem said while people all around them turned to stare.

"Don't worry, they won't know me. Not without my wig and pounds of makeup," Kacey told Jem. She didn't lean over, didn't make eye contact. But it wouldn't matter.

He'd be leaning in her direction any second now.

"Tell him," Levi said. "You said you're on TV…"

"I said Lacey and I both were on TV."

Lacey could feel the heat creeping up her skin. Kacey knew she hated to be outed.

"But you aren't anymore." Jem's half question was aimed at her.

"Kacey is. She's Doria Endlin from *The Rich and Loyal*."

He shook his head. "I'm sorry, I don't watch daytime television." He smiled at Kacey.

That was that. Lacey glanced at Levi, then prepared to relax and enjoy lunch with the little boy.

"What show were *you* on?"

It took her a second, and a miraculously well-placed kick from under the table, for Lacey to know that Jem had been directing the question at her.

"Me? I wasn't ever on a show."

"We did commercials mostly," Kacey said. "From the time we were two. Mom cashed in on the whole blonde twin thing."

"She never pushed us, though," Lacey quickly pointed out.

"Nope, we loved it and wanted to do it," Kacey said.

Jem was studying her. "I find it hard to picture you loving being in front of a camera."

"I loved playing make-believe with Kacey," she said, shocked that she'd been quite that open. "I loved the different places we got to go and the things we got to do..."

"Lacey got to be on a race car one time, Dad," Levi said.

While Jem cocked his eyebrow at her, Lacey noted that Levi had remembered a minor detail from weeks before. Not normal developmental stage for a four-year-old. Usually their memories didn't stretch back much beyond a week or so, if that. They were too busy moving forward to hang on to what was behind them. And...

"Lacey," Kacey said, laughing. "Tell him about that commercial..."

They'd burned their fannies on the hot metal, sitting on the hood of that car. Lacey had quickly figured out that if they took the labels off the cans of motor oil they were there to sell, they could sit on them. Only problem had been when the prompt came to hold up the cans in front of the camera and all they had to sell was blank tin cans.

"You're the one who got to ride in the car," she said quickly and turned to the child at her side.

"Remember, Levi? I told you my twin sister got to ride in the car..."

Because Kacey had asked; Lacey hadn't wanted to be a bother.

"What happened at the shoot?" Jem was half grinning as he watched her across the table while Kacey told Levi all about her trip around the track in a real race car when she wasn't much older than him.

Just to kill time, Lacey told Jem about the short little dresses and Mary Jane shoes they'd been given to wear. About the hot metal on the hood of the car. And taking off the labels to save their backsides. When he laughed out loud, drawing attention to their table again, she ducked her head.

Because she'd wanted to laugh right along with him.

CHAPTER TWELVE

"KACEY'S PRETTY LIKE MOMMY, and Lacey's nice like Amelia." Levi's words blasted into the silence that had fallen when their food came.

Tressa and Kacey were pretty and Lacey was nice? Implying that Lacey, who was identical in looks to Kacey, didn't appear pretty to a four-year-old?

Jem had taken a bite of burger when Levi's voice first hit him.

And then Jem blurted, "Don't talk with your mouth full." His own words didn't do much better, following a full twenty seconds behind his son's.

It was, by far, the most embarrassing moment of Jem's entire life. And considering how many times his older sister had tried to humiliate him when he was growing up, that was saying a lot.

"Well, thank you for the lovely compliment, Levi." Kacey recovered first, leaning forward to smile at the boy and hand him another French fry. Probably in an effort to fill the little mouth to prevent it from uttering another word. Jem figured she was onto something.

And that his son absolutely was not. Lacey was far more beautiful than either Tressa or Kacey.

Wait. Lacey and Kacey were identical twins. Both of them were far more beautiful than Tressa.

But then when Jem looked at his ex-wife he saw the sense of entitlement that had her walking out on perfectly good jobs because things weren't going the way she'd deemed they should. The drama that made life's challenges so much harder to handle than they had to be.

"I'm sorry." Jem leaned over to say the words quietly to Lacey. He couldn't just let his son's misspoken words hang unaccounted for. "He…"

Shaking her head, Lacey smiled at him, taking another bite of her grilled turkey and tomato sandwich. "He thinks I'm nice," she said. "You have no idea how much of a compliment that is to me, considering how we met. A lot of my kids hate the sight of me."

Yet she obviously cared so much about them. She had about Levi. And he wondered again about her job. About her. How did she do it? Giving her all to people who didn't want her around? Why did she?

"It's just the clothes," he said and then wished he'd bitten his tongue instead. Literally. "You probably noticed that Tressa puts a lot of emphasis on fashion…"

"She told you I went to visit her?"

Right, because all he'd heard from Lacey after that was that the case had been dismissed. Jem had no idea what all Tressa might have told her, which was why his usual way—to tell the truth—just worked best.

"I was on the phone with her when you pulled up out front of her house."

"Did you tell her who I was?"

"No."

She took another bite of sandwich, seemingly unaffected by Levi's unintentionally hurtful comment.

"Why not?"

He'd just reminded himself that he was a truthful guy. "Because I didn't want her to freak out on the phone." He popped a French fry into his mouth. The mushroom burger was good today. Talking to her was better, even if he *was* having to make up for his son. "The whole drama thing I told you about," he continued as she chewed.

"And also because I figured that if she had been the one who called you, she'd already know who you were. I kind of wanted to see how she handled you coming to the door."

"To see if you could figure out if she knew me?"

"Something like that."

"What was your conclusion?"

"Tressa didn't call you."

He watched her carefully—very carefully—
and still couldn't discern if he'd hit on the truth.
He was sure he had, but not because of any indication he'd gathered from her.

"So what do you think?" Lacey nodded toward
Kacey's half of the sandwich they'd shared.

"Really good," Kacey answered. "You?"

It was as though something tangible passed
across the table. Jem almost felt as though he was
intruding as he sat there.

"Fine. Good. I'd order it again," Lacey said.
And Jem knew they weren't talking about food.

Which meant what? That Kacey was asking
her sister if she was okay?

He hoped so. Because based on Lacey's answer, she wasn't as bothered by Levi's comment
as he still was. But he was still rational enough
to realize he was stretching things. She'd probably just liked the sandwich.

And really, what woman could take offense at
someone saying her sister was beautiful when
she was an identical twin?

Kacey and Lacey were still speaking. Silently.
But it was palpable.

"So, I was thinking…" Kacey said, swinging
her head from Lacey's direction to his. "You said
you're in construction, right?"

This was in answer to a question she'd asked
while they'd been waiting for their waitress to
take their orders.

"Right."

"Is that the bill?" Lacey asked, turning as their waitress approached. "I'll get this."

"I'll get it," Jem said, already reaching for his wallet. "A gentleman doesn't invite pretty ladies to eat with him and let them pick up the tab. Even when he's only four."

Their waitress passed them by without stopping and Jem looked up from his wallet to see Lacey giving her sister a steely-eyed stare.

He had to admit, he was curious as hell. So he said directly to Kacey, "You were asking about my business..." Just because... Well, he wasn't sure why.

"That's right, I was," Kacey said, turning so that she faced him completely. Body and all, giving her sister her right shoulder. "Our birthday's coming up in another month and I've already decided what I want to give Lacey."

"Kacey..." Lacey sounded pained now.

"What's that?" he asked. Somehow the woman of his fantasies was getting hot about something. He had to pursue this.

"An enclosed sunroom and garden," Kacey said. "She's got this piece of land off the side of her house that's virtually unusable. Wasted space. She's always loved fountains and flowers and loves to read. And now that I'm going to be visiting on a regular basis, I'll use it, too."

"There's no way in—" Lacey glanced at Levi

"—no way you're going to pay for an addition on my house."

Kacey shrugged. "I can always just transfer the money into your account…"

"And it will sit there unspent."

Chins were jutting. Jem sat back, fascinated. Even Levi, who'd been eating French fries and playing with the golf tee board, stopped to watch.

"I'll call Dad and tell him—" Kacey started.

"Stop right there." Lacey spoke sharply enough that once again their table got a few looks from patrons at other tables. "Seriously, I'm not going to let you do this, Kace."

"You were just saying a couple of days ago that a sunroom would be the perfect use for that space."

"I know, but I wasn't being serious."

"You don't want a sunroom?" Jem did his part to keep the conversation going.

"No!" Lacey looked back at Kacey after a brief glance in his direction. "At least, well, yes, I'd love one, but you are not paying for it." That last bit was directed at Kacey.

"Then I'm giving the car back to you," Kacey said, and there was no doubting that she meant business.

"What car?" Jem asked, enjoying himself far too much.

"We did a shoot three years ago," Lacey said, looking at Jem again briefly. "It was for a major car manufacturer. The commercials aired for a full quarter and they wanted us to be seen driving in the car."

"A red convertible sports car," Kacey told him. "Lacey said she couldn't possibly drive to work in a car like that and my car had just been totaled, no fault of mine, so I ended up with the car. We were both in the commercial and people can't tell us apart, anyway, so it didn't really matter which one of us was driving it."

"You did a car commercial when you were little, too," Jem mused, fascinated by the turn the day had taken.

"That was for motor oil," Lacey said. "And you are not giving me the car."

"Then I'm giving you a sunroom with a garden. Or calling Dad."

"You wouldn't."

"I think you know I would."

Another stare-out ensued. Levi was playing with the tees, but Jem could tell his son was getting restless. Instead of putting the little wooden pegs in and out of the holes, he was lining one up and using another to kick the first one off the board. If they didn't end this, tees could be flying soon...

"Let me get this right," he jumped in, because a guy knew that when he had a possible opportunity at his door that he didn't want to miss, he should reach out and grab it if he could.

And a dad knew when he had to move quickly. "You want to pay me to build a room on Lacey's house?"

"And a garden," Kacey said, looking only at him now.

Out of the corner of his eye, Jem saw Lacey reach over and put all the pegs back in their holes, putting the board in front of Levi so that he could jump pegs again. Expecting his son to push the board away, he was surprised to see Levi turn back to his task.

"I think she means hire your company," Lacey said. "And it's not going to happen."

Kacey reached for the small pouch she'd unclipped from her waistband and put on the table, pulling out a cell phone.

She pushed a button. "Hey, Dad!" she said, her expression completely serious as she looked at her sister.

"Hang up." Lacey's words came out with a bite. And a look that he was pretty sure could mean that he'd just won himself an excuse to be around his fantasy woman for a good part of the summer.

Lacey filled Levi's board again, this time leaving a different hole empty from which he had to start.

After a few minutes of chatting about the weather, the shopping she and Lacey had done, what they'd eaten and what they'd watched on television, Kacey asked after her mom and dad, talked about an ankle brace and the broccoli they'd left in the fridge at the cottage and rang off.

Levi took the pencil Lacey had pulled out of her purse and was pressing it to the napkin she'd put in front of him.

"So we're agreed?" Kacey said in the same breath as "Bye, Dad."

"Fine."

"So." Kacey turned to him. "I'm giving my sister a sunroom and a garden for her birthday…"

"Only a sunroom."

Kacey stared for a minute. And then said, "Fine, only a sunroom." She turned back to Jem. "Would you like the job?"

"His company," Lacey said. "Jem's the boss of foremen. Who are the bosses of the men who actually do the work."

He didn't see any point in arguing the point. He hadn't always been the boss. He was fully licensed and proficient in every aspect of the framing, drywall and electrical work his men did. And occasionally, he kept a smaller job for himself. To keep himself sharp. Or because he wanted the excuse to spend more time with the first woman who'd captivated him in a very long time.

"I'm happy to come take a look," Jem said, using his professional voice. "I'll give you a quote and see what you think."

"Good!" Kacey smiled.

Lacey's face was completely straight.

Levi burped.

"On one condition," Jem said, prolonging the high he was on for another second or two.

"What's that?" Kacey didn't look bothered. In spite of the hopeful rise of Lacey's brow.

"Tell me why Lacey didn't want you calling your dad."

"Oh," Lacey said, her tone dry. "I can answer that. Dad fancies himself a self-made do-it-yourselfer. He gets the jobs done, but there's always something a little off about things. Like a floor that's not quite level..."

"A door that doesn't close right."

"Trim with a bit of a gap in the corner."

"Electrical outlets that aren't live."

"Switches that you have to turn up to turn off and down to turn on."

Both girls were chuckling. Jem was grinning.

"Remember the time he put that sink out in the shed, and when Mom mentioned that it was dripping, he said he knew and it wasn't a problem—they'd just keep a bucket under it?"

"And your mother's okay with all of this?"

"Heck, no!" the women answered in unison. Same words. Same intonation. And he still heard Lacey's voice. "Anytime Mom needs something done, she calls a professional before she tells Dad," Lacey told him.

"He doesn't take offense?"

"Probably. But he still putters, has his projects.

He's building a shed, complete with electric and plumbing, at their beach cottage in San Diego..."

Her parents had a beach cottage. So did his. A place for family to gather.

For some reason the thought bothered him.

CHAPTER THIRTEEN

IF LACEY DIDN'T love her sister so much, she'd strangle her.

"Face it, Lacey, you're glad I did what I did."

She wanted to argue, but knew it was pointless. "Part of me is still angry with you."

"I know, but that part of you needs an attitude adjustment."

"Offering to take Levi to the park while Jem and I go over the plans was overkill."

"To the contrary, it gets me out of here."

"I don't need you out of here, Kace. It's okay. I'm not twenty anymore. You and I are connected at the hip, which means that any guy who likes me is going to see you, too. If I can't trust him in that situation, then what's the point in liking him?"

"So you admit it. You do like him?"

"No! I'm telling you that the things I said when Ramsey dumped me for you as soon as he met you...they were wrong. It wasn't about you. Or me, either. It was him. That was more than ten years ago, and I can't believe I brought it up last year. I am disgusted by and so sorry for the horrible and stupid and childish things I said."

She'd hoped, at least, that the memory had faded with time. She wasn't proud of herself for going off on her sister, her soul mate, when it was herself and the world's reaction to her that had really had her upset.

"But you were right, too," Kacey said. Her eyes clouded over as she tucked her heels up to her butt on the side of the hot tub, where they were ending their Saturday night with a glass of wine. They'd walked back to the beach. Watched a movie. And still hadn't been ready to turn in.

Lacey's next-door neighbor was out of town for the summer and, in exchange for her watching the house, she'd been granted unlimited use of the hot tub.

"I was the one who got to ride in the race car. Every single time we went on a job where they could only take one of us, I was the one who was chosen. There wasn't one boy in high school who asked you out first. And when you brought your college boyfriend home to spend Christmas with the family, he met me and dumped you. It all happened, Lacey, just as you'd said. There were things that you left out, too. We walk into a room, people reach out to shake my hand. Not yours. I feel guilty as hell. I hate it. But I don't know how to change it."

"You aren't going to change it," Lacey told

her. "You aren't meant to. Your personality is just different from mine. More bold. You're outgoing. I'd rather stand in a corner. You always know the right thing to say. I tell the truth even when it's best to keep my mouth shut. You shine, Kace. I don't."

Silence fell for a time. They both sipped their wine. And then Lacey chuckled. "Remember the time you insisted that I put glitter all over my skin so that I'd stand out more than you would?"

"That was a disaster," Kacey said. Lacey's skin had had a reaction to the spray; she'd itched like crazy and had welts all over by the end of the evening.

"But it made senior prom memorable!" Lacey really could laugh about it now. She hadn't liked the guy she'd been with any more than Kacey had liked her date. But they'd loved the chocolate ice cream their dad had gone out to get for them as a consolation prize. It had been waiting for them when Mom had finished rubbing the topical antibiotic all over Lacey's welts after the twenty-minute shower she'd insisted Lacey take.

"Mom and Dad were going to ground me for that one," Kacey said now.

"Which wasn't fair. You were only trying to help."

"And you ended up coming to my rescue. Like usual."

Funny that Kacey would say that. Lacey had

always felt like Kacey was the sister who solved their problems. But maybe she hadn't been. Maybe Kacey's bright light, her always coming in first to Lacey's second, had blinded Lacey to a truth or two.

And maybe this new sunroom, this attempt of her sister's to do something big for Lacey, was as important for Kacey as it could be for her.

"Anyway, it seemed like the decent thing to do, offering to take the little guy to the park, since Jem's coming out on a Sunday to look at the project. It's not like there's a day care open or anything."

It was all highly unusual. A contractor making a nonemergency house call on a Sunday. A woman buying her sister a room for her birthday.

Lacey being so obsessed with Jeremiah Bridges.

"Just make sure you don't stay gone too long," she said. And hoped she hadn't just given her sister any more bad ideas.

JEM HAD NEVER been more energized giving a quote in his life. Nor had he cut his costs quite so much. He had one goal in mind—to make damned sure he got the bid. And he couldn't even explain that.

He hardly knew the woman, had spent less than one full working day with her all told.

But she had a hold of him.

And he wasn't fighting it.

It felt too damned good.

So good that his mood didn't sour when Tressa called to tell him that she really wanted to quit her job. Even after he'd stuck his neck out for her. She didn't think it was right that she'd had to apologize when she was the one who'd been slandered.

It also wasn't right, according to the thirty-minute tirade he listened to, that she had to smile and be gracious when people were rude to her. It wasn't fair. She'd been hired to make the bank money while keeping customer interests in mind. She was doing that. Brilliantly.

She felt underappreciated and that was no way for a person to have to feel every single day.

Plus Mick was watching over her too much now. She felt like she was on trial and the stress was getting to her.

He asked her what Amelia had to say about it all.

She said Amelia was her rock.

And then told him, again, that she wanted to quit her job.

He told her she needed to stick it out, reminded her that he'd put his reputation on the line at her request and added that her alimony was ending. It had to end, he told her.

At which point she surmised that he was having financial difficulties and rang off before he could tell her about them.

Or tell her she was wrong. Which he wouldn't

have done, even though she *was* wrong. The defensive tongue-lashing that would ensue wasn't worth the satisfaction of pointing out the obvious.

Good news was, she no longer had the right to view any of his financial data.

Tressa could drain blood from a turnip.

But not from him. Not anymore.

FOR THE FIRST time in...ever...Lacey had to fight an urge to leave work right on time that next week. She did her job as well as always. She took time for casual conversation with her coworkers—keeping connected to what mattered most—and volunteered for extra duties.

But while she gave her all to these activities, as usual, she struggled with the idea that she had a sister at home who had to be kept under control. Now that Jem was in the picture.

He was there three nights that week when she got home, as she'd known he was going to be—Kacey's arrangements, not hers.

Her sister was paying for the job Jem had been hired to do. Technically he was working for her, and she wanted things well under way before she had to get back to Beverly Hills and the taping of the next season of *The Rich and Loyal.* Hard to believe that they were already well into Kacey's second week in Santa Raquel.

Lacey's driving need to be home had nothing to do with keeping her sister from being alone with Jem. She swore that fact to herself every single day as she refused to give in to the drive to get home before Jem arrived. She only wanted to make certain that she was a part of the choices being made for the home she owned and would be living in.

A couple of times she acknowledged to herself that while Jem's guaranteed eventual response to Kacey didn't matter to her, she didn't trust Kacey not to tell Jem more about her than Lacey wanted him to know.

That her sister was on a mission to get Lacey hooked up with a man she was truly hot for went without question. Kacey openly admitted to the plan to Lacey.

That didn't mean she was going to be successful. She wasn't. Kacey had no control over men's reactions to her. Or to Lacey.

Which was why there was no need for Lacey to try to minimize Jem's alone time with her dazzling sister. Nothing was going to change the fact that Lacey just didn't measure up in the exuding department.

At least not practically speaking.

What the week did do was show Lacey how much her sister loved her. She knew, anyway, but, still, it filled her heart, and broke it, too, to see Kacey trying so hard to be invisible. Didn't matter what she wore in the makeup or clothes department, didn't matter what she did with her hair, Kacey entered a room with her eyes open and people were drawn to her.

It wasn't her fault. There was nothing either of them could do about it.

Maturity had brought that knowledge to Lacey's heart.

Moving away, having a life of her own where the two of them weren't being compared, where she wasn't always seen side by side with her sister, had been her way of dealing with reality. Of finding her own peace. Her sense of self and a chance to be truly happy.

And a chance to let Kacey be happy, too. Feeling guilt for something you couldn't help was excruciating. Hurting the one who was a part of you from the womb wasn't something you could ever be at peace with.

Jem measured and brought computerized drawings. Lacey signed city permit forms. Twice that week Kacey had pushed the two of them—Lacey and Jem—out the door to go look at flooring, screens, paint swatches, while Kacey entertained Levi at Lacey's house.

She'd chattered about the house. Asking questions about the framing process. Pouring the floor, leveling it. Running electric. Keeping her mind focused so it didn't run away with her.

He cooperated nicely. Answering questions. Explaining in detail—with utmost patience with her ignorance. Making suggestions, based on what she said she wanted, not on his own tastes.

She didn't even know his own tastes.

Or anything new about him. Other than that he was a very patient man. And clearly very knowledgeable about his business.

And that was as it should be.

They didn't mention Levi. She couldn't. Not for any ethical reason, but because it didn't feel right to her, discussing a former investigation. He didn't mention his son, either, which she found a bit odd. Parents generally went on and on about their youngsters, finding every normal developmental advancement a miracle and oftentimes accomplished better than anyone had ever done it before.

She put his reticence down to the fact that she'd represented a chance that Levi could be taken away from him. But in his shoes, she'd have been glad for a chance to mention the boy in the nonthreatening setting, conveying the sense of normalcy that Jem wanted her to know existed within the walls of his home.

"How long is your sister staying?" He broke protocol—asking a personal question—as they left the home repair superstore he'd taken her to just before closing Thursday night, after she'd been more than an hour late getting home. He'd wanted her to take a look at retractable shades, and to consider windows, as well, for the two screened sides of the new room, so that she could use the space year-round.

He'd already talked her into including a heating duct. She'd have to have heat and air to include the square footage in her home's value assessment.

It also meant raised taxes, but not enough to make the trade-off a bad idea.

"I'm not sure," she said now, feeling suddenly deflated in spite of the fact that she'd been expecting questions about Kacey. It had only been a matter of time. "She's got another couple of weeks until she has to go back to work. I'm hoping she'll be with me that long."

"You two really lived together until you were thirty?"

"Yep."

"What about relationships?"

What about them? Defensiveness sprang forth, but she wasn't susceptible to it anymore. "We had them," she said, assuming, she hoped, a Kacey smile as she answered lightly.

"But neither of you married."

"Not yet."

"Why not?"

"That's a bit personal, don't you think?" She could be Kacey when she needed to be. Like a lot of identicals, they'd done their share of switching places and fooling people as they'd been growing up. She just had to make sure she didn't make eye contact.

It was the eyes that gave them away.

"It's just… You're both so beautiful and…"

Lacey actually got hot from the inside out. Which brought to mind the complaints her mother had made a year or two ago as she'd gone through middle-age flashes.

"Why this sudden interest in our love lives?" Her tone held authority, not come-hitherness. She was Lacey again. Because there was no point in trying to be anyone else.

"My interest isn't sudden."

Head whipping to the side, pins pulling against her scalp as the twist she'd put in her hair that morning moved, Lacey looked at him.

Her question had clearly *not* been an invitation. If he was making fun of her…

He wasn't smiling. Not even close.

What was going on here?

"I don't have a love life," she said slowly. Was he seriously interested in her love life?

No. It was Kacey's he wanted to know about. Wow. Crazy that it took her a second to figure that out. The year and a half living apart from Kacey had softened her brain.

And…Jem was a nice guy. A truly nice guy. He'd pay attention to Lacey out of genuine interest. There were a lot of nice guys out there. They couldn't help gravitating toward Kacey…

"I don't believe you." He'd stopped at a light and was looking directly at her. Kind of like

Kacey did when her sister was telling her something without words.

She'd given him the perfect opening to ask about what he really wanted to know—her sister's love life.

"It's...true." She stared back at him.

The light turned green. He pushed the accelerator.

And her heart sped up.

CHAPTER FOURTEEN

By Friday Jem had a building permit in hand and was looking forward to the project at Lacey's like he used to look forward to working on his boat. He'd be doing the work mostly by himself. He hadn't put labor in the bid.

Which meant he was going to have to work after hours.

It also meant that Lacey would be home while he was there. He'd like things just to have worked out that way, but couldn't kid himself. He'd planned the entire venture, down to starting while Lacey's sister was still in town. Kacey seemed hell-bent on spending time with Levi.

That left Lacey to Jem. It was only going to take him a couple of weeks to get the work on her room done. Which gave him that long to get her to go out with him.

For some reason the goal—which generally took him seconds to accomplish when he met someone he wanted to date—seemed out of reach.

He showed up unannounced Friday night, just

to tape the clear plastic envelope containing the permit to the front of the house.

Levi stood beside him as he stuck the envelope to the front window, where he was required to leave it displayed from before the job began until after it was complete and inspected by the city.

Before Jem could stop him, Levi reached up on tiptoe and pushed the doorbell. He didn't even know the kid could reach that high.

"Levi!" he said. "We aren't here for a visit."

"I wanna see Kacey and Lacey. And they want to see me." He stood there, arms folded against his chest, staring at the door.

It didn't open.

"They're not home." He stated the obvious, his mind filling with an immediate picture of the two beauties walking side by side on the beach just blocks away. That gave him an almost undeniable need to get his ass down there before any of the hundreds of summer visitors—of the male beach-bum variety—hit on them.

"But I wanna see them!" Levi's wobbly voice gave warning to a brewing storm.

"They aren't home, son. There's nothing we can do about that."

"Why did we come now?" Instead of when the sisters were home, Jem filled in the blank.

"Because we had to drop off this permit so I can start work tomorrow morning..."

He knew as soon as he said the words that

they were a mistake. He walked down one of the two steps from Lacey's small porch to the paved walkway leading up to her house from the tree-lined street. Arms still firmly crossed, Levi stood his ground.

"I wanna come with you."

He'd known what was coming as soon as he'd mentioned the next day's work. And was now picturing two beautiful blondes coming home to a helpless construction worker on their front porch being worked over by an unhappy four-year-old in the throes of a tantrum.

Not a pretty sight.

Or something he needed his ex-caseworker to witness.

"Let's go get some hamburgers for dinner and talk about that." He cringed as he heard the bribe come out of his mouth. Levi loved burgers. And was allowed only one a week. He'd already had two, counting the one he'd had the previous Saturday at Uncle Bob's.

"No." Levi didn't yell. He just shook his head and stood firm.

Jem considered picking him up at the waist like a sack of potatoes and carrying him kicking to the truck. Anything to get him out of that neighborhood before he caused a scene.

"Look, Levi. You know there are some things that I can't change. No matter how much you want me to. Like having to go to the doctor once in a while for checkups."

"He gave me a shot." The boy's opinion of that move was clear in both the tone of his voice and the way his nose scrunched and his chin got hard.

"And going to school is another one. You have to go even if we both want to stay home."

"You have to go to work," Levi said. Jem fell in love with the boy all over again. Levi was repeating the lesson Jem had given him when they'd had the tantrum about going to school. Everyone, no matter what their age, had to do their jobs. Either work or school. No one was allowed to just stay home, because then there would be people who needed help and no one to help them. And there would be no money to buy food for families.

"That's right."

"'Cause people die if they don't eat."

Close enough. "Right."

"But Kacey and Lacey have food."

"Kacey and Lacey aren't home, Levi. That's what I can't change right now."

"But I wanna see them."

"They don't know that. And they're busy somewhere else." He took Levi's noncasted hand and gave it a gentle tug, breathing a silent but very big sigh of relief when the boy didn't snatch it back.

"Where?" Levi joined him on his step.

"I don't know." He and his son took the next step together.

"We can find them."

"Can we discuss this in the truck?"

"I want a hamburger."

Of course.

"Then we'll discuss it over hamburgers."

Walking with purpose the rest of the way to the truck, Levi climbed into his seat as soon as Jem had the back door open.

"Dad?" he said as Jem climbed into the front seat, dreading the possibility of Kacey's car coming around a corner. It hadn't been parked in the drive. He'd known when he'd stopped that the women weren't home.

"Yeah?" Jem asked, not sure he was going to like whatever had put the serious look on his son's baby face again.

"Can you tell them not to put the pickles?"

He always did. Every single time.

"Yep."

"'Cause I don't like the pickles," Levi stated emphatically, as though Jem didn't already know, in great detail, every single one of Levi's likes and dislikes.

Jem knew, which was why he could also expect—when Levi found out this was his weekend with his mother and that he was going there after dinner—the full-blown tantrum he'd just avoided.

"ARE YOU SURE?" Lacey walked beside her sister on the beach, staring at the sand their bare toes were kicking up. Her sandals hung from the fingers of her right hand. Her left hand was clenched.

"He said exactly those words." Kacey's tone was as subdued as it ever got. "'Mommy shook me up and I threwed up.'"

Feeling the heat rising to her face, Lacey moved to the left and let the water wash over her feet as she walked. "Why didn't you tell me this last night?"

"Remember that time on our birthday when Dad was whirling us around in the yard by our feet and you threw up?"

She did. Of course she did. Her stomach settled.

"And then right after Jem left last night, he called, remember? Because he'd had a message from the permit people and they needed an exact color match for the siding before they could approve the permit..."

And they'd talked for an hour. She'd felt bad about the fact that he was planning to work through his weekend. He'd told her he'd have been working, anyway. Then she'd felt bad for taking him from someone else's job and he'd told her about the boat in his garage.

She'd wanted to know if it was a ski boat. He'd said it was a catamaran—so he could take it on the ocean—but told her that his family had had a ski boat when he was growing up.

Which had led to where he was from, and from there to the fact that he had a close-knit family back in Georgia. It painted a picture of him that she liked. But was way too much information.

"You were asleep when I got off the phone," she said now, remembering. Kacey had had a headache the day before. Lacey hadn't been surprised to see her sister in bed early.

"Then today, I remembered something he'd been talking about earlier in the week and it's clear that the two go together."

Lacey made a mental reach to find her professional self. "What did he say earlier in the week?"

"He asked me if I'm mean when I wake people up. I said no, of course not! He'd been talking about that show he's so into. We really need to see that at some point, by the way. He's got me curious. Anyway, I thought that was why he was asking. Then he says that Mommy shakes him awake when he has bad dreams. But Whyatt on *Super Why!* didn't do that when someone had a bad dream…"

Levi thought his mother's actions were mean? And he'd been looking to Kacey for confirmation?

"You think he had a bad dream and she shook him until he threw up?" She had to call Jem.

She couldn't call Jem.

There was conflict of interest written all over that one.

She had to call Sydney, the social worker she shared cases with most often. They had the same philosophy, and Sydney was a newly added member of the High Risk Team started by the Lemonade Stand and would have access to immediate high-risk assistance from all professionals who could possibly be needed. Doctors, psychiatrists, police, hospital records.

If Lacey had screwed up and put that little boy at risk...

She'd called Ella Ackerman, the High Risk representative from the children's hospital, too.

But Tressa could have taken Levi to other hospitals.

Or Jem could have.

She'd met Tressa.

There was no way that kind, gentle, self-deprecating woman would hurt her son. She'd given him up so her penchant for drama didn't negatively affect his emotional stability...

People prone to drama were also prone to overreaction. Tressa had said she overreacted. To everything. Which made Jem crazy. Or something to that effect...

"We have to get back," she said now, spinning around so quickly she almost lost her balance in the sand. "I have to make some calls."

"I could just be overreacting here. This isn't my business and I don't want to get anyone in trouble.

But it's been bothering me all day and Jem said Levi's spending the weekend with his mother."

She hadn't heard that. "When did he say that?"

"A couple of nights ago. You were in the bathroom and he and I were talking about timing for the project in relation to when I have to leave."

Lacey didn't have time to deal with completely inappropriate jealousy.

She might be overreacting. And Levi might be in danger.

She'd risk one to prevent the other.

Pulling her phone off the clip on her shorts, she dialed Sydney's private cell.

FUNNY HOW LIFE could turn on a dime. In twelve hours' time, Jem had gone from looking forward to the weekend with great anticipation, to dreading the job he had ahead of him.

He could call one of his teams to build the room, but he'd take a loss for all labor costs if he did so. Just to save himself some discomfort.

His comfort wasn't worth that amount of money to him.

"I love you, Dad."

Looking in the rearview mirror, he saw the far too serious expression on his son's face and said, "I love you, too, Levi."

He'd never been comfortable saying the words, not with anyone, until his son was born. *I love you* were some of the first words he'd taught the boy.

If there was some good out of the events of the night before, Levi back at home with him would be it.

All of it.

"Are we going to see Kacey and Lacey now?"

"Yep."

"Can I play with them while you work?"

"We'll see." If they didn't want to watch his son, he wouldn't be working that day. Even if he'd been able to find a sitter at the last minute, he hadn't felt inclined to do so.

He was working for free. The least the traitor could do was provide free child care.

As soon as he'd had the thought, Jem gave himself a mental admonishment. Lacey was doing her job, because she cared about Levi.

He knew her well enough to know the truth about that statement. Even if there did exist a social worker who was hooked on his or her own power and got some kind of adrenaline rush out of lording it over a dysfunctional family, she sure didn't exist in Lacey Hamilton.

The woman was true blue.

She was also dead wrong about Tressa.

As he was going to tell her, the first opportunity he got.

CHAPTER FIFTEEN

"HE'S GOT LEVI with him." Kacey turned from the front window to look at Lacey, her expression filled with worry.

"That's good." Truth be known, she was relieved.

"It's good that he's here, too, huh?" Kacey asked, coming closer. In a sundress with ballet slipper flats, she was as dressed down as she got. But she needn't have bothered.

Any hope Lacey might have secretly held that there could possibly be a chance for her and Jem to explore whatever she might have been feeling between them had just been quashed.

"He's been around all week, Kace." Before she'd ratted him out.

Well, technically, she'd ratted out his ex-wife, but Tressa and Jem seemed to be pretty close. Closer than any divorced couple she'd ever known. And in her course of business, she'd known a lot of them.

Lacey had dressed down, too. In her newest pair of six-inch navy shorts and a white tank top.

Kacey had tried to get her to put on one of her sundresses. She just hadn't wanted to do so.

It wasn't her.

And if nothing else, she was honest with herself and others about who and what she was.

And wasn't.

Kacey was the "movie star." Lacey was her shadow. And a damned good social worker.

He was on his way up the walk, with Levi, in jeans and a white T-shirt just like his father, skipping along beside him.

"A whole week and he doesn't even see me most of the time," Kacey said. "He's been too busy looking at you."

She wanted to tell Kacey she was dreaming. Or lying. But she'd noticed, too. She'd been afraid that she'd been fooling herself.

In a week's time, with her sister right there every single day they'd seen each other, Jem still looked at Lacey first. And most often. He smiled at her, directed his conversation to her. Of course, it *was* her house.

But Kacey was paying the bill…

"Looks like I get to babysit today." Kacey was smiling—and heading toward the front door. "See, it all worked out fine."

Her sister never had been one to see the trouble in her path.

Which could be why she was still living alone and dating losers.

Not that Lacey was doing any better.

As soon as it became obvious that Jem planned to put in a full day of work as long as he could count on the sisters to take care of his unexpected charge that day, Kacey offered to take Levi to the beach. Jem gave his permission.

Without hesitation.

First, because he knew how much his son would enjoy the outing and Levi's emotional health was his first concern at the moment.

And second, because he knew he needed to have a word with Lacey Hamilton without Levi anywhere near enough to hear.

"His suit's in that bag," he said, indicating the backpack he'd carried in with him. He'd loaded it that morning with snacks, a swimsuit, change of clothes, juice boxes and a *Super Why!* video. All with Levi's input as the boy stood there supervising.

"I'll show you," Levi said, taking Kacey's hand. He turned back before he got to the bag, though, grabbing Lacey's hand, too. "Come on, aren't you going with us?" he asked, looking between the sisters.

"Lacey needs to stay here, Levi," Jem said. "She's the homeowner and I may have some questions as I get started." Levi wouldn't know what he meant, but he wouldn't question the tone of voice, either. The words were for Lacey, letting her know that if she wanted the work done, she best stay put.

Right or wrong, he was angry with her and needed to let her know before he started work on her house. It wasn't too late for her to change her mind.

Or for him to change his.

He didn't miss the long glance the sisters exchanged, and that silent communication, like they were speaking a foreign language right in front of him, purposely, so he wouldn't understand, pissed him off, too.

Deathly silence fell as soon as Kacey and his son vacated the house.

Jem waited for Lacey to apologize. To explain. To say anything at all. He got angrier every second that she just stood there.

To her credit, she didn't attempt inane conversation, talk about getting started or leave him to his work.

"You could say something." After he bit back what he really wanted to say, he got the words out.

"No, I can't."

"What does that mean?"

"Ethically, I can't."

"Oh, no, lady, you aren't going to play that card

with me. No way. You think it's fine to pretend to be a personal friend to my son and me and then turn on us and not be personally accountable for having done so?"

That hadn't come out right. He was beyond caring at the moment.

"Sounds to me like you have a pretty skewed sense of ethics."

He hadn't meant to say that, either.

"I can, personally, discuss with a friend anything a friend wants to discuss with me, personally. I cannot bring up or speak to state matters that involve my employment with social services."

He wanted to ask her how long she'd worked on that one, or if it was rote. Maybe she'd done this before—befriend someone just to spy on them because she couldn't find proof of wrongdoing in the usual way.

The thought shamed him. And hung around, too.

She hadn't negated his "friend" claim. She'd kind of supported it.

The realization calmed him. Not much, but some.

"You're waiting for me to bring it up."

"I can speak to you as a friend if you have something you want to discuss."

He held his tongue and called it a victory.

"Do you have any idea what happened at my ex-wife's house last night?"

"Literally, none at all. I can guess, though, based on what I do for a living."

"They didn't rescind his mother's visitation rights, if that's what you're thinking."

"I didn't know."

"But you were thinking it."

"I knew a temporary request for supervised visits was a possibility."

They were standing in her kitchen a few yards apart. He wondered if they should sit. But she didn't offer.

Maybe he should just get his tool belt and get to work. Have the conversation later. Or never.

"There was no evidence to substantiate another look at her. Tressa's a good mom. And an incredibly protective one."

"Then why is he with you, and not with her for the weekend as planned?" He'd have thought the question a challenge, if not for the fact that she could only be asking as a friend.

He'd never had a friend feel less like one at the moment.

He'd never cared more.

"Tressa lost it when Sydney Gardner showed up at her door last night, asking questions about nightmares, shaking and throwing up."

"Did Levi have any nightmares recently that you know of?"

"That sounds, Ms. Hamilton, like a professional question, not a friend one."

She sat with her hands clasped together on her cute little oak kitchen table—a set for two, which was all that would fit in the small space.

When she didn't say anything, he pulled out the seat opposite her. Far enough that he could scoot down, lean back and look as though he didn't have a care in the world, without bumping his knees against the table leg.

"Let me explain something," she said when he'd assumed his position and grown still, staring at her. It occurred to him, as he waited for her to continue, that he could be mirroring his son from the night before with his jutting chin and arms crossed against his chest. When Levi had found out that he had to go to his mother's for the weekend.

"I made a call, as any concerned citizen should do, when my sister told me something that made me afraid for Levi's safety. After relaying only what I'd been told, and nothing more, I hung up."

"Obviously you told whoever you called that you'd had Levi's case, but closed the investigation."

"I did not."

He wasn't sure what to do with that.

"The minute I became personally involved

with you, I ceased being a social worker," she continued after he'd grown greatly uncomfortable with the silence.

"So you didn't tell your coworker about Levi's case."

"I did not."

Okay, then, maybe he'd been wrong.

"I knew she'd find it, though. And know exactly why I called. That's why I called Sydney at home. We've worked together a lot over the past eighteen months."

If she was trying to tell him something good, he missed it.

She'd set him up and was playing semantics.

Now he was more than just pissed. He was... disappointed. To the point of...he didn't know what.

"Sydney's a professional through and through. She's as dedicated to these kids as I am."

Her hole was getting deeper.

"She won't speak to me of this case ever again. And I won't mention it, either. I can't. That's what happened when I called her."

She was looking him in the eye, and he saw a sunset again. The kind that brought you to your knees.

Calmed you. And invigorated you at the same time.

Which pissed him off all over again.

"You're telling me you can't speak on my behalf."

"I'm telling you I have no power whatsoever. Either way."

She couldn't speak *against* him, either.

And she hadn't. She'd simply called in a private citizen concern.

"Tressa's a mess."

And that was Lacey's fault.

"Did Levi have a nightmare at her house recently?"

"The weekend after his meeting in your office. It was because of you. Not Tressa."

Well, not her, Lacey their friend, but Lacey the social worker who took him from his father to play games he really didn't want to play.

Still, Lacey was a woman. Tressa was a woman, and Levi's mother. She was the one who'd experienced the nightmare firsthand and knew what it was about. She was the only one who'd talked to him about it.

"Is it possible she 'lost it' then, too, and shook him to make him stop screaming out?"

"She couldn't wake him up. She called me and I talked her through it. She did not shake him. He was flailing around with that cast on his arm and she was afraid he was going to hurt himself."

"Maybe he accidentally hit her with the cast and that made her angry. Maybe…"

He shook his head. "No way."

"He told Kacey she shook him until he threw up."

Jem didn't move. Not even so much as to allow his expression to change.

"You didn't know, did you? That he threw up?"

He scrambled to make sense of what was going on quickly enough to hold his own and protect his family. "I know that he threw up when he was over there for Easter. He ate an entire chocolate bunny."

"Was Tressa playing with him at the time?"

"I don't know. I know he threw up on her." Tressa had called him then, too. Because she was a drama queen.

"He was upset and she thought he'd be happier if I came to get him."

"Did you?"

"Of course."

And Levi had come home weepy because he didn't feel well.

He'd been fine the next day, though. His usual self.

"Did you go get him the night of the bad dream, too?"

"No. Tressa called back and said it was all under control. I talked to him. They were having a late-night snack and he sounded happy."

He'd been weepy, though, once he'd come home. Because home reminded him of Lacey's visit?

But then why did his son welcome the woman's return to their lives, to the point of not wanting to go to his mom's so he could see Lacey and Kacey?

Because of Kacey?

"Did Levi ever tell you about the nightmare?"

"No."

"Did you ask him about it?"

"No. I didn't want to make it into some big deal if he was past it. Didn't want to make it more of a big deal than it was." He heard the defensiveness in his tone. Damn her.

And her job.

"Yet he told my sister about it."

He didn't like that part. Didn't really understand it. But he couldn't see how he could work out such an omission with a four-year-old.

"Tressa's a good mom." He heard himself sounding repetitious, but didn't know any other way to help her understand, *make* her understand, for God's sake.

This was his life she was messing with.

And she was making any possibility of something between them more remote. Didn't she get that?

"She called me last night as soon as she knew why Sydney was there. She was upset and didn't want to upset Levi. She asked me to come get him immediately and asked Sydney to sit with them, and not ask her any more questions, until I arrived. That's how conscientious she is of our son's welfare. Sydney called me after speaking with Tressa. She wanted to speak with Levi."

"I'm assuming you let her."

"Of course."

She didn't ask the outcome, but he told her, anyway. "She said that she's going to keep an eye on Tressa, stopping in now and then during her weekends, but that she wasn't overly concerned. Just being careful. I'm assuming because you were the one who'd made the call."

She'd overreacted. It was obvious to him. And while one part applauded her level of conscientiousness, another part of him resented the fact that she hadn't just called him, as a friend, and asked him about it. "We could have had this conversation last night, you know. Without involving social services."

He could swear a look of pain crossed over her face. Or remorse?

"I'm a social worker, Jem. You have no idea the things I see—day in and day out, over and over—with different kids, different families. I will always err on the side of better safe than sorry."

Everything inside of him slowed down and came to a halt.

He was as bad as Tressa, making it all about him. Which wasn't like him at all.

"Fair enough."

"I can't speak to anyone officially now," she said. "I'm off the case. But I have to tell you…

from where I'm sitting, I'm concerned about Levi. Are you absolutely certain that your ex-wife isn't hurting him?"

"Absolutely." Tressa was a lot of things, but she loved Levi. "She'd die for him."

"That doesn't mean that, in a fit of drama, she wouldn't hurt him." She was looking at him deeply. The thought was inane. And still there. She was trying to tell him something, but he wasn't getting it.

"Tressa isn't the violent type."

She didn't look any more satisfied with his answer than he was with the entire conversation.

But at least he knew one thing.

She was, officially, completely, off the case. He had nothing more to fear from her.

And for that, he was glad.

CHAPTER SIXTEEN

IT ALL STARTED because he had to eat. Levi, that was. And, well, Jem, too. When Lacey and Kacey had returned home Friday from their walk on the beach, and she'd seen the permit taped to her front window—the moment when she faced the fact that she really was getting her new dream room—she'd insisted that Kacey show her how much the room would cost.

She was going to contribute at least half of it. They settled on Lacey's half being her birthday gift to her sister, because Lacey was getting truly upset, and that was when she'd seen how little Jem was making on the deal.

Not because he'd broken out his labor costs, but because she'd done the math on the choices she'd made. And while they'd been in the home improvement store, she'd seen how much lumber cost.

Kacey had pointed out that he'd have a pretty substantial contractor discount, but the wood wouldn't be free.

He was doing this as a favor to Kacey.

So they were going to have to do favors for him—like watching Levi, and feeding them both.

As soon as she and Jem had reached their somewhat tenuous truce Saturday morning, she'd left to make a grocery store run to get more tuna, chips, fresh fruit and peanut butter and jelly just in case.

When Kacey and Levi returned from the beach, she served lunch in the dining area off the kitchen. She didn't eat in there often, preferring her table for two in the little nook in her kitchen.

But there were four of them.

For dinner, too.

On Sunday Jem showed up with a booster seat in hand. "I had an extra out in the garage," he said as Lacey stared at the thing and Kacey took it from him.

"It goes in my chair," Levi said, walking straight up to the chair he'd knelt in the day before, his good elbow helping to prop him up on her dining room table.

The booster chair move-in was unexpected, except that she figured she knew Jem's real motivation. Kacey. She'd seen guys do some pretty crazy things over the years to get to her sister.

Like walk a mile each way to get her the fish tacos she was craving. They'd been fifteen. The guy was their next-door neighbor at the time. Lacey had asked for regular tacos. He'd forgotten and brought fish for her, too. She hated fish tacos.

There'd been the jeweler who'd designed a necklace just for Kacey. Of course, he'd also then used her name to sell a mass-produced version of the original. With her permission.

She'd once had a man sail a yacht from Florida to San Diego just to pick her up for a two-hour date because she'd mentioned that she wanted to see his yacht.

Lacey had been the first one to express an interest in seeing the seventy-foot yacht with a swimming pool on the deck. Mostly because she didn't really believe there was one. He'd shown her a picture, and she'd introduced him to her sister. He was fascinating, had done a lot of things with his life and was still in his midthirties, but she hadn't felt any sparks. She'd known Kacey would, though. Kace went for flashy guys, the ones who wore all the right clothes.

And jewelry. She liked guys who wore rings.

Jem had a class ring on his right hand. Even when he worked.

Maybe none of the things Lacey could currently bring to mind were as crazy as building a room, but they were close.

Kacey had fallen hard for the yacht guy. They'd been hot and heavy for more than a year. She'd wanted to get married, start a family. He'd had more pressing matters. Like sailing around the world, buying into a casino in Monte Carlo and looking for a summer home in Greece.

Jem was the marrying kind, a family man.

And gorgeous.

He was also successful. He wore a tie to work when he wasn't giving away his labor for free. His jeans were designer, even when wearing a tool belt, and his work shirts looked like they came straight out of a high-end men's fashion magazine.

He wore the glint of success well; it might be understated, but it was still there.

Lacey almost felt sorry for him when Kacey wouldn't give him a second look.

And so, on Sunday, when her pager went off, a callout to any available case agent to see to an emergency, Lacey pushed the callback button immediately. Her coworkers wouldn't be surprised. Lacey was most always the one who took after-hours calls. Unless she was already on one.

Jem didn't seem all that put out, either, when she stepped outside to tell him she'd been called into work. He'd been measuring and stopped. Looked up at her.

"The child in danger is lucky to have you on the way," he said and then smiled at her.

She nodded and left him alone with her sister and his son. Let Jem and Kacey work out whatever would or would not be between them. Lacey had learned a long time ago she couldn't fight nature.

No matter how much she might like a guy.

And there was another issue at hand, too. She wasn't working Levi's case anymore—couldn't go anywhere near it professionally—but she cared every bit as much about his safety as she had when she had been his caseworker.

Being a friend didn't mean that she lost her work skills. Just like Jem building a room for her at slave labor wages didn't mean she'd get a second-rate room.

Sydney had Tressa covered. And Lacey had access to Levi. Easy, natural, uninstitutional access.

The call she'd received involved two girls, aged six and seven, who'd been left alone for at least two days. A neighbor had called the police.

Law enforcement was at the scene before she was. Lacey caught a hint of what they feared—that something had prevented two normally attentive parents from returning home to their girls—but her job wasn't to solve the mystery.

The neighbor who'd called the police had already fed the girls. She offered to keep them with her, but when neither girl seemed inclined to seek the woman out for comfort, Lacey decided to take them with her.

Helping the girls pack a couple of days' worth of their favorite clothes, pajamas and toys, she took them back to her office, where she set them up with a snack in the playroom, and then, leaving the door open and taking a monitor with her, she headed down the hall to her office to make some calls.

The girls had an aunt in Santa Barbara. They'd both told her so on the way to the office, in between asking if she was taking them to their mommy and daddy. The aunt was fairly easy to trace down, but didn't answer the phone number listed for her on the internet.

She didn't answer her door, either, after Lacey made a call to local police to make a well-check run. There was no sign of disturbance at the home and neighbors said she'd gone on a trip up the coast for the weekend.

They also said she had a brother in LA, an uncle to the girls who was married with a couple of kids of his own. He'd already heard from the police, was distraught to find out that his sister and brother-in-law were missing, and he and his family were on the way to Santa Raquel.

The overall prognosis for the family didn't look good—a sudden disappearance of seemingly conscientious and loving parents. The girls were in good hands, though. And for the night, at least, back in their own home as, after investigation, Lacey released them to their aunt and uncle.

But Lacey couldn't help thinking that their lives were going to change forever after that day. Just as she couldn't stop thinking about the one thing the police had also wondered...

If the parents were so loving and conscientious,

why were both cars gone, and the girls left home alone?

It wasn't for her to figure that one out. All she could do was wonder, and wait. And worry, if she let herself get in too deep.

That wasn't her job, either.

But the not knowing, and her inability to do more for the children in that moment, left her pensive.

Missing lunch with her sister and Jem and Levi didn't improve her mood, but she knew the day had transpired as it was meant to do.

Her life was dedicated to helping children.

Which was why, Sunday afternoon, while Jem was getting ready to pour cement in the trench he'd dug with a backhoe around the perimeter of the new room—not that she'd been paying attention earlier in the week when he'd explained the process to her—Lacey suggested that she and Kacey build a puzzle with Levi. She'd picked a couple of them up at the store on the way home, just to make certain that she didn't walk in on the tail end of lunch. She'd chosen one-hundred-piece puzzles and was fairly certain that Levi would not only take an interest in them, he'd be able to do them without help.

Jem had already been back at work, and the kitchen had been cleaned up, by the time she'd walked in, and rather than disturb him—or hope to glean any change in his demeanor that would indicate whether or not he'd enjoyed lunch alone with her sister—she joined Levi and Kacey in her craft room, at the multipurpose table she'd set up. Levi sat on his knees on a chair, leaning his elbows on the table—his fist, and cast, pointing straight up to the ceiling—and picked up puzzle pieces as soon as she'd dumped them.

She took to her own task, as well. Leading his conversation, and letting him regale them with his imaginative tales. The puzzle was almost done and Levi was a happy, well-adjusted boy without a care in the world.

If all they talked about was his life with his dad. Things he liked to do. And cars.

"Did you notice that when you mentioned his mother his little lips got thin and he quit chattering?" Kacey asked softly when Levi left the room after announcing that he had to go potty.

"Of course I did," Lacey said. There was something about Tressa. The woman was genuinely caring. Sweet and loving. And volatile on occasion. A toxic mix.

Of course, Lacey was also in the process of fighting the hots for Tressa's ex, so she'd be more apt to find fault with the other woman. It was natural. Human nature. It was a good thing she was off the case.

"Can we do another one?" Levi asked twenty minutes later as they took apart the car puzzle and put the pieces back into the box.

"Sure!" Kacey told him. Lacey went to check on the pasta casserole she'd put in the oven, and to see how much longer Jem was going to be, and then went back to join them.

Levi and Kacey were talking about their trip to the beach the day before. About sharks and boats and little-boy things.

"Do you like to swim?" Lacey asked, rejoining them at the table. They already had the perimeter of the puzzle a quarter of the way done.

Kacey seemed to be having as much fun as Levi was. She was a natural with him and would make a great mother. And...

"Uh-huh." Levi had answered her question about swimming.

"Did your daddy teach you how?" Kacey asked. "Do you have a pool in your backyard?"

Lacey could answer that one for her—they didn't. But apparently they had a goldfish pond she had yet to see.

"Mommy does," Levi said. "She teached me." Nice. Normal. Conscientious. Good mothering.

"And you like it?"

"Uh-huh." The boy nodded while he picked up a piece and put it in its proper place. They were making a train with a smiling face on the front of the engine.

He was concentrating. Showing no signs of discomfort or stress. But he was back to the same one-word answers he'd given her when she'd questioned him in the playroom at work. Not chattering on as she'd come to recognize as his normal way.

Because he didn't like being questioned? Was she making problems where there were none?

The little cast came into view. And she thought of the unexplained bruises on his torso. Nightmares. A mother who chose to have her son immediately taken away when a social worker showed up at the door. The day care's report of changed developmental performance and personality. One and a half known hospital visits for each year of his life.

Normal or not?

On a hunch, she asked, "How old were you when you learned to swim?"

She didn't expect him to know. Four-year-olds didn't usually catalog in a time sequence.

"I dunno."

"Did you take lessons besides with your mom?"

"Nope." He placed another piece.

"Do you swim at your mom's a lot?" Kacey asked, her tone completely different from Lacey's.

"I dunno."

Feeling guilty for the interrogation, Lacey decided to let the whole thing drop, to trust Sydney to do her job.

She found an eyeball for the engine's face and handed it to Levi. "Here, I think this goes in over there," she said, not saying where "there" was.

He put it immediately in place. "Did *your* mommy teach you to swim?" His soft *r*'s grabbed at Lacey.

He wasn't looking at either sister. They looked at each other. "Yes," Lacey said when Kacey shrugged her shoulders like she didn't want to answer.

"She taught both of us at once," Kacey added then. At which Levi looked up at her, cocking his head and frowning. "Does twins' moms have four hands?"

"Of course not, silly." Lacey grinned at that. He was a normal, sweet little boy. She was giving him too much credit, thinking he was so completely advanced and purposely holding back.

His face didn't clear. "How does she hold two under at once?"

"Hold two under?" Kacey asked the question. Lacey's heart thrummed in overtime. She told herself not to jump to conclusions.

"You know, hold you under so you don't suck in your nose and then you come up again." Kacey's eyes widened.

"Oh, you mean holding on to you and dunking you under to help you glide through the water and then bring you back up?" Lacey said, breathing easier. Toddler swim classes, at least in California, where children were around water frequently, were common. Drowning deaths among young children were, statistically, a high cause of death and the best protection for them was knowing how to swim.

Levi had been placing a piece. It didn't fit, though he tried to force it, and he finally gave up. Climbing down from his chair to stand on the floor, he said, "No, you know, like this." He grabbed hold of his ribs and then squatted down, paused several seconds and then jumped up with both feet leaving the ground. As though springing up out of the water.

"Oh," Lacey said, glancing at Kacey and shaking her head.

"No, our mom didn't do that with us."

She was no longer on Levi's case, but as a concerned citizen she could make another call. She could call every day if she had more to report.

"Did you like it?" Kacey asked.

"Nope. I cried." His babyish *r* sounded more pronounced to Lacey. Could someone be mistreating him?

"Then what did your mom do? Did she stop?"

He shook his head. "She did this." He put his hands back on his ribs, scrunched up his face like he was straining, and the knuckles on his good hand turned white at his ribs.

She remembered the bruises Mara had noticed on Levi's torso. Bruises Jem surely would have noticed when he picked the boy up after his weekend visit. Could it have been from the swimming "lesson"?

"Was she mad at you?"

"I dunno."

"Did you tell your dad about learning to swim?"

"Uh-uh." Levi shook his head, climbing back up on his chair to lean over the puzzle again. "Mommy did."

"When he came to pick you up?"

"Uh-uh. On the phone. Dad was gone away a long time and we were playing a game."

"Who was playing a game?"

"Mommy and me. After swimming we played a game and it was fun."

"Then your dad called and your mommy told him you'd learned to swim?"

"Yep!" He put a piece in place—the nose of the engine face.

"Did you tell him that you cried when you learned to swim?"

"No." Levi's chin did a chest plant.

"Why not?" Lacey's instincts were driving her now. She gave them free rein.

"I dunno."

Why wouldn't Tressa have told her ex-husband that the swimming lesson made their son cry? A lesson that was memorable enough that a four-year-old could recount it months later.

"It's okay, sweetie. You can tell me why you didn't tell your dad you cried. You won't be in trouble, I promise."

"No, I can't."

"Why not?"

"I dunno."

"Did someone say you couldn't tell?"

He shook his head. "I don't wanna do this any-more," he said, climbing down from the table.

"Hey, squirt." Kacey grabbed him around the waist as he passed and pulled him up onto her lap. "You know that you can trust us, right? I promise you, we won't let anyone hurt you. Ever. Okay?"

Not at all what Lacey would have said, because the promise was empty. Sometimes she couldn't prevent the hurt. And children in abusive situations were generally lied to. They needed honesty if they were ever going to learn to trust and grow up to have a healthy relationship...

"I wanna go home."

"I thought we were having fun here." Kacey smiled at him, gave him a little bounce on her knee.

He just sat there.

"Don't you like me anymore?"

He nodded.

"Do you like Lacey?"

He nodded again.

"So what's the problem?"

"If I tell you, she can make me not live with my dad." He whispered the words, looking Kacey straight in the eye. His lower lip trembled, but he didn't cry. Then he turned a fearful gaze on Lacey.

Had Tressa told him that Lacey was trying to take him away from his parents? Or was he asking Lacey for help?

Either way, she was going to get it for him.

Something was very, very wrong here and she wasn't going to stop until she knew for certain that Levi Bridges was not being abused.

CHAPTER SEVENTEEN

JEM WAS SITTING out back with the fountain on at the fish pond Sunday when his cell phone rang.

Levi was asleep, exhausted from the weekend at Lacey's. The monitor sat on the table beside him. His ringer sounded again, and a third time.

His son was safe. He didn't want to deal with Tressa. And there was no one else who'd be calling him on a Sunday night.

Bridges Construction did not work on Sundays. Ever. It had been part of the policy under which he'd gone into business for himself.

A throwback to his days growing up in the Bible Belt. The ringing stopped and then started again.

He glanced at the caller ID and picked up.

"What is it, Tressa?"

"Did you talk to her, Jem? Did you talk to that Sydney woman?"

"The office doesn't open until tomorrow. I told you I'd call her then."

"She came here on a Friday night. She could have come to your house."

True. "I'd have called you if she had."

"So where were you?"

Feet dropping from the boulder he'd had them resting on, Jem sat up. "What do you mean, where was I?"

"All weekend. I stopped by. It *is* my weekend to see Levi, remember?"

And Tressa had agreed never to come to his house. He'd needed space where he could be away from her drama. That was their agreement. If she needed him, she was to call and he'd come there. Not that he still didn't half expect her to show up unannounced.

"You were here?"

"Yes."

"When?"

"I don't know... Saturday."

"I thought you were going to the city with Amelia."

"We had a fight."

His gut clenched and he longed for the beer in his refrigerator.

"I had errands to run yesterday." The words burned his tongue. He couldn't stand to lie. Ever. But to tell her the truth was just plumb dumb. He was not a masochist.

"And today?"

"You came by again today?"

"Twice."

"Tressa."

"I know. But I needed you, Jem."

"You didn't call."

"I wanted to see Levi."

She was feeling insecure because she'd panicked and called him to pick up her son. She was afraid that it made her look like a bad mother. He understood. He just didn't have patience for her at the moment.

He had real problems to deal with.

Like the fact that he was falling for a woman who didn't appear to want a relationship with him.

And a son who'd been clingy again that night, wanting Jem to lie with him in his bed until he fell asleep.

Because of a weekend spent with Lacey?

Tressa had intimated that Levi's nightmare had been because of his visit with the other woman.

But he begged to go see her. Hell, he'd practically thrown a tantrum on Friday when Kacey and Lacey had been gone.

And while he was spending a good deal of his time with Kacey, he seemed to like Lacey equally...

"Where were you, Jem?"

"On a job. I thought I had the weekend free, remember?" He'd lived with her a long time. And knew that the only way to deal with her sometimes was to go on the defensive.

"Where was Levi?"

"At a sitter's."

"Who? What sitter? I thought we talked to each other about his sitters. You don't want me leaving him with just anyone, you said."

Shit. He stood up, paced the pond. He'd gotten soft. All this time spent with Lacey and her sister, he supposed. "The woman whose house I'm working on has a sister. She watched Levi while I worked. I was there the entire time." Levi hadn't been, but she didn't need to know that. If she'd seen the boy out with someone else, he'd already have heard about it.

"A woman? How old is she?"

The tornado was back in his gut. He'd thought divorcing her would get rid of that at least. "I don't know how old she is," he said, letting his irritation show. Sometimes she'd back down if she knew she was pissing him off. "I don't ask those kinds of questions. She wanted work done. I'm doing the work."

"*You're* doing the work?" She squelched. "Why isn't one of your crews doing it? What's wrong, Jem, are you having problems with the business? You need to let me take over again."

When he'd first started the business, Tressa had been in charge of his finances, of investments and payroll. He'd run quotes through her, too, as together they'd found the most cost-efficient way of doing quality work. That had been a long time ago. He'd still viewed her as a life partner then.

Before she'd started keeping tabs on every woman he talked to, seeing affairs where there were none. Before she'd accused him of taking cash from clients so he could go to strip clubs without her knowing where the money was going.

As if he'd ever do either.

"The business is doing fine," he said now. There was no way she was coming back to work for him. Ever. "I'm doing this job on the side. As a favor. It's just one room."

"A favor? Who is this woman? What do you owe her? Levi knows her, too? Who is she?"

The string of words that went through his mind, self-directed, weren't pretty. Or kind. "I don't really know her," he said now, thinking of Kacey. "We just met the day she asked me to do the job. She's paying for a room to be built for her sister. As a birthday present."

"Is she young?"

"You know I'm not a good judge of age, and I haven't paid any attention, in any case."

"What does she look like?"

"Definitely not one of a kind, I can tell you that. I don't know, Tress. If you want me to take notes next time I'm with her, I will. I really just want to get the work done and get out of there."

"Is she pretty?"

He thought of Kacey. "Not that I've noticed." Not like Lacey was.

"Do you like her?"

"I don't know her, Tress. Please, can we stop this? I'll call Sydney tomorrow and find out what's going on. I'm sure it's just a routine follow-up," he lied again. "Last time they visited both of us within hours of each other. I'm sure they'd have been here to question me this weekend if there was a problem."

Tressa's silence was a blessing. Not only because she wasn't coming at him, but because it meant she was calming down.

Then she said, "I wonder what happened to that Lacey woman. Can you ask to have her put back on our case? I liked her."

He had a headache, thinking he'd forgo the beer for a couple of aspirin and bed. "I'll ask," he said and softened his tone. He told her to take a sleeping pill and get a good night's rest. They knocked her out for a good eight hours.

And then he went in for that beer. He'd gotten off lightly. She hadn't accused him of screwing his client. Or called members of his crews to tell them that he was screwing a client. Both of which she'd done before.

Not that any of that was her business anymore. She just thought it was, and went ballistic anytime she thought he might be seeing anyone.

Unless she was in a relationship. Then it was okay.

Shaking his head, he went back outside to his

backlit pond and sent a silent plea to Amelia to call Tressa. She would. Eventually. She always did.

He just had no idea why.

AFTER A BRIEF conversation with her sister about whether or not Lacey should call Jem—Kacey's vote was an absolute yes—Kacey stopped Lacey before she picked up her phone Sunday night.

"You didn't ask about lunch today," she said.

Because she didn't want to know the details. What was, was. She was okay with that.

It wasn't like she and Jem had done more than spend a little time together. He'd never led her to believe for one second that he was interested in her in any way other than a friend. One he wasn't even sure he completely trusted.

It wasn't his fault she was drawn to him like some kind of pathetic groupie.

"What's there to ask about?" she said, wishing Kacey wasn't standing in the archway that led from the living room to the hall. She wanted to be in the hall—walking down the hall—away from this conversation. And her sister's discerning, loving gaze.

"He didn't eat with us," Kacey said.

She knew Jem was under Lacey's skin. Lacey didn't have to say a word and she knew. She just didn't seem to get that it didn't matter if Kacey was interested in the guy or not; it didn't stop the guy's gaze from straying.

Kacey also wasn't quite as good at accepting that she couldn't make things happen as she thought they should.

"While I was making grilled cheese, he came out and asked if I'd mind overseeing Levi's meal so he could keep working."

"He didn't eat?"

"He ate. But outside, studying drawings and walking around the space he's framed off."

"He needed to get the cement poured today so it would have time to cure." He'd told her so. "He was probably just running behind."

"Or maybe he didn't want to eat alone with Levi and me. Maybe he ate outside because you weren't here."

Maybe. But if that was so, it was probably because Kacey was giving him no encouragement whatsoever.

And even if it wasn't, she couldn't really believe it wasn't.

Besides, at the moment they had a much bigger issue on their hands. Jem believed in his ex-wife. Lacey didn't. And Levi's future rested in the middle of the dispute.

After Kacey went to bed, Lacey took her phone into her craft room, sat at her sewing machine and started working on a quilt she was making for one of the shelters that housed kids on a temporary basis. After a minute she stopped, put her Bluetooth earbud in place and called Jem.

He picked up on the second ring.

"I'm sorry to bother you. I know you've already given up your entire weekend for me, but this is important." She'd spent a good twenty minutes practicing that and was pleased overall with the delivery.

"What's up?"

He didn't sound bothered. But he probably would be as soon as she told him the reason for the call.

"I'm not interrupting anything, am I?"

"Nope. My bottle of beer, the fish and I are happy to have you join us."

"You're sitting outside?"

"Yep. It's a nice night."

She hadn't been out, but had an overwhelming sense of wanting to be in that backyard with him at that moment.

"Is Levi with you?" They couldn't have the conversation she needed to have if the boy was sitting right there.

"Are you kidding? He was worn-out. He's been asleep for more than an hour. And before you wonder, Miss Social Worker, I have a nursery monitor right here on the table beside me."

"Believe it or not, I wasn't concerned." She told him the truth. She'd seen the nursery monitor in Levi's room and had noticed receivers around the house, too. Those were some of the types of things she was trained to see.

"Well, then, I apologize."

"For what?"

"Accusing you of…"

"What, being on guard and working even when I'm not at work? You don't have to apologize for that. It's true." He wasn't going to take this well. She just knew it. She wished she didn't have to make him upset with her.

She liked him. And wasn't impartial. Which was why she was no longer on his case.

"I wanted to ask you something," she started, lowering her voice in hopes of softening the impact of the coming inquisition.

"Yes, I'll have dinner with you, all alone, any night you choose."

Her stomach jumped. Making room for the liquid heat flooding her lower belly. "What?"

"I said yes, I'll have dinner with you, all alone, any night you choose."

Where on earth had that come from? The thought was quickly followed by another. He was drinking beer. And it had softened his brain.

"Really." The word was a statement. One meant to show him she knew he was egging her on and she wasn't falling for it.

Not that Jem was the type of person who toyed with people. At least, not in what she'd seen of him in the few weeks she'd known him, but what did she know?

"Of course, really."

He sounded completely sincere. Kacey had pointed out on more than one occasion that he was paying as much or more attention to Lacey as he did Kacey. She'd even caught him looking at Lacey over the dinner table that night, when Kacey had been the one talking.

Of course, Lacey had noticed, too. All the way down to her toes. But she didn't think it meant all that much.

So, he wanted to have dinner with her.

"Why?" She'd never have asked if not for the distance afforded by telephone communication.

He half sputtered, half chuckled. Like he was choking on a sip of beer. "What do you mean why? You're a beautiful woman. I'm a normal male with normal urges and I'd like to spend some time alone with you."

"Okay."

"If you're worried that I just want you for the sex, then…"

"I wasn't," she interrupted as her panties started to get moist. What in the hell was the matter with her? She didn't have those kind of reactions. Even in her fantasies. She had too much control to let anything get that far.

"Don't get me wrong," he continued, his voice lowered. "I do want to have sex with you. As soon as possible. But I want to have dinner with you, too. And this late-night phone conversation is pretty cool, too."

"You're nuts." She laughed. The fantasy he was building was going to consume her if she'd let it. And he was teasing her. He *had* to be teasing her. "You hardly know me."

She couldn't afford to believe he really liked her even half as much as she liked him.

Because something told her that losing him in the end would hurt far worse than any pain she'd ever known before.

"You're wrong about that." How a voice could sound so sexy she had no idea. But just listening to him talk was making her want to go to bed with the man. Which was not a good thing. At all.

Maybe in the secret recesses of her mind. But nowhere else.

Of course, these days, people had sex without even dating. Or dating exclusively. They had sex without love. Or even a great deal of affection.

People. Not her.

But he didn't know that…

"We might not have known each other long," he continued, "but the way you came into my life was pretty intense."

Sure was. She'd told him he was under suspicion because there were reports his son was being abused. "I suppose."

"I had the hots for you the second I saw you standing on my doorstep."

If that had been a confession, he'd sounded way too proud of himself to be seeking forgiveness.

And she was too busy accepting the fact that he'd had the hots for her when she'd been all Lacey. On the job. Completely herself. Her heart fluttered.

And then slowed.

He'd had the hots for her before Kacey came to town.

Other guys had chosen her, too, before they'd met Kacey. Before they'd known a larger-than-life rendition of her, one who was equally nice, existed.

He wouldn't be the first guy to settle for her when Kacey made it clear she didn't want him.

Her high school prom date had that distinction. The one who'd taken her home early because her skin was breaking out in glittery welts.

"I've spent a few evenings with you, getting to know your tastes."

She'd purposely kept things completely business. For both their sakes. "I...guess."

"I've just spent the entire past weekend in your home. I know what kind of housekeeper you are. What kind of cook. I know you put the toilet paper on the roll with the end on top instead of on the bottom, which makes it easier to find when one needs to pull..."

"Okay, now you're embarrassing me."

"I noticed because I do it the same way."

She was even more embarrassed.

"I know that you have a genuine fondness for

my son, that you're a natural around him and that he likes you."

"He adores Kacey." She wasn't going to pretend otherwise. Fantasy or no.

"When he asks for one of you, he always asks for the other, too."

"And do you, too?" Growing up in Hollywood, they'd had their share of come-ons from men who wanted to take them both home.

They'd even had an offer for a B-rated movie deal once. Kacey had fired the agent who'd passed that one on to them.

"A guy might fantasize," Jem said, his tone sobering, "but I like to focus on one woman when I'm making love. There's only one of me."

Were they really having this conversation?

She needed to stop it, but didn't want to. She was kind of enjoying herself. Because it didn't really mean anything.

And because it was better than pissing him off, which was what she was about to do.

"So…if I agree to this dinner thing…does it mean I have to have sex with you?" The line was more Kacey than her, but she pulled it off.

She hoped he'd say yes. She knew that if he did, she was going to end things right there.

"Sex is not a requisite for a dinner date."

"You're sure."

"Absolutely."

Wow. What man gave up sex, even in jest?

"Okay, then." She called his bluff. Because the conversation was beginning to matter.

"Did you just agree to have dinner with me? Alone? As in a man and a woman on a date?" He showed no signs of distress. Or humor, either. He sounded like he really and truly wanted to have dinner with her.

She wasn't sure why he was pursuing her like this, but she would not let herself get in so deep she'd get hurt. But...

"I think so. Yes. And I'm not having sex afterward." She needed him to understand that right up front. It couldn't get that far. She couldn't have sex without falling for him. And she absolutely could not fall for him.

She had no idea what made him different from any other guy she'd ever dated. A couple of whom she'd had enjoyable sex with, without heartache when the relationships ended. Regret, sure. Who liked to share an intimate relationship and not have it work out? But heartbreak? Not since college, when she'd brought her boyfriend home for Christmas and he'd dumped her for Kacey.

Jem was discussing nights for their proposed date. Lacey was scaring herself to the point of wondering if she should back out.

"Is Wednesday okay?"

"Yes. Kacey and I don't have any plans."

"Do you think we could talk her into watching Levi?"

"I don't think we'll have to twist her arm." If her sister had still been up, she'd be sitting there eavesdropping and nodding her head emphatically.

He suggested a couple of places they could go. She told him to surprise her, because she truly didn't care where they went. And if she knew, she'd start looking forward to it, picturing the evening in detail, building it into more than it could be.

But she couldn't let him hang up. Not yet.

Because he might be canceling that date before he'd ever made a reservation.

CHAPTER EIGHTEEN

GLAD THAT HE'D changed his mind and taken a beer back outside rather than going to bed on a Tressa low, Jem stretched out in his seat, bantering back and forth with the woman on the other end of the line.

He'd forgotten what a natural high that could be. He'd been into Tressa. Really into her. But he couldn't remember the sound of her voice ever wiping away everything bad in his world.

He'd been into other women, too. A few of them.

Nothing compared.

He'd asked Lacey Hamilton out on a date. And she'd actually said yes.

She said yes! He felt like his junior high self, ready to race his bike to the top of the mountain that stood just outside his hometown and scream at the top of his lungs.

Instead, he sat there sipping beer, unable to wipe the goofy grin off his face.

"Jem?"

"Yeah?" Had she changed her mind about

going to bed with him after dinner? Okay, it might be a little premature, but…he was ready. More than ready.

If she was…

"On another note, I still haven't told you the reason for my call."

Thinking back, he figured she was right about that. He'd hijacked the conversation to talk about dating.

She said yes!

Maybe she'd changed her mind about the tile or paint color in the room he was building for her—a common phone call in his line of work.

"It's about Levi."

His feet came back down to the ground with a flop as he reminded himself that she was off the case. She couldn't take his boy away from him.

And then he realized that she wouldn't take his boy away from him. He'd just talked about how well he'd gotten to know her.

It seemed he really had. If he were abusing Levi, she'd take him in a heartbeat. And he'd expect her to. Otherwise, they were on the exact same side.

"What's up?" His tone was even when he finally spoke. Coming from a place of confidence, knowing Lacey was his partner on this one. Not his adversary.

"Has he ever talked to you about learning to swim?"

"Yeah, of course. He loves the water," he answered and then tried to remember specifically what Levi had told him. "There's a pool at Tressa's place and she was adamant about making sure he knew how to swim so there wouldn't be any danger of accidental drowning. I told you how she overdramatizes everything. But she handled it. She taught him to swim all by herself."

He'd been proud of her. She'd taken control of herself, been positively productive and done something good for their son without Jem's help.

Lacey's silence left him room to say more and he added, "He's not ready to join a swim team or anything, but he's proficient. He can get from one side of the pool to the other without taking in any water. It's only seven feet across, but the point was to know that wherever he fell in, he could get to the side."

Again, Tressa's plan had been good, well thought out.

"But you weren't there to see the actual lessons?"

"No." He remembered that with a little regret. He'd have liked to have been included. But he got so much of Levi to himself, he certainly couldn't begrudge his ex-wife her share of big moments alone with him. "I was in San Francisco for a California contractors' convention and also to meet with a potential client and work up a bid for me to send one of my crews up to work on a complex of condominiums."

"You were gone awhile, then."

"Yeah." He leaned back, put his feet up again and took another sip of beer. "A little over a week. It's the longest I've ever been away since Levi was born, and I gotta tell you, it wasn't easy. I called him every day. Twice. Morning and night. I think he handled the separation a lot better than I did."

Wow. Talking to someone about his personal stuff, one-on-one, felt good. Damned good. He hadn't realized how much he'd missed that part of having a companion.

"And by the time you got back, he knew how to swim?"

"Yep. But that's kind of been the story of Levi's life. He masters new skills as soon as he puts his mind to them. Like walking. When he was ten months old, he took one step, holding on to the chair he'd pulled himself up on, and within two days, he was walking from the chair to the couch."

Suddenly he was back to doubting again. Kacey and Lacey had been alone with Levi that afternoon. And the boy had been subdued at dinner. Because he was exhausted, Jem knew, but...

"Why the questions about him learning to swim?" he asked now. "Was there a situation with him when Kacey took him to the beach? Did she tell you something I should know?"

Levi could have run off toward the water—though if he had, it would surprise Jem. Levi knew the consequences—no beach for the rest of the summer—if he didn't respect the dangers inherent in being near the water alone.

He started to sweat until Lacey said, "He was perfect at the beach. Kacey didn't tell me something you should know, Levi did."

Everything inside Jem slowed down. Feet firmly on the ground, he sat forward, staring in the dark toward the pavers he'd laid himself.

"What did he tell you?"

"He asked Kacey and me how our mother held us both underwater at the same time when she taught us to swim."

That could mean any number of things.

"He demonstrated to us how his mom held his ribs and squeezed as she held him under the water."

Four-year-olds exaggerated. Levi told him impossibly outrageous stories all the time. And Tressa did have a tendency to panic. She could have had too tight a grip on him, but only to keep him safe.

Was everything they did going to be under scrutiny now? And for how long? What in the hell had that anonymous phone call gotten them into?

"He said that he cried."

"He told you that?"

In the version he got, Levi had had great lessons. He'd excelled as usual. When he'd made it across the pool by himself, Tressa had bought a little plastic basketball hoop and basketball for the pool and they'd played with it and had a blast.

Levi had taken him by the hand out to her pool to show the little plastic basketball hoop to him as soon as he'd gotten back to town.

"He also told me that he didn't tell you, which is why I'm telling you. It seems significant that he not only didn't tell you, but that its magnitude is such that it's still in his data bank."

He didn't disagree with her.

She was telling *him*. Talking to him like a friend would. Or someone who also cared for his son.

The immediate defensive traffic in his brain slowed. Allowing Jem to process information calmly.

"When did this happen?" Her question broke into his thoughts.

"March. We had those few warm days and Tressa keeps her pool heated."

"Here's the thing, Jem…" He waited through her pause, wanting to know her thoughts. "I don't want you upset with me, but this is what I do for a living, and I can't just turn it off because I'm not working."

"I want to hear what you have to say." As she

said, she dealt with kids every day. He'd value her input.

"You remember I told you about a report of bruising? And you were adamant that if there'd been any, you'd have noticed?"

His blood ran cold.

"After I interviewed you—and Levi—I knew you were right. There was no way you'd have missed the bruises, and I believed you hadn't seen them. It's partially why I closed the investigation. There was no evidence to substantiate the claim, so I had to believe someone had simply been overzealous."

He wondered if she should be telling him all of this.

"But now... The timing's right, Jem. I think that Levi's torso *was* covered in bruises. And that they'd faded before you saw him."

Tressa wouldn't hold Levi so tight, for so long, that his torso would be covered in bruises. She'd... No, she just wouldn't. She was his mother.

A drama queen, yes. Unpredictable and self-absorbed a lot of the time. But not when it came to Levi. She always put him first.

His almost-full-time custody of their son was a case in point. Tressa was missing so much, and she knew it. Innumerable tearful late-night phone conversations were testimony to that fact.

She planned everything else around her weekends with him—never canceling or going out when it was her turn to care for their son—unless she absolutely couldn't help it. She was agreeable anytime Jem asked her to keep Levi for an hour or two if he had a business dinner or association meeting to attend.

"Say something."

He didn't know what to say. "I'll talk to her."

"You think she'll be honest with you? If she was going to admit to hurting him, don't you think she'd already have told you?"

He had to remind himself that Lacey didn't know Tressa. Or how her mind worked. If she'd done something she wasn't proud of, she wouldn't come out and tell him. That served her no benefit and could cause her discomfort. But lying to him when he asked a direct question could cost her more.

Bottom line was, she needed him. And the divorce—the fact that he'd gone through with it—had shown her that there were some things he just was not going to put up with. No matter how much he understood her inner workings.

And sympathized with her very tough past.

"I think she'll be honest," he told her. "I'd like to give her that chance. Are you agreeable to that?"

"What do you mean? It's not up to me if you talk to your ex-wife."

"I assume that since you made one report as a private citizen, you can make another." He'd figured that out shortly after he'd breathed a sigh of relief that she was off his case. And thought there was nothing more to fear from her.

Truth was, he *had* nothing to fear from her. Not because she was off the case, but because she cared about the exact same things he did.

"And it also stands to reason that with your position, a report you might make would carry more weight than one another, unknown citizen might make."

"So what are you asking?"

She didn't deny the fact that she might call her coworker.

"I guess I'm asking you to be my partner in this," he said. "Let me talk to Tressa. I'll get back with you and let you know what she says as soon as I do. And then, if you feel that you need to make your call, you let me know that, and you make your call. Nothing behind your back and nothing behind mine. Does that work for you?"

This was bigger than asking her out for a date. Way bigger. And yet, in some ways, it seemed to have the same implications.

"Levi's not going to be spending any time with his mother in the next couple of days, is he?"

"Nope."

"Then it works fine for me."

"All of it?"

"You talking to Tressa, you mean?"

"That. And the not going behind each other's

backs part. I tell you everything Tressa says or does. You tell me before you make any calls you feel you need to make."

"Yes. That works for me."

"No matter what you think, or what, professionally, your instincts are telling you, you'll let me know before you report any concerns."

"Yes, as long as Levi isn't in immediate danger. But you have to know, Jem, I will report concerns even if you don't want me to."

"Good." His feet were back up on the rock. The goofy grin was gone, but something more substantial, and just as good, seemed to be taking its place. "Because rest assured, Lace, if you ever think my son is danger, I want you to move hell and high water to help him."

She didn't say anything. He wasn't sure why.

"You called me 'Lace.'"

He hadn't realized. But...

"You'd rather I didn't?"

"No, I kind of liked it. It's just...only Kacey and my parents have ever called me that."

"She says it all the time. I guess it just stuck with me."

A ridiculous conversation, but he liked it, anyway.

Almost as much as he liked her.

CHAPTER NINETEEN

LACEY WAITED ALL day Monday to hear from Jem. He'd be working, for sure. And Tressa would be, too. Still, she was on edge. In a queer sort of way. Levi was perfectly safe for now. If Tressa was abusing him, in any way, Jem would keep the boy away from his mother even before the state could intervene. So Levi wasn't the immediate concern.

Which left...Jem.

She was concerned about Jem contacting his ex-wife and getting into an emotional discussion with her.

Because she was jealous?

He'd asked her on a date. No more. She had no ownership over him in any way. No matter how much she was drawn to him.

Or how perfect he seemed to her.

And even if she did feel a little like she was sending a steak into a lion's den, it was more than that. If Tressa had fooled Lacey so completely, then was it possible that she was doing a number on Jem, too? It wouldn't be the first time she'd seen a woman be manipulative.

Not that Lacey knew Tressa at all. Jem knew her. Lacey had spent a couple of hours with the woman.

But after ten years of living her job, her instincts were usually spot-on.

Which would mean that Tressa wasn't hurting her son. And yet, Levi's story the day before had been true. She was sure of that.

And clearly it was significant enough to him that he was talking about it almost three months later.

She'd meant to tell Jem about Levi's last comment, too. About being afraid that "she" would not let him live with his father.

Whether the "she" was Tressa, or Lacey, or someone else entirely in the little boy's mind, Jem needed to know that his son was harboring the fear that he could lose his home with his father, at an age when the little boy needed security more than anything else. Security was the freedom that allowed kids to grow. To think they could do anything. Explore. Learn. Reach out and take life on...

Jem wasn't going to be working on the house that night, or at all that week. He wanted the footer to cure for a week. And also had to have it inspected before he pulled out the metal frames, backfilled the holes and poured the cement that would become the floor of the room.

Any other time she'd have thought the whole

process boring as hell. Funny how fascinating it all was to her now.

Funny, too, how Tressa was blonde, decorated her home like Lacey did and liked the same kind of tea.

She brushed the thought aside. Jem had wanted the divorce from Tressa. Wanted to live apart from her. Lacey was definitely not a "second" choice where the other woman was concerned. She wasn't something he was settling for because he couldn't have what he really wanted.

At least not where his ex-wife was concerned.

Growing up in her sister's shadow was making her paranoid. And it had to stop.

His call came in while she was on her way home from work. He was home already and had Levi watching a video, which gave him roughly twenty-two minutes to have a conversation without Levi paying attention.

He was speaking so softly she could barely hear him—even with her car's Bluetooth feeding his voice through the speaker system.

"I talked to Tressa before I picked him up from preschool," he was saying.

Lacey's heart thumped so hard she could feel it. She hated that. Also hated that she couldn't read anything in his tone of voice or see his face.

Her interest in him was more than professional. She couldn't pretend otherwise.

"And?"

"He did cry when she was teaching him to swim."

"She told you that?"

"As soon as I asked." He sounded...calm.

"Why was he crying? Was he afraid of the water?"

"He wasn't listening to her. She was trying to get him to put his face in the water, then lift it back up, and move his arms in a front crawl. But he kept jumping around and splashing. He slipped and went underwater and she panicked. She was scared to death he was going to drown and she overreacted. She reached down and grabbed him as tightly as she could and hauled him up out of the water. And then she yelled at him and made him cry."

As most parents might have done.

"And I can tell you right now, the reason he wouldn't have told me was because he hates me to know when he misbehaves. He's always so eager for me to be proud of him, so eager to get things right..."

She wanted to address that, too, just because she spent her days counseling parents in raising healthy children. Too much of a need to please Jem could result in some real problems for Levi later.

Thing was, she hadn't noticed him putting any undue pressure on his son. He wasn't overly harsh with him. Nor did he require anything out of the ordinary of him.

"Levi doesn't act like a child who fears disappointing you."

"I don't think so, either. But Tressa's right. He never tells me when he's been in trouble over there."

"Maybe it's her he fears disappointing."

Or maybe she was giving the little boy reason to fear. What if she was threatening him? Telling him he'd have to leave his father's home if Levi told about the times she lost her temper with him? Not that Lacey had proof of that. Just a supposition.

"I can't imagine that he fears disappointing Tressa, but I suppose he could think that the reason she doesn't live with him, like most mommies live with their kids, is because of him. We've both talked to him a lot about it, about the fact that Mommy and Dad have a problem between them and that they can't live together anymore. He's seemed quite happy living with me..."

"You sound hesitant." She was almost home, so she pulled off at the beach, parking with a view of the incoming tide, to finish their conversation. Kacey would be waiting with a grilled chicken salad ready. Lacey wanted to get this settled first.

"It's just... He's been a little more clingy lately."

All senses on alert, she pushed her twist to the back of her head and asked, "Like when?"

"Most recently, when we came back from your house last night."

That one was easily explained by the conversation that had taken place in the puzzle room.

"And?"

"He had that nightmare at Tressa's. He was particularly clingy the next day when I brought him home."

"Was that the first time?"

"No. The first couple of days after he broke his arm he was off."

"And no other times?" Mara had said his demeanor had changed noticeably over the past months.

"Not that come to mind. Kids change every day, it seems. One minute he's a baby wanting to be held. The next he's pushing away from me to get down. He wants me to cut his meat, and then suddenly it's all about him doing it himself. His personality is changing, sure, but nothing that seems alarming or abnormal."

She didn't see Levi every day—or hadn't until recently. Mara had known him since he was a baby. Mara was around developing toddlers and preschoolers every day. She'd know about normal developmental personality changes.

Still, Mara wasn't a professional counselor. "Have you talked to Tressa about the clinginess?"

"No. But she's talked to me about him being upset. Mostly because of the nightmare."

"What does she say about it?"

"That he's afraid you're going to take him away from me. That he won't be able to live with me anymore."

She'd known. Her instincts were still honed—in spite of her personal involvement. But there were a couple of things off...

"How would he have known why I was in your house? Or why he came to my office? Did you tell him?"

"Of course not. Absolutely not. He's a four-year-old. There's no way he'd understand that on any level that could be okay for him."

"Agreed. But you'd be surprised what some parents do. Kids, even ones with advanced intelligence, still believe pretty much everything their parents tell them. Some parents, those with something to hide, will manipulate their kids into believing or hiding things."

And someone had told Levi why Lacey had first come into their lives.

"Tressa didn't tell him, if that's what you're thinking."

"You didn't. And I didn't. Who else is there?"

"I don't know, but I'd bet my bank account and future earnings that it wasn't her."

He had her attention. "Why do you say that?"

"Because he told me that she told him you were a friend of hers. That you just wanted to get to know us because she'd talked all about us and made you want to know us."

She frowned. Watched as a lone surfer rode a lame wave in the waning sun. "That doesn't sound like something he'd have made up."

"He didn't. I asked her if she'd told him who you were and she was as shocked at the idea as I was. Seeing it as cruel. Which was why she didn't want him there when Sydney showed up on Friday night. She was afraid she'd get upset, or cry, or say something, and he'd catch on. If she'd told him that you all were trying to take him away from me, she could have just let him stay. Sydney was just there to talk, like you were at my house with him present the first time."

He was right.

"So maybe she's wrong and this doesn't have to do with me at all." Which brought up the second thing wrong with the theory. "If he thought I was out to separate the two of you, wouldn't he be panicked at the thought of us alone together? Wouldn't he want to keep the two of you away from my house? And certainly shun me as a friend?"

"He'd move into your house if I'd let him."

The words brought a vision to mind she hadn't allowed herself to focus on. She was the woman who found good and loving homes for children. Not the woman who brought them home.

"I guess we'll just have to keep a watch on

things and see what brings on the episodes," Jem was saying. And she figured they'd used up fifteen minutes, at least, of their twenty-two.

"It could just be that he's clingy when he's tired," she said against her better judgment. If there was even a slight chance that Levi was in danger, she couldn't be giving his father reason to put his guard down.

Yet she cared about Jem and wanted to soothe him if she could. He was a good father. The best. Doing a job solo that usually took two people. And doing it better than most, in her admittedly prejudiced opinion.

"I'm still bothered, though," she had to add. "Tressa's story about the swimming incident. One grab to haul Levi out of the water wouldn't have caused bruising all along his torso."

"No, but the fact that she'd held on to him for dear life every second he was putting his head underwater, then picking it up and learning to move his arms and kick his feet, would certainly do so."

What healthy parent held their kid so tightly they were bruising him for that length of time?

"Do you think it's possible she was pissed at him for his noncompliance, and forcing his head underwater over and over?"

The scenario fit exactly what Levi had described.

"I don't," Jem said. "There are just some things

Tressa wouldn't do. Purposely hurting Levi is one of them."

"You sound so sure."

"I am sure."

"Can I ask why?"

"Because my ex-wife thinks she needs me. And she knows that if she ever...*ever*...does one thing to hurt my boy she will never see either one of us again."

He believed what he was saying beyond the shadow of a doubt. Lacey was convinced of that much.

She wanted to believe him, too.

But she drove home with a heavy heart.

Sometimes people couldn't see what was right under their noses.

Was it possible that Levi wasn't the only Bridges male that Tressa had been manipulating? Was Jem a victim, too?

She told herself she was being ridiculous, that Tressa's drama was wearing off on her. But once the idea had been planted, she couldn't seem to escape it.

CHAPTER TWENTY

JEM DIDN'T TALK to Lacey on Tuesday. There'd been no real reason to. While he could have made an excuse to call, he purposely chose not to do so. He didn't want to tempt her, in any way, to call off their date. Or tempt fate, either.

He talked to Tressa, though. She called him Tuesday right after work. And Wednesday, too. Seemingly to check on Levi, to ask how his arm was doing—a few weeks late on that one. They were due to have the cast off in another week or two.

Amelia was still out of the picture and he had to wonder if she'd finally had enough. He'd seen the pattern with Tressa often enough not to be surprised by it. She had her way of seeing the world. Knew what she needed. What she thought was right. And if someone didn't meet her expectations, she didn't go easy on them.

In their early days, that had been a good thing for him. She'd encouraged him to work all the hours in the day. To certify in all of the fields in his profession. He'd been planning to do so.

Wanting to do so. She'd paved the way with evenings spent helping him study. Quizzing him. Learning his trades with him so that he could focus almost exclusively.

And she'd made some good investments with the money he was making. He got his contractor's license and she'd encouraged him to seek out a small job, on the side, separate and apart from the electrician he was currently working for. He was a certified framer. And plumber, too.

He wasn't sure when he'd quit pleasing her. Lord knew he'd tried his damnedest to keep her happy. A failed marriage didn't sit well with him. Because a marriage took two—to succeed or fail.

He was about to fail her again, he knew, as he pulled up to Lacey's little house Wednesday just before six.

"We're here!" Levi called from the back. Jem had planned to feed him before bringing him over to play with Kacey until bedtime. Kacey had insisted that dinner was part of their date.

Tempted to tell his son not to mention this outing to his mother—ever—Jem refrained. He wasn't going to start down that slippery path, no matter how justified he might feel in doing so.

He knew why Tressa was calling so much all of a sudden—besides the fact that Amelia wasn't in her life at the moment. She was afraid that Jem was interested in another woman.

Because of the conversation they'd had Sunday

night. He should never have told her he was doing the job as a favor. Or that the client's sister was babysitting their son.

She'd always been afraid that Jem would fall for someone else. Every day of their marriage, she'd doubted his fidelity. It didn't matter that he'd never, not once, given her any cause to doubt him.

Cheating wasn't his style.

But this time she was right. He *was* interested in another woman. Very interested.

And he wasn't going to let her screw up his chance.

Shrugging aside guilt he had no reason to feel, he helped his son down from the truck and followed behind as Levi ran up the walk, climbed the two cement steps without holding on to the rail and rang the bell.

"YOU WORE YOUR hair down." Maybe not the best first line for a first date, but as he glanced at Lacey before pulling away from the front of her house, it's what came out of his mouth.

Her hair being down was significant.

"I'm on a date." Her smile was mysterious. He kind of liked it.

"You always wear your hair down on dates?"

"No." He started the car and pulled away from the house, where her sister and his son watched from the window, waving at them. He didn't want any intruders on this conversation.

"What's the determining factor?" Might as well get straight to the point.

"There isn't one."

"But you have done it before." Suddenly he felt like they weren't just talking about her hair.

"Once or twice." He made a turn. And then another.

"Did it go well?"

"One did, one didn't."

He pondered that. Wondered if she knew they were really talking about sex.

"We didn't talk about where we were going to go," he said. Wanting badly to go with what he'd mentally termed option B sometime during the past couple of days.

She was in nice quality white capri pants and a red, white and blue crop-sleeved cotton tunic, with blue sandals and a big red, white and blue cloth purse.

If she thought the ensemble in any way hid, or detracted from, the lovely curves she was hiding, she was dead wrong.

"I told you, it doesn't matter to me."

So…option B, it was?

"You want to go back to my place? I've got a couple of steaks, some potatoes we can put on the grill. And veggies, too. We could sit out at the fish pond, have a glass of wine…"

He'd wired the backyard for music. They'd be alone. His bed was close by. No chance Tressa would find them out and about if she happened to be scouring Santa Raquel eateries.

He didn't think she'd go that far. Not anymore. She'd learned her lesson on that one.

But he'd be able to relax more if she could see his truck in his driveway in the event she did another drive-by. He knew she was checking up on him, so it just made sense not to rev her engines if he could help it.

"I'd actually prefer that," Lacey said. "In case you haven't noticed, I'm not as much into having a lot of people around me as my sister is."

There it was again…her comparing herself to Kacey. Funny how people couldn't see themselves as they really were.

INSTEAD OF THE usual blue jeans and various work shirts she'd seen him in, Jem was wearing black jeans and a white polo shirt for the evening. It looked like he'd shaved, too. The nights he'd come to her house to work he'd had a very definite five-o'clock shadow. His dark hair was as natural looking as always…

Good thing he didn't wear the polo shirt to work. It was lethal. Not only did it accent the breadth of his shoulders and chest, it showed off the dark hair beneath it. Made her want to run her fingers through it.

People slept together on first dates all the time. She never had. And wouldn't. But if this was going to be her only chance, if she did it before she was in too deep...

Stop it.

"You like your steaks rare?" he asked, standing by the impressive outdoor kitchen he'd built. It had a sink with running water, a small refrigerator—from which he'd taken a bottle of wine—and a bottom cupboard that contained not only the two wineglasses they were using, but various other drinking vessels, as well. Small plastic ones included.

And there was the grill. Infrared. With two burners off to the side.

"I like them medium," she said. "Kacey's the rare girl."

He closed the grill. "You did it again."

"Did what again?"

"Compared yourself to your sister."

She hadn't noticed.

"Why do you do that?"

She shrugged and took a sip of wine. She was having a good time, was alone with a man who was affecting her like none other, was filled with anticipation and a tad bit of naughty. Something more in tune with Kacey than herself...

She'd just done it again.

"It's natural, I guess, when you grow up side by side with another human being who looks exactly like you do."

He sat down, touching his knee to hers. Could

have been an accident, but he kept it there and took a sip of his wine. A light merlot.

"The curious thing is that you always seem to come off on the bad end of the comparison."

She could have been back onstage with lights shining so brightly on her that she couldn't see anything in front of her. He saw too much.

She felt naked. Raw.

A tad bit defensive.

"You know Kacey," she said, sipping more quickly than she otherwise might have done. "She glows. It's not her fault. Not anything she even wants. But it's always been that way."

"She's the sunrise. You're the sunset. Both are equally spectacular."

Oh, my God. Had he just said that? She stared at him. She loved sunsets, thought them the most stunning of all the natural wonders...

She was going to cry.

"In case you haven't figured it out, I'm a sunset guy."

Lacey blinked. And blinked again. He got up to turn the steaks—on purpose, she'd bet, giving her a second.

"I like my steak medium, too, by the way."

She knew what he was doing. And if she hadn't already been falling in love with him, as Kacey kept asserting, she started right then. Falling hard. And fast.

People fell in love at first sight. And she...

Afraid, she knew she had to stop the downward hurtle. "People have always preferred Kacey to me," she told him. If he was going to be blind, she at least needed to tell him what he wasn't seeing. Better now than later. "From acting directors to the high school prom committee—both junior and senior years—to...men."

"Or maybe it was just that she was the easier one to reel in."

"What does that mean?"

"If you see a doughnut right up on the front of the tray, and there's another equally delicious-looking one in the back, which one are you going to take?"

"The one in front."

"Exactly."

"Kacey and I aren't doughnuts on a tray."

"She's accessible. You aren't so much."

She sipped and eyed him, wanting so badly to fall under his spell. To believe what he was telling her. "You're saying I'm hard to get."

"I'm saying you're more discreet. Which makes you more interesting to a discerning guy like myself."

She was in severe danger of adoring this man.

And his wine, of which she helped herself to a little more, with hands that shook.

"When Mom and Dad called for us, they always said her name first."

"Who was born first?"

"Believe it or not, I was. For six minutes and ten seconds, I was the only one of me."

"You're still the only one of you."

She knew that. More now that she'd moved out on her own. And she was lonelier since then, too.

"I love having my sister around," she said. And was just discovering how much. When her resentment of Kacey had begun, she didn't know, but she knew it was gone. "I miss her like crazy." The wine had to be loosening her tongue.

And her brain, too.

"I didn't realize how much coming second all the time had affected me."

"Who got better grades?"

"I did."

"So you didn't come second there."

"Yeah, I guess, but grades were never that big of a deal in our household." She and Kacey were already earning enough to support themselves before they'd entered high school. "You know, it's one thing if your sister is taller than you, better endowed, with prettier features...you get that fate gave you other graces. Hopefully. But to have your looks be exactly the same—from the same egg—and still be overlooked..."

She sounded pathetic and wouldn't blame him if he was second-guessing his choice of sisters. A part of her almost hoped he was.

It would make life so much easier. Safer.

"Would you rather be Kacey?" He was studying her.

"Of course not. Her life would drive me crazy."

"Plus you prefer softer shades to brilliant white." Information gleaned from their paint-chip expedition the week before.

"Yep."

"Just think how unhappy you'd be, then, if you'd been the sunrise."

Something new and beautiful flowered within her. In spite of herself.

Lacey smiled at him over the top of her wineglass.

CHAPTER TWENTY-ONE

HE THOUGHT ABOUT having sex with her. About once a minute. Interspersed with keeping his mind on their conversation. More when they weren't actually talking, like when she bent over to look in the pond to meet Levi's goldfish—all of which had names. She learned them, too.

He thought about sex with her a lot as they ate and she slipped the fork between her lips and back out again.

But he thought of a lot of other things, too. Like how much he wanted to ask her out again, to have her over again.

Alone. And when Levi was home.

They talked a little bit about the world, society. Mostly in terms of bringing up a child in tumultuous and rapidly changing times. Her views mirrored his, and he hadn't even told her where he stood. Not that that surprised him.

He had no idea who up there was in charge of this stuff, but he actually had the thought that maybe she had been picked especially for him.

He also knew that he was getting way ahead of himself.

She'd agreed to have dinner with him, not get married.

Not that he was getting married, either. He just wanted...more.

Sex, yes, but even more than that.

The sun had set. Their dishes were empty— Jem had eaten the last couple of bites of steak from her plate. They each had a little wine left in the bottom of their glasses. There was some in the bottle, too. Enough to take inside with them.

"What time did you tell Kacey we'd be home?" Levi was going to bed at Lacey's and probably wouldn't even wake up when Jem transported him to his car seat and then to his bed at his house. Even if he did, he'd go right back to sleep.

"I didn't. She said stay out as late as we want." She smiled in the way that made him think she was hiding something. Or enjoying a private thought.

He wanted in.

"What did she really say?"

"That she didn't want me to ruin the evening with a timetable. I'm supposed to relax and just let everything flow."

He nodded. "I like that."

"How am I doing?"

"You tell me."

"I think we're flowing along pretty well."

He grinned. He knew. But it was still good to hear.

"Do you ever get angry?" He just had to ask.

"Of course! Everyone does."

Watching her beneath the soft outdoor lighting he'd installed, he said, "I want to see you in a bad mood."

The words didn't sound anything out loud as they had in his mind. He just couldn't imagine Lacey screaming trash like Tressa did. Like his older sister, JoAnne, had when he'd been growing up and their parents went out and left her in charge.

"What? You want to see me in a bad mood? Why?"

The look she was giving him could have made him feel odd. Except that it seemed warm somehow. Maybe he needed to slow down on the wine.

"They say you don't truly know someone until you've seen them at their worst. I want to really know you." Now, that had come out as he'd meant it to.

"So...you show me your worst and I'll show you mine."

He grinned. "I don't think I can find it right now."

"Me, either."

Leaning forward, he reached for her and pulled her toward him. She stood, and so did he. They were just standing there, looking at each other.

"You are the most beautiful thing I've ever seen," he said.

She shook her head. "You've seen..."

With a finger to her lips, he silenced her.

"But it's true, Jem," she said softly, her gaze seeming to implore him to understand. "Life's hard enough to deal with without hiding from the truth. One of the things you learn as an identical twin is that you are not original."

"But you are individual, Lacey. I know Kacey. I've seen her. Spent a lot of time with her. And she's beautiful. Sweet. Kind. But I look at you, I see into your eyes, and there's...more. Your eyes show me the essence of you, the person. Not just the body with features identical to your sister's. You could dress like Kacey and she could dress like you and I'd know you instantly."

He had no doubt of that. He just wasn't sure how to convince her. And sensed it was vital that he do it.

With both hands, he pushed the hair back from her shoulders, let his fingers trail down her arms to her waist. Beneath the loose tunic. To the smooth skin he'd yet to see.

Lacey's hands were on his hips, almost on top of his belt. And when he moved forward, she tilted his way, into him, touching his lips as he touched hers. Pressing into him. They were melting. Her. Him.

He'd imagined starting off slowly—testing her

waters, moving cautiously through the waves of desire. Tasting her lips and pulling back. Instead, her mouth opened—or his did—and their tongues were meeting as if they'd known each other their entire lives.

His penis almost exploded. Hands shaking, he held on to her, thinking that he'd sit, pull her onto his lap. Ease a small bit of his excruciating pain.

Or masochistically make it worse.

And his doorbell rang. The sound came to him faintly at first. Almost something he could ignore. Until his brain computed what it had been. His lips left Lacey's.

"That was my doorbell."

"You expecting someone?" Her smile definitely belonged in his bedroom.

"No."

The dread in his gut told him who it could be.

If he left Tressa standing outside, with his truck in the drive, where he'd left it so she'd know he was home and relax and leave him alone, she'd keep ringing. Or worse, come around back. She couldn't get through the privacy fence. But she could find a knothole to look through…

"Probably just a neighbor, maybe with some misdelivered mail," he said inanely, feeling like a two-timing jerk in a bad comedy. "I'll be right back."

The absolute last thing he wanted to do right then was leave Lacey standing out there alone.

The second last thing was to face Tressa.

So maybe it wasn't her.

He hoped to God it wasn't her.

He'd warned her about showing up at his place.

If she was there, it meant she was in a bad enough mood that she didn't give a damn.

And that was not on his agenda for the evening.

Or any evening.

He knew before he got to the door that it was Tressa. He saw her car parked behind his truck in the driveway. Her way of blocking him in. Holding him captive to her.

Hurrying to the door, before she got more upset and insisted on searching his house to see what he was doing with their son there, he hoped to God his lips didn't look kissed as he pulled open the door.

"What's wrong?" he asked the second he saw her.

"Nothing. I just...wanted to see Levi."

"He's in bed, already asleep."

"So, I can peek in on him."

"No, Tressa. You know our agreement. My home is my space." He was not going to let her drama into his world.

"I just want to see him, Jem. He gets his cast off soon and I just... I feel horrible that it happened, and..."

Her tears softened the steel around his heart.

Tressa really did care. She loved Levi. And he knew how much she let things eat her up inside.

"You'll wake him up, and since he knows he only sees Mommy at her house, he'll be confused. Hasn't he already been through enough?" He hated to use her own tactics against her, feeling dirty, like he was becoming her, but since he obviously couldn't do as she wanted—mostly because Levi wasn't in his room—she left him no choice.

A chair scraped against a paver outside. He realized, too late, that he'd left the sliding glass door open in his haste to prevent a Tressa meltdown.

Turning her sharp gaze from behind him, to Jem, she said, "You have someone here."

Not now, Tressa. For God's sake, not now.

"A buddy is out back sharing a beer with me."

"Don't lie to me, Jem."

"Fine. I'm on a date. We just finished dinner."

"With Levi in the house?" Her voice had already raised an octave, the sharpness growing more acute.

He wanted to help her. To make her see how she looked when she got this way. To hear how she sounded. He knew she didn't mean it. And would be sorry later. She'd make it up to him.

Except that it just wasn't possible anymore. Because he knew that no matter how sorry she was, there'd be another time. And so—God help him—he'd taken their son and walked out on her when she'd thrown out the divorce challenge one particularly exhausting Sunday afternoon.

"Single father's date, Tressa. And it's just dinner. Outside."

"No. Don't you pull that bullshit on me, Jem Bridges." Tressa's voice rose another octave. "You forget, I know you."

He hoped none of his neighbors had their windows open. One of the reasons he'd made the stipulation that Tressa couldn't come to his house was because he couldn't stand the way people looked at him after one of her screaming episodes. Like he should somehow be able to stop her.

Like he must have done something pretty heinous to have upset her like that.

"You can't wait to stick it in her, can you?" she spat. Literally. Her saliva landed on his chin. "You're nothing but a whore, Jem Bridges. A whore! I worked like a dog, helping you get where you are, supporting all the long hours, the responsibilities I had to take on alone, while you climbed up in your world. And now that you're the boss, what do you do? Do you take care of me? The one who had your back during the hard years? No. You walk out on me. On our family. So you can whore around. You think I don't know what's going on?"

"It's not what you think, Tressa." It wasn't a one-night stand, a cheap liaison. But she'd like the truth even less. Because if Jem had another woman in his life, she'd lose even more control…

"I see that twinkle in your eye, Jem," she said. "It hasn't been there in a long time. I'd actually forgotten it. Until suddenly—ta-da!—here it is. Just like you to rub my face in it."

"I have no idea what you're talking about."

Tressa had no right looking into his soul. He'd taken all rights back from her when he'd left their marriage.

"You're a damned loser, Jem. You know it, and so do I. She's welcome to you."

She turned to leave and Jem breathed a sigh of relief. Until she turned back. "Don't you think you're going to get away with this, Jem." Her voice was lowered, but not enough. "I came over here to make love with you. Because I know it's been a while for you and I know you have your needs, and how do you repay my kindness?" If a guy could die of the cringes, he'd be gone. "This is how you repay me? By tramping around on me? Well, forget it, buddy. You better hope you get some from her, because you sure as hell aren't getting it from me. This door is closed."

He'd heard that one so many times it didn't even faze him. He only wished it were true. When was Tressa going to figure out that he couldn't get it up for her anymore? Not even if he'd wanted to.

"I hate you," she said. "If Levi weren't asleep, I'd take him out of this house right now. He's way too good for you, Jem. I wish to God you weren't his father."

She'd been back down the walk as she spoke. Reaching the grass, she turned and fled to her car.

But not before he'd seen the tears pouring down her face.

She was hurting. More than she could bear.

And he was sorry.

SHE HADN'T WANTED to overhear, had tried her best not to. But then, when she'd resigned herself to her fate, she'd tried to hear every word so that she could know what they were dealing with. She'd expected him to reappear as soon as the screaming stopped. She heard the front door shut and heard Tressa's car starting up in the distance.

It was another two or three minutes before Jem reappeared. His gaze sought hers. And then moved away.

"I'm assuming you heard that?" he asked almost nonchalantly as he stacked their dirty dishes, silverware on top.

"Most of it." All of it. But having counseled many people on the victim end of abuse, she wanted to spare him as much humiliation as she could.

Instead of sitting and talking to her like she expected, he carried their dishes into the house and came back for their wineglasses.

"Sorry about that, I just wanted to get them

rinsed and in the dishwasher before stuff hardened."

Since when did steak juice harden? But she understood. He'd needed time to collect himself.

He might be forgetting, but this wasn't her first rodeo. Or even her fiftieth.

"And I'm sorry about back there, too."

"You have no reason to apologize."

Their wineglasses sat on the table, untouched. The bottle looked forlorn next to them.

"You ready to go?" He was still just standing there.

"If you want me to," she said, not sure what was going on. Weren't they going to talk about what had just happened?

He knew what she did for a living.

"Of course I don't want you to, but I'm sure you want to. Come on, I'll take you home." He reached out a hand to her.

She ignored it. "If I wanted to go home, I'd say so, Jem."

Even if he wanted her to go, she didn't feel like she should. What she'd just witnessed... It had strengthened the suspicions she'd been having since Sunday. Mara was right. Levi was being abused. By his mother.

The woman was clearly out of control.

She thought Jem was going to argue with her, insist on taking her home. He surprised her when he sat down.

"Kind of ruined the evening," he said.

"Not unless we let it."

His grin was forced.

And Lacey wasn't sure what to do. She was too close. Couldn't find her boundaries…

"Can I bring back the twinkle to your eye?" she asked. And immediately hated herself for the question. As if this was in any way about her.

He tilted his head. Looked at her. And smiled. A real smile. "You already have."

"I'm glad."

"Believe it or not, I am, too."

He needed time. She didn't like it, didn't want to not help him, but she wasn't a professional when she was with Jem.

She was a woman tuning in to the heart he was starting to show her. Or, if nothing else, a friend tuning in to a friend.

"You want to call it a night?" she asked then.

"No, but…yeah." His gaze was direct, touching her as intimately as his lips had and far more deeply.

Lacey nodded, picked up their wineglasses and walked into the house, leaving him to follow with the bottle.

She couldn't take away what had happened to him. Not just that night, but for however long he'd been a partner in an abusive relationship. But she could tend to him now. By listening to what he wasn't saying.

Giving him what he seemed to need. Time to himself. To assimilate. To recover.

He collected his keys. She grabbed the over-size red, white and blue cloth bag Kacey had presented her with that evening when she'd returned from work. Her sister had spent at least part of the day shopping.

He turned off lights as they moved to the front of the house. She let herself out. He locked the door as he exited behind her.

He didn't touch her. She didn't walk close enough to him to risk contact.

Neither said a word as they drove home. Lacey wondered if their first date had been their last. If one perfect kiss was all she was ever going to know.

She wondered if he'd send a crew to build her birthday present.

She wondered what she was going to tell Sydney. And knew that she had to let Jem know that she'd be calling her coworker in the morning. She'd given her word. He'd tell her everything Tressa said, and she'd let him know before she called in a report.

When he pulled up in front of her house, she had the words ready to spill. She was going to call Sydney in the morning.

"Will you have dinner with me tomorrow night?" His question forestalled her.

"Yes." Her answer came without forethought.

But even if she'd taken time, she knew it would have been the same.

"We don't have a lot of time before Kacey has to leave."

"A week."

"I very much want to share you with Levi," he said. "But I need you to myself."

"I understand."

It was too much, too soon. And there didn't seem to be any way to stop it.

"I'm sorry."

Leaning over, she touched her finger to his lips. "You have nothing to apologize for."

He looked like he was going to say more, but leaned over and kissed her instead. An intense, tongue-joining promise of a kiss. And then he walked her up to her front door, made small talk with her sister, collected his son so tenderly the boy didn't stir in his sleep and was gone.

Lacey spent the night wondering how much of what she thought had happened really had or if she'd read too much into things, been clouded enough by the wine that she'd only felt as though she'd actually walked on cloud nine.

And knew that until she had a chance to talk to Jem again, she wasn't going to say anything to anyone. Levi wasn't going to be with his mother during the next twenty-four hours.

She had a little time to figure everything out.

CHAPTER TWENTY-TWO

JEM CALLED TRESSA Thursday on his way home from work. He'd learned a long time ago that it was best to be proactive with her.

He knew it was vulnerability behind her crazy words, her need to try to control those she cared about. Her own little piece of the world.

She'd been abused from the time she was a toddler. Her parents had withheld love anytime she didn't meet their expectations. And worse. She'd been hit regularly, locked in the laundry room for a couple of days at a time, even burned with her father's cigarette once. But the worst, for her, was the emotional starvation.

He figured that was partially what made her so prone to drama. She had too much stored up inside of her. A lifetime of emotion that had had no outlet.

And now that she was no longer held captive, now that she was free, she had a desperate need to do all she could to keep her world the way she thought it should be.

He also knew that if he called her, she'd calm

down. And it was best for Levi, for his overall development, if the mother who loved him, and whom he loved, was calm.

"Are you going out with her again tonight?" That didn't bode well.

"Do you want to talk or do you want me to hang up?" He left the control up to her, but his message was clear, too. He wasn't going to go through a replay of the night before.

"I want to talk."

In his truck, on his way to pick up Levi, he nodded.

"I'm sorry, Jem." The apology was a bit fragmented through his Bluetooth, but he'd known it was coming, too. Maybe had even called to collect it.

"I know."

"It's just... I don't know what I'd ever do without you."

"You keep by our rules and you'll never have to find out."

"But what if—and I'm not saying this is even a remote possibility in your life right now—but what if you ever do meet someone and want to marry again. She'll have a say then, and I'll lose..."

"Any woman I would ever marry would know, before she accepted my proposal, that you are my son's mother and will always be a part of our lives."

The words left a heavy weight on his shoulders. One he didn't want. But he'd promised her a lifetime. For better or worse.

His son needed his mother because he loved her, had bonded with her, and because she loved him in a way no one else ever could.

"And I spoke the truth," she was saying now. "I don't mean to be so harsh, but I did give up everything to help you get where you are."

He understood that.

"And you are a lot looser than I am. Since our divorce I haven't slept with anyone but you, while you've had at least two other lovers that I know of."

He'd had one. But that number could change soon. And was none of her business.

"I understand," he said, because he did. She wasn't going to admit how awful she'd been or take accountability. In her world, people used your mistakes against you. But he also knew that she was sorry.

"I need you to honor our agreement and stay away from my house, Tressa."

"Why, because I ruined your little tryst with your whore friend?"

Every nerve in his body tightened. "I had dinner with a woman, period. That was all I had intended and all I did. You are the one who made it seem like something more."

"Wait…" she said before he mustered the

composure to hang up. "I didn't mean that. You know I didn't mean that."

He took a deep breath. He needed peace more than he needed to be right.

"I'm sorry. I'm guessing you didn't get much sleep last night."

He hadn't.

"I'm not saying that as a dig or an innuendo. I know that my drama unsettles you. I really do try to rein it in for you, Jem. We're just so different, you and I."

"That we are."

"But that's not my fault."

"I never said it was."

"I know. You're so good to me, Jem. And I… just need you to know that I know that. And that…I appreciate you so much."

He started to relax. "I need you to stay away from my house."

"I know. And I will. I promise. Amelia and I are going to the city tonight. She's got tickets to a Broadway play. We're going to spend the night in Beverly Hills and treat ourselves like queens."

Thank God. Amelia was back in the picture. *And* Tressa was going to be a hundred miles away. A double gift. He could relax and give himself completely to his night with Lacey. Without worrying that he'd be bringing the wrath of Tressa down on her.

"What about work tomorrow?" He wasn't

going to keep supporting her. Alimony was up and he was done.

"I took a vacation day. But I do want to talk to you about that," she said. "But not today. I've got to get packed and…"

"I have a question for you." He was just curious.

"What's that?"

"Did you call Amelia or did she call you?"

"She called me. And apologized, too."

Tressa used to make him apologize for everything that happened between them, too. Until he'd finally refused to do so.

"So now I have a question for you," she said.

And he wished he'd kept his mouth shut.

"This woman from last night…are you going to see her again?"

"Considering what she overheard last night, what do you think?" He could have out and out denied that he had another date. But the words stuck in his throat—as though they were somehow disloyal to Lacey. With his luck, fate would sic karma on him for the lie and take Lacey away from him.

"She was a little upset with you, huh?"

"It was a first date, Tressa. Wouldn't you have been?"

Which made it doubly miraculous that Lacey had taken the whole thing in stride.

"I'm sorry," she said again.

He didn't think she meant it that time.

He hoped to God she didn't ruin the best thing—next to Levi—that had ever happened in his life.

IT WAS JEM'S idea that Kacey and Levi spend the evening at Jem's house, leaving Lacey's home for the two of them for their date.

Kacey, who was like a saint on a mission, was ready to move her things over there and trade places with Jem. As it was, she jokingly threw her toothbrush in her purse. At which time Lacey told her she was being ridiculous and said they weren't planning on a late night.

Kacey didn't know how little chance of success her date with Jem had that night, because Lacey hadn't mentioned Tressa's visit the night before. Or the talk they'd put off.

She'd texted Jem and asked him if it was a good idea that Kacey and Levi be at his place, in case Tressa showed up again. Jem had texted back that Tressa was in LA overnight.

But that didn't mean his ex-wife wouldn't still be there, too. Between them. Because she had to tell Sydney about the outburst she'd witnessed.

The things Tressa had said…they bordered on psychotic. And if Jem didn't see that, if he was too blinded by the smoke to see the fire…

If he'd been living with Tressa's episodes so long they seemed normal to him, chances were that he couldn't be relied on to see the dangers to Levi, either.

Not that the boy was in any danger at the moment. Tressa didn't have him again for another week.

He just had to see that even though Tressa loved her son, if she had times when she was unable to control herself, she could also be hurting him.

If he could see. But then he'd have to see that he'd been a victim, too. It was a hard enough fact for women to face. Because of the stigma it carried, men fought seeing that particular reality even more.

But even if Jem was a victim, it didn't make him any less desirable in Lacey's eyes, or any less manly. If anything, it showed her his backbone— that he'd survived, had gotten out. Ran a successful business and was raising an adorable and mostly well-adjusted kid.

She didn't find him any less sexy, either. Most particularly when he showed up at her door in board shorts, a T-shirt and flip-flops. She'd let Kacey talk her into one of her ankle-length sundresses. It was tie-dyed and had spaghetti straps but was loose and flowing so she could still feel as though she wasn't flaunting something she wasn't willing to share with every guy who looked her way.

Her hair was down again. And she'd put in the

pearl-and-gold flip-flop earrings she'd bought on a trip to Hawaii with Kacey a few years before.

Jem stopped cold and stared when she opened the door to him.

"Your sister said to tell you she forgot to move the wine from the freezer to the refrigerator." Kacey had driven over to Jem's. She didn't want to be without a vehicle in case of emergency.

He was still standing on her stoop.

"I already found it and moved it," she told him, then added, "She made a grilled chicken and vegetable casserole for us, homemade rolls and peach cobbler for dessert. All on her own. I thought we were going out."

Kacey had set the table, too, with linens and wineglasses and candles. Lacey wanted him to know it wasn't her doing.

That, after the night before, she wasn't presuming anything.

"Can dinner wait?" he asked.

"Of course." Her heart sank and she felt a little stupid in the dress. She might just be on the shortest date in her history.

"I thought we'd take a walk on the beach. Enjoy the sunset…"

The glance he gave her as he said the last word robbed her of the doubts that had been plaguing her since she'd left him the night before. She hadn't imagined that this…intense whatever this was…was forming between them.

Dinner was in the refrigerator. Just needing to be warmed up.

"I'd like to take a walk," she told him. And locked her front door behind them.

CHAPTER TWENTY-THREE

ONE THING JEM had learned from his years with Tressa was that it was better to get things out in the open than it was to avoid them hoping that they'd go away. They never did. They just festered and eventually exploded into something more than they'd ever needed to be.

He wanted the beach and the ocean to help ease them back to where they'd been before Tressa's interruption the night before.

He'd been back and forth on his chances. They hadn't looked that great in the middle of the night. By the time he'd left his house with Kacey and Levi happily visiting with Levi's goldfish, he'd been feeling a bit more optimistic.

He took her hand as they set out from her house, and liked the feel of her fingers intertwined with his. It was a turn-on. And an odd kind of reassurance, too.

"So, let's talk about what happened last night," he said as they turned a corner and could see the beach a block ahead of them.

"Okay."

He waited for her counselor stuff to come at him. It wouldn't be anything he hadn't heard before— like each time he'd encouraged Tressa to get help and then had been asked to join in for a session so the counselor could explain his wife to him.

Again.

Lacey wasn't talking. So he told her a little bit about Tressa's upbringing. About the abuse and the way she'd gotten herself out, paid her way through college and not looked back. "She's been to counseling," he assured her. He knew the ropes. "She's one of those who chose to rise above instead of fall in."

Those had been the words of one of Tressa's counselors. He'd never forgotten them and had hung several years of marriage on them.

"She just gets…scared…sometimes. She's petrified of being alone. And she and her best friend had had a fight."

"Amelia?" Lacey asked. And he remembered that she knew a lot more about Tressa than he'd given her credit for. She'd investigated her, interviewed her, toured her home and…

"Yeah, Amelia."

They were at the corner, waiting to cross the street to the beach. There was no light, just a four-way stop on a two-way street, and they had to wait for the traffic to clear.

"Anyway, she apologized. And she's agreed not to come to my house."

"She's not allowed at your house?"

"Just as part of our personal agreement. I need my space from her drama."

Lacey nodded and he looked at her.

"She mentioned it," she said, stepping off the curb as the traffic cleared.

As they made their way to the sand, dropping hands to take off their flip-flops, and then rejoining them, he pondered what she'd said.

"Tressa told you about me? About our relationship?"

"Only in terms of her. She said the divorce was because her drama was too much for you day in and day out."

He bit his tongue. Life was cleaner that way. He absolutely was not going to be dragged into the "he said, she said."

Lacey was looking at him. "That's not true?"

Just like that, life changed. Jem was at a crossroads, and nothing was going to be the same again. He had a choice to make. If he remained loyal to Tressa, he was committing himself to a lifetime of having her come before anyone else, other than Levi.

If he didn't, he couldn't go back.

He had no idea what a life of not taking care of Tressa looked like. The sun was setting, but that didn't account for the red he was seeing. This is what Tressa had meant. What she'd known. He'd thought she'd been telling him that his future wife would try to tell him what he could and could not do.

That wasn't it at all.

It was him. He had to decide. Where did his loyalties lie? With Tressa and the family they had created? Protecting the mother of his child from herself, or being completely open and honest with a different life partner? What was best for Levi? Not a life with Tressa. He knew that. Clearly.

In the end, it didn't feel like it was his choice to make. Whatever hold Lacey had over him had taken control.

They were walking along the sand. Them and many others. Joggers. Couples. Kids.

Jem remembered a summer at Myrtle Beach with his family. They'd built some killer sand towns. Not just castles. Modern-day towns.

He wanted to build one with Lacey. Right then.

The rest of the world be damned.

Her question still hung between them. He'd never met a woman who was more about listening than talking.

After Tressa, Jem found solace in the comfortable silences he could share with Lacey.

"We divorced because Tressa called a client and told him that I was screwing his wife. Her word—*screwing*—not mine."

"Were you?"

The question was fair. She'd heard Tressa call

him a whore. Not that she'd have taken that literally, obviously, but it had implied infidelity.

"The woman was seventy years old. So was the man, but that didn't preclude him from having a much younger wife I could have been screwing. In Tressa's mind."

"Oh."

Yeah. "When Tressa found out how old the wife was, she told him I was doing it with his daughter."

Lacey missed a step, held on to his hand tighter and said nothing.

"The couple had their sixteen-year-old granddaughter living with them. She had cerebral palsy and I'd carried her out of the car and into the house one day because the battery on her chair had died. Unbeknownst to me, Tressa had been driving by the place because I'd been spending so much time there. But also, she said, because I smiled a lot when I talked about them."

"So what happened?"

"I apologized, profusely, for my wife's paranoia. The man took me aside. He told me about his own indiscretion, back when he'd been serving in the Korean War. How he'd spent the past forty years making it up to his wife. He told me to have patience, to love my wife and to understand that I had to do whatever it took to rebuild trust."

"Had you been unfaithful?"

The question disappointed him. "What do you think?"

"I doubt it, but I've learned recently that I'm not impartial where you're concerned."

And just that quickly he was soaring above the waves again. He'd best be careful lest he even begin to resemble his ex-wife with her emotional bursts.

But, again, the question was fair.

"I was never unfaithful to my wife. Not once."

"So why did she think you were?"

Her question sounded curious. Almost clinical. Not challenging. And he said, "I've tried like hell to figure that out. I think, in my wholly unprofessional opinion, that it stems from the way her folks withheld love as a means of discipline. I don't think Tressa ever really feels like she can trust anyone to care about her. To be true to her."

"Not a bad analysis."

He was glad she thought so.

"You were telling me about your divorce."

"It turned out that Tressa's phone call was so ludicrous that no one gave it any credence. Except for me. When I thought about what could have happened... What if that girl hadn't had a disability? Or the wife had been closer to my age? What if she'd seen me talking to a sixteen-year-old in a pool? What if she'd called that girl's father? Not only could I have lost a lucrative client, but I could have been charged with statutory rape."

Lacey walked beside him in silence, still holding his hand.

"I couldn't live like that anymore." He told her his shame—that he'd left his wife because she'd been abused as a kid and he couldn't handle the backlash.

"You shouldn't have had to live like that at all."

God, he loved those words. Soaked them right up. And knew that, as she'd said, she wasn't impartial where he was concerned.

"Tressa admitted to what she'd done, admitted that I'd never been unfaithful to her. In writing. She sent a letter to my clients, taking full accountability for her inappropriate behavior."

"And she told you she'd never do anything like it again."

"That's right."

"Has she?"

He hesitated. She'd come close. But... "No."

"So last night, saying you whore around, when she knew you had a date in the backyard, you don't think that was similar behavior?"

He could see how she'd think so. "She was just having a rough night. She's fine now." Tressa was a pain in his ass, but he could handle her.

Lacey stopped to pick up a shell and show it to him. A perfect, unchipped half clam with a beautiful rainbow of colors inside and beige swirls outside.

She put it in the pocket of her dress. A memento

of their date, he hoped. The first of many keep-sakes they'd collect together.

"Has she ever been violent with you?"

"Of course not." He was a six-foot-tall one-hundred-and-ninety-pound male in excellent shape. He could carry his weight and then some. Tressa weighed one hundred and fifteen pounds and couldn't lift even half that.

"She's never thrown anything at you?"

Not *at* him. There'd been the time she'd taken toast out of the toaster and thrown it across the room. A wineglass she'd thrown against the wall once.

"No."

"Never slapped you?"

He'd stopped her arm midswing, holding on for the brief second it took for her to collapse against him, sobbing, begging him to love her.

"She's never physically harmed me in any way," he said quite succinctly. He wanted Tressa out of his life, but he wouldn't throw her under the bus. She had enough problems, enough people who'd trampled her heart and who'd been dis-loyal.

He wasn't going to have her pay for something that wasn't on her. He couldn't live with himself if he did that.

"I don't go for Tressa's drama," he said slowly. Double-checking the honesty in his words. "But Amelia, she can handle it better than I can. And she's an attorney. She'd know if there was something in Tressa that pushed the boundaries of legal or not."

"Have you talked to her about it?"

"Yes."

"And?"

"She says that Tressa's her friend and she's not going to talk behind her back."

The lawyer was loyal. He respected her for that. And trusted her to care enough about Tressa to have done something if Tressa was in real trouble.

"I have no desire, whatsoever, to spend any more time than I absolutely have to with my ex-wife. At the same time, I don't want her paying for my issues."

"*Your* issues?"

"I'm not good with drama, with emotional outbursts." Of the female variety. Give him a guy's anger twenty times a day.

"Jem, I'm sorry, but I just have to say. What I heard last night…those things Tressa said to you…they were abusive. It's not *your* issue. People don't talk to each other that way."

Her tone had changed. Completely. He was holding her hand and still felt as though he'd been cut adrift.

Not because she was against him. But she'd become…impartial. He didn't like it.

So he was going to set her straight right then

and there. She and Kacey might have had the perfect family, but most weren't. No matter how great your parents were, or how close you were to them and your siblings. No matter how many grandparents were in and out all day long, or how many cousins and aunts and uncles filled church pews with you.

"You're wrong." He'd tried to soften the blow, but there were some things that just were...what they were.

"Tressa is a walk in the park compared to my sister, JoAnne."

She stopped in her tracks, only inches from him as she stared up at him in the growing dusk. They really should turn around, even though there were enough homes, restaurants and resorts lighting up the beach that they'd be fine even when it was fully dark out.

"Your sister talked that way to you, too?" she asked softly, studying him. He allowed it because she was back with him. Friend more than professional. The softness in her gaze was completely personal.

"My sister was the devil herself when I was growing up."

Every family had one. You just did everything you could to make certain it wasn't you.

Unless you were JoAnne. She'd had no reason. Not like Tressa...

"How so?"

She was his sister, his only sibling. Family. He wished he'd been a little more circumspect in his word choice.

He looked for a way to explain without coming off like a complete jerk.

"JoAnne was five when I was born," he said. He'd probably gone back a little too far. "Up until I arrived, she was it. My folks' whole lives revolved around her. They'd had a tough time getting pregnant and she was like a gift from heaven to them."

And then he'd come along. A son.

"After I was born...my folks probably weren't as sensitive to her needs as they could have been," he said, thinking back, aiming for fairness. "She had some jealousy issues."

That went unattended. Forever.

"And she took it out on you?"

She'd locked him in a closet once when their mother was making cookies, so that he didn't get to lick the bowl. He was five. He'd turned on a light and looked at the pictures in the books that were stored on a shelf next to him.

"My folks had this thing," he said. "If we were bad, we weren't spanked or put in time-out. We had perks taken away from us. If I back-talked my mother, I'd lose the fishing trip my father had promised me for the weekend."

Lacey's silence left him far too much room to say more than he wanted to.

"So JoAnne had this game. When we were in the car, she'd pinch me. Over and over. If I told, we'd both get in trouble, which meant that we'd both lose a perk. Her contention was that she'd lost all perks she'd cared about when I was born."

"Did she?"

"I have nothing upon which to base an opinion. I don't know what life was like for her before I was born. My parents were great to me. I don't remember them being bad to her. But I was five years younger than she was. I have no clue what went on after I went to bed at night."

He turned them around and headed back up the beach the way they'd come. Wondering if Kacey was a good cook. And wishing, completely selfishly, that Lacey had had time to make their dinner.

Not because she was a better cook. As far as he'd been able to tell, both of the sisters were well schooled in the kitchen. He just wanted to eat Lacey's cooking.

Which probably made him a sick puppy. Or just weird, at the very least, a weird dude.

"She used to tell me that I wasn't wanted. That I was a mistake. That I was ugly and everyone laughed at my sorry ass. She'd pull my hair just to see if she could make me cry. And then mock me if I did. And if I told our parents, she'd make life twice as miserable."

He'd learned how to stay out of her way. And

later, how to placate her. Because life wasn't perfect and wasn't meant to be easy.

They'd switched hands when they'd turned around. Lacey's palm was cool from the night air. He wanted to hold her. To lie on the beach with her and lose himself in her, to pleasure her so thoroughly that she forgot the bad parts of his world existed. And hers, too.

To help them both forget that people weren't always kind to one another.

In a perfect world, maybe they were.

But in reality, everyone had a bad side. Issues. Hurts that didn't heal as well as they could have.

"When I grew taller than she was, stronger than she was, she resorted to tears," he said, remembering out loud under the cover of the darkness that was falling. "She'd use tears as a threat and point out to me how our father was a sucker for her tears, giving in to her every single time she cried."

"Was she right?"

"About Dad? Pretty much." And he understood that. Every single time Levi cried, it took a piece out of him.

"After that I gave her whatever she wanted most of the time. It was easier than dealing with the muck she'd conjure up."

"Was she nicer to you?"

"Tressa's words last night were kind compared to the things JoAnne continued to say to me. But they were only words. I learned to deflect the barbs for the nonsense they were, and to pity her."

"Didn't Levi say she's coming to stay with you?"

"Right. Yes, she is. Later this summer."

"So...things have changed since you grew up?"

"Nope..." He grinned. Because life really was kind of a joke sometimes. "She's pretty much as bad as ever."

"Then why...?"

"My folks asked me to put her up." He let his shrug finish that sentence.

"Did they also tell her she had to stay with you?"

"What? No, of course not. It wouldn't do any good if they had. JoAnne has no problem defying our parents."

"She wants to stay with you."

"I guess." He hadn't given it much thought. "It's a small thing," he told her. He stopped, turning her until they faced each other, touching, front to front.

"You want to know what I know?" he asked, gazing down at her in the moonlight—and in the glow from the lights farther up on the beach.

"What?"

"That I have so much to be thankful for I'd be a fool to waste my energy crying over the things I can't change. I've got a boy that brings me joy every single moment of every day. A job I love and that provides a better than average income. I'm my own boss. I can make my home whatever I want it to be because I'm the guy who knows how to do that kind of stuff. And I'm on the beach with a woman who I never thought I'd meet..."

He stopped himself.

"I never thought I'd meet you, either." Lacey filled in his silence, understanding.

And, with those words, sealed his fate.

CHAPTER TWENTY-FOUR

THEY WENT OUT again on Saturday. Kacey was back at Jem's, though Lacey hated that her sister was spending so much time babysitting. Not that Kace seemed any the worse for wear. She looked more relaxed and was laughing out loud a lot more than Lacey could remember her doing.

Hard to believe that in another week she'd be gone—back to the craziness of her Hollywood life.

Lacey had worn another one of Kacey's dresses that was loose fitting and just a bit shorter and fancier. Jem had told her he wanted to take her out someplace nice.

And he had. On one of their city's dinner cruises. They'd had steak and lobster by candlelight, seated outdoors at a balcony table with live music playing softly in the background. She remembered asking for honey mustard dressing on her salad. And liking the bread. She probably would have a hundred little image memories when she looked back on the night. But as they drove from the harbor back to her house, all Lacey could think about was Jem.

The way she'd caught his eye in the candlelight. The sound of his laughter when she'd been telling him about the time she and Kacey had hidden behind a sign in a subway station and had taken turns popping their heads out from behind it on opposite sides without leaving enough time for a person to have moved from one side to the other...

He'd put a tie on with dark pants and a white shirt and she just couldn't stop consuming him with her senses. The musky scent. The slightly rough working-man hands that held her hand or touched her cheek so tenderly. The intense way he looked at her.

She ate dinner and left the boat hungry.

For him.

Life wasn't perfect. And might not be easy. But there was no doubt in her mind anymore that Jem Bridges was more to her than just a man she'd met. More to her than any man she'd ever met.

They hadn't talked any further about Tressa, other than for Jem to say that his ex-wife and Amelia were spending the weekend at the beach with a couple of Amelia's friends.

Lacey also hadn't talked to him about her suspicions regarding Tressa as a perpetrator of domestic violence against Levi. And Jem, too. She wasn't his counselor and couldn't be objective.

She didn't want to say something that would do more harm than good.

But she hadn't forgotten. She knew that sometime before Tressa's custodial visit the following weekend, she was going to have to let Sydney know about the scene she'd overheard between Jem and his ex-wife. The verbal abuse she'd witnessed. *After* she told Jem that she was going to call Sydney.

She just kept hoping that he'd come to the realization on his own, after everything that had happened with Levi—social services bursting into his life, the talks they'd had.

He was a thinker, someone who faced things head-on rather than avoided them. A doer. He didn't run away from problems.

She wanted to give him time.

In the meantime, she wanted to give him... her. Not just her body, though she wanted that, too...but...

They reached his truck and he held the door open for her, pulling out the stepstool he'd surprised her with earlier so she didn't have to step up so high in her dress.

Always the gentleman. A man's man who'd protect those he cared about with his life. And yet...one who also seemed to respect a woman's abilities as equal to his own. His willingness to look at his ex-wife as a whole person, to see her

good, her value, had shown her how he respected
women in a way nothing else could have done.

She fully believed now that Jem was a victim
of domestic violence. But he was the least likely
victim she'd met during the course of her career. She had no doubt that he had scars, mark-
ers from the damage done to him—psychological
and emotional—and yet he was a well-adjusted,
emotionally alive, functioning adult. This spoke
to her of his strength of character, his determination to be the best he could be.

She watched him walk around the truck. His
ass looked the best in those pants.

God, she had it bad.

They were about two blocks from her house
when he said, "I want to make love with you."

"You're welcome to come in for a while." Her
tongue practically stuck to the roof of her mouth.
She'd never made an appointment for sex before.
Or talked about doing it beforehand.

"I'd kind of planned to. I just want my inten-
tions clear before I enter your home."

The look he sent in her direction made her feel
like a puddle on his seat. The trembling of her lips
was her giveaway and she gave him a weak smile.

Good thing the inside of the truck was dark.

"I don't think you do this lightly," he said.

Was that going to be a problem for him? So...
she'd change. Immediately. She could find a way

to be casual about sex. Because she didn't want to live without knowing what sex with him felt like.

"I don't, either," he told her.

Desire raced through her veins, but her mind slowed. "I didn't think you did," she said.

"What Tressa said the other night…"

She didn't want his ex-wife there, but she experienced a moment of thrilled relief with the confirmation that he was thinking through the situation they'd left hanging openly right in front of them. But she still didn't want her there.

"We already talked about that…" Unless Tressa was a problem for him. It was pretty clear that the woman still considered him her property.

Lacey had assumed the problem was Tressa's. Was it Jem's, too? Was he feeling guilty?

The darkness was her friend, hiding her humiliation.

"The thing about Tressa is…there's usually a grain of truth in the things she says. That's why her words can be so lethal. She hits her mark and then screws it all out of proportion."

"I don't know what you're telling me." If he wanted her to believe he'd been a male prostitute, she just wasn't going to buy it. He'd told her he'd never been unfaithful to his wife.

"After my divorce…I went out with a woman I didn't know. Slept with her. And never saw her again. Tressa…found out about it."

"You slept with a woman you didn't know was safe?" The thought stopped her in her tracks.

"Hell, no." The disgusted tone of his voice had her wishing she hadn't asked *that* question. He pulled up in front of her house and put the truck in Park. "She was a perfectly respectable woman—a nurse. The sister of a colleague. She was open to having a relationship. I wasn't."

She nodded. Waited.

"I am now."

Oh. God. Okay. Well…

The silence took away her ability to exhale. Or speak. And then all the air left her in a gush that had been building. And building.

She opened her door and jumped down, grabbed his hand as he met her on her side of the truck and walked with him, unsteadily, up to her door. "My bedroom's this way…" she said as the door closed behind him, pulling him along down the hall. She'd changed her sheets that morning…and was ashamed for a moment, like she'd been planning this.

"Wait…" He didn't move.

She didn't want to wait. Afraid that the moment would pass, that this…thing…would end. And she'd never know… Looking into his eyes, she wanted to know exactly what he needed. So she could give it to him.

"I don't want to rush," he told her. "I have a feeling this is going to be something we're going to remember for the rest of our lives, and I want to savor every second of it."

"In that case, sir, could I tempt you with a glass of wine?" She'd never felt so stupid, so out of control and immature. And so...needy.

They'd held themselves to one glass a piece at dinner in deference to the fact that he'd be driving as soon as they docked.

"You can tempt me any way you'd like." He followed her into the kitchen and pressed his hardness up against her backside as she reached for the glasses. With shaking fingers she poured the wine, managing to get most of it into the glass.

She turned, handing him a glass. "Here's to a first time we'll remember forever," she said.

He clicked his glass against hers. "To remembering forever," he said in return.

That was the moment Lacey admitted to herself that she was falling in love.

HE HAD NO idea he could feel as though he was making love without undressing. Or touching.

Wineglass in hand, Jem wandered outside to the footer he'd poured where Lacey's dream room was going to be. He wrapped himself up in the feeling of being in her home. Her space. Alone with her.

He wanted to strip off his pants and bury himself in her. And he wanted to keep them on and enjoy knowing that he was *going* to bury himself in her.

"I heard from the inspector today," he said, toe to toe with her in what was going to be the middle of the room. He pushed himself into the V between her thighs.

"Why didn't you say so?"

"As soon as I saw you in that dress tonight, all I've been able to think about is getting you out of it. I completely forgot my good news."

"We have the go-ahead?"

"I planned to pour the floor tomorrow, if that works for you."

"I think it's pretty clear that anything you plan works for me."

Her fingers skated up his thigh, stopping just below his ass.

"Why do I get the feeling we aren't just talking about building a room here?"

"Maybe because we aren't?"

Their wineglasses were full...and in the way. Taking hers from her, he set them down on the newly inspected footer. On his way back up, he grabbed the bottom of her dress, pulling it up with him and dragging it over her head.

And things were almost over before they'd begun. Her panties were lace. Her skin the same honey golden color all over. Her thighs went on forever...

She put one thigh forward and a hand to her

waist, drawing his eye to the curve of her hip, a flat belly.

His penis throbbed. Painfully, but he ignored the irritation.

And now he could no longer even pretend to ignore the fact that she hadn't been wearing a bra.

"You aren't playing fair." He groaned, reaching for the button at his waistline.

"I'm not playing at all," she told him in such a sultry voice he had to try to capture it. With his mouth.

His fly was unzipped as he planted his mouth on hers. Finding her tongue with his. Immediately. Hungrily.

He still wasn't touching her with anything other than his lips. He didn't trust himself. Didn't want everything to end. He wanted a beginning that lasted forever.

"Oh, my God..." he whispered raggedly, pulling the tie from around his neck to drop it in the dirt. His shirt followed right afterward.

"Time is money, you know," she told him.

"There is no amount of money that could pay for this time right here," he told her. He stepped out of his pants and briefs all at once, left them puddled on the ground and approached her. He'd take her on the wall. In the dirt. Any way he could think of.

"I like how eager you are," she whispered, her gaze on his crotch. She stood up, turned her back to him and, leaving her dress where he'd dropped it, walked into her house.

Unable to tear his gaze from the white lace-covered backside, Jem grabbed a packet out of his pocket, dropped his pants again and sauntered slowly in behind her.

Two could play her game.

CHAPTER TWENTY-FIVE

LACEY HAD NEVER had a thing for muscled working men. Had had no idea how sexy construction workers could be. She and Jem were in her room. She was a lady. A queen. He was strong. Solid. Gorgeous. And he wanted her. She touched his chest. He rubbed his penis against her leg. She kissed him. He picked her up off the ground and held her suspended against his rock hardness.

He hadn't touched a single erogenous zone and she felt as though every one of them had been loved repeatedly.

Her nipples were hard. She was moist. And he prolonged the misery by running fingers down her back and stopping just above her tailbone. Licking her belly button, but no lower. Or higher.

"Jem," she finally moaned. "I need you."

"I know, Lace. I need you, too."

"Then…"

"Shh." Standing, he let his jutting maleness slide between her legs as he touched a finger to her lips. "The longer we hold out, the higher we'll fly."

She didn't know about that. If he didn't hurry, she might very well fly without him.

And this from a woman who had a history of being grounded.

HE KISSED EVERY part of her that he'd seen over the past couple of weeks. Her hands. Her arms. Her calves and feet and knees. Her ears and neck. Her chin and cheeks.

He kissed her shoulders, sliding himself over her body.

"You're going to know me all over." He heard the words at some point and realized he'd said them aloud.

"Please, Jem."

But he helped her bear the pain and gave himself a pleasure he'd been imagining for weeks. With two fingers he touched her nipple and rubbed gently across the tip. She cried out, moving her hips.

Lowering his head, he took her nipple into his mouth. Not for too long, though. Just long enough to keep her wanting.

He moved to the other side and played with that tight bud with his fingers and lips. Then gulped when she grabbed his penis.

"If this doesn't happen soon, I'm not going to be responsible for..."

He kissed her before she could finish the sentence, eased her back against the edge of the bed and spread her legs. Standing in front of her, he grabbed the packet he'd dropped on the bed when they'd come in, opened it and slipped it on. Finally, he ran his finger along her moist center and positioned himself.

He looked into her eyes before he moved any further. "This is only the beginning," he told her.

"You are my man." The words sounded like a promise.

He gave a slow push, still holding her gaze.

"Can you feel me?"

"Oh, God, Jem. Yes."

"I can feel you, too." He barely got the words out. The effort it was taking not to ram himself home and find relief was more than he'd ever imagined.

But he'd made a promise—to her and to himself. Love with Lacey was going to be different than it ever had been before.

He was marking his forever.

LACEY COULD HARDLY meet her sister's gaze when Kacey came in the door a couple of hours later. It wasn't her reticence that gave her away, though.

Nothing as momentous as what she'd just experienced with Jem would have been missed by her identical twin. You couldn't have a change that magnanimous and not have your counterpart feel something different about you.

"How was Levi?" she asked.

"Perfect as always. I have to tell you, if I was going to have a nephew, I couldn't pick a better one."

Lacey, in thin cotton pajama pants and a matching T-shirt, had been watching a rerun while waiting for Kacey and, reaching for the remote, turned the sound off as her sister dropped her purse and joined her on the couch.

Kacey felt peaceful, but somber, too.

"I didn't talk to him about…you know…" She couldn't bring herself to say Jem's ex-wife's name in her home so soon after…

"I didn't figure you had."

"Did he say anything to you?" Her lover had left her bed to go to his home, where he and her sister, her spectacular look-alike, would be home alone. And she hadn't worried. Not even a little bit.

"Just asked after Levi, then told me the night was a complete success and thanked me about a million times over. He also asked if I was up for any more babysitting before I head home."

One week was all they had left. She didn't want to think about that.

"I'm going to need a chance to tell him about talking to Sydney without Levi present," she said when she'd just been thinking that she didn't want to saddle Kacey with babysitting during her last week of vacation. "I don't want to do it over the phone."

She needed to be able to reach out and take his hand. To see into his eyes. To know that they were going to be okay.

"You made love with him."

There was no point in denying it. And while the sisters didn't kiss and tell, they usually let the other know when they were in a physical relationship. Up until a year and a half ago, they'd shared the same house. And it was polite to let your roommate know when a man was going to be at the breakfast table.

"Yeah. Without telling him that I'm going to make his life uncomfortable if he doesn't do it himself."

"You went with your heart." Kacey knew her well.

"You think I should have told him first?"

"I'm not saying that. You know your stuff, Lace. You've always known when to let others figure things out for themselves. And when they do, there you are, sitting right beside them. Ready and waiting."

They weren't talking about Jem. Or domestic violence.

"We've both been kind of cast off at sea, haven't we?" she said, not regretting a second of what she'd done with Jem that night, but not gloriously happy about it, either. There were hurdles in front of them that couldn't be ignored.

"I thought it was just you," Kacey told her,

taking Lacey's hand in both of hers and holding it on her knee. Something she hadn't done in years but used to do often, Lacey remembered. Usually when they were waiting to go on camera. In their pubescent days Kacey had started to get nervous sometimes before going on air.

"I thought you were running away when you came up here, because you were so convinced you were second best."

"In some ways I was," Lacey said. If they were going to clear the air, really clear it, and be as connected as they'd always been—and she hoped they were—then she had to be honest. With Kacey, of course, but also with herself. "In a lot of ways I was," she said now.

"I know. And sometimes…I liked it that way. It's like I was the star and you were my sky."

Kacey's eyes filled with tears. "Like that old song…you were the wind beneath my wings."

And if that was all she'd ever be, it would have been enough because Kacey's wings were lovely. When she spread them, she brought joy to so many. Not just by entertaining them, but with her kindness, too. Her open heart.

"And I focused far too much on not having my own wings," Lacey told her. "When in reality, I never really wanted them. I didn't want to come in second, to lose my boyfriend to you, and every solo job offer…" She stopped. They both knew all the ways in which Lacey had been passed over through the years. "But I also didn't want to be in the spotlight. To have people fawning over me. I'm not good at it."

"I like that I can shake someone's hand, or smile at them, and make their day," Kacey said. And somehow managed to convey heart, not conceit.

"You're living the life that you were meant to live," Lacey said. Knowing that as great as it had been sharing a home with Kacey again, they were going to have to separate. Because just as Kace belonged in Beverly Hills, Lacey's life was in Santa Raquel.

In a very short period of time, even before Jem, the little town had become home to her.

"Not completely." Kacey shook her head. "But you knew that, too, didn't you?" She met Lacey's gaze and Lacey couldn't look away.

"This is where you shine far brighter than I do, Lacey, and it's worth far more than shiny lights. You get life. You get the big stuff. The small stuff. The real stuff. You see what most people are too afraid to look at. And you find ways to make it okay. From the time we were little you were always making life okay."

Kacey had been the acrobat. She'd been the net. It wasn't a choice either of them had made. It just was.

"I date the wrong type of men," Kacey said now. "I love my work. I'd go so far as to say I need it. It completes something in me."

A fact that had been obvious to Lacey since they'd been about eight. "I agree."

"But I'm not enjoying clubbing. I get bored at the parties. I want...more."

"You *need* more."

"You knew."

"I suspected."

"And you waited."

"And prayed." A lot.

"I'm excited to get back to work," Kacey said tentatively, as though the news might upset Lacey.

"I know, Kace. It's okay. You've got a gift."

"I'm going to miss you."

"I'm going to miss you, too."

"So, I was thinking...there's no reason why I can't commute on weekends. At least on weekends when I don't have an event to attend."

"Your room is your room. Anytime. Leave clothes here. Things in the bathroom. You have a key. Show up whenever you want." She had things at Kacey's condo. And still had her key, too.

"I'm not going out with anyone who doesn't seem like someone I'd want to marry someday," she said.

"Good."

"You knew I'd get to this point, didn't you? That's why you never took me seriously when I tried to introduce you to a new guy."

"I hoped. But if you ended up marrying one of

your fancy-pants but empty-hearted suitors, I'd have welcomed him into our family."

"This time with Levi... I want kids of my own."

"I want to be a mother, too." To Levi, some-day, if she and Jem made it to that point. And to children of her own.

"Did you notice number thirty passed us by last year?"

"How could I miss it?" Lacey's grimace prob-ably wasn't the prettiest look she'd worn that night. "There had to be five hundred people at that party."

"And you were a hit."

"Because I drank too much."

"Me, too." Kacey's expression sobered. "Be-cause I couldn't figure out why I wasn't happy when I had it all..."

"Me, too," Lacey told her.

"So...you want some cobbler while we watch *Lucy*?" Kacey asked, nodding toward the old black-and-white sitcom rerun that was just start-ing.

Lacey turned up the sound while her sister dished up the dessert Lacey and Jem had never gotten around to eating. They sat up for another couple of hours. Watching television. Talking. Eating second helpings of cobbler.

It was only when she made it to bed that Lacey remembered the wineglasses out on the footer.

She'd pulled on her robe to run out and gather their clothes so Jem could get dressed. She'd forgotten the wine.

She smiled. And fell asleep that way.

Overall, it was probably the best night she'd ever spent.

CHAPTER TWENTY-SIX

AFTER REMOVING THE metal frames and backfilling around the footer, Jem called a couple of employees, who brought in a truck and poured the concrete for Lacey's floor on Sunday afternoon while Lacey and Kacey took Levi back to the beach to play in the sand.

For a good bit of the time they were gone, he was jealous of a four-year-old kid. And happier than he'd been in...maybe ever...as his son came skipping back up the walk just before dinnertime, a sister on either side of him holding his hands.

"I'm the luckiest guy on the beach, Dad!" Levi said, letting go of their hands to run up to the front door of the house. "Can I put my hand in the cement?"

It was their ritual. Anytime Levi was around when cement was poured, he got to leave his mark. In a place that would be built upon. He was leaving little parts of his son all over Santa Raquel, but in a way that was not a bother to anyone.

"Hold on, buddy," he called. "You know the

rules." If Levi didn't wait for Jem, if he even touched wet cement without his father's say-so, he lost the privilege. "Why is he the luckiest guy on the beach?" he asked the sisters.

Lacey was back in baggy cotton shorts and a blouse. Kacey in short shorts with a T-shirt that showed her figure to perfection.

"Some guy told him so," Kacey said. "I think he thought Levi was his way in, but that kid of yours set him straight."

Not at all happy with the surge of real jealousy that sparked through him at the thought of someone hitting on Lacey at the beach, Jem looked her way, his brow raised in question.

"Levi told him to please go away because we weren't supposed to talk to strangers."

Jem burst out laughing. Gotta love that boy!

SHE DIDN'T REGRET making love with Jem Bridges. Not even a little bit. She'd thought of him during her first seconds of consciousness Sunday and had taken him with her through all of the moments of her day.

And the more she thought of him, the more vulnerable she became. Because this wasn't just a trial—a maybe—for her. She'd given him far more than her body for a night. If he walked out of her life, she was going to be damaged.

She'd spent her entire adult life preventing herself from being in that position.

"Let's play the game," she said to Kacey as the sisters left Jem to change Levi out of his sandy, wet beach clothes in the spare bathroom and headed to the other side of the house, to their rooms, to clean up before they all had a quick dinner together.

Kacey glanced her way and frowned.

"What?" Lacey forced a big grin. "Come on. It'll be a hoot."

"Lacey..."

"What?" she asked again. "You're the one who always wants to play. Now one time I do and..."

"I'm up for the game, Lace. I'm just not sure why you are."

Of course she was. Kacey knew, just as Lacey did. She was being an immature, self-absorbed little kid.

Paranoid and frightened, too. But she couldn't seem to stop herself.

"Please, Kacey? I know it's stupid, but I have to know. Too much is at stake here." Possibly her heart. Maybe even the rest of her life.

Maybe she'd let go of a lot of the residual feelings she had about having always been second best and often passed over for her more radiant twin. Maybe someday she'd even be able to laugh at how much she'd taken it all to heart.

But she wasn't there yet. Intellectually she was. But emotions...they were a bit trickier.

"You think it's going to help you relax?" Kacey

asked her. She didn't seem to even consider the fact that Jem might go for the wrong sister. That he might not "know" Lacey as well as he thought he did. Or said he did.

It could just be that, until now, every single time he'd seen the sisters together they'd been easy to tell apart just by their clothes.

"That's my plan." Or at least to know if she was believing in something that didn't exist, making more of it than it was. "I hate being so damned insecure."

"The game isn't going to change that, Lacey. Only you can. By believing in your own worthiness."

She did think she was worthy. Very worthy. She also believed that most people found her sister worth a little bit more.

"Please?"

"Okay, fine, but I get to pick out the outfit," Kacey said, heading into Lacey's room and going straight for her closet. "Seriously, Lace, you need to quit hiding behind this stuff."

She turned, a look of shock on her face as she looked at Lacey. "No, you don't," she whispered, looking stricken. "God, Lacey, I'm so sorry. I'm as guilty as everyone. This is your look because it's who you are. And, oh, God, I'm so sorry. I do it to you, too, with all my nagging, trying to make you look more like me, as if you don't look as good as I do... I didn't even know..."

Lacey's eyes filled with tears as she stood there accepting her sister's hug. Drying Kacey's tears. Telling her it was okay. That they were okay.

And hoped to God that Jem was as good as his word. That he didn't just see the clothes and shape and skin, but could really see the woman inside the body just by looking into her eyes.

Ashamed of her weakness, feeling sick to her stomach for needing reassurance, she let Kacey make her into an off-work television star.

SHE SENT KACEY in first. Jem was in the kitchen, heating up the pulled pork the girls had brought home from a stand on the beach. After dinner, he and Levi were going home because Levi needed a bath before bed, Jem had said.

Lacey hated that she wasn't going to have his hands on her body again, but figured he was probably right to take things slow until they knew where they were going.

Neither of them could afford a big crash.

"Hey, Kacey, is Lacey almost ready? We got a hungry boy here." She heard Jem's voice and figured he hadn't turned around yet, hadn't seen her sister.

But…if he'd smelled her, her scent would have been Lacey's. They'd played this game before. Hundreds of times.

Knew how to do it down to every detail, including toenail polish.

"She'll be along in a second," Kacey said, un-nerving even Lacey with the toned-down note in her voice.

And suddenly she didn't want to go in, didn't want to play the game. She wasn't being fair to Jem.

And maybe not to herself, either.

"You can come in now," Jem called just as she was turning around to go change. "I just heard you take a step in the hall."

She froze. Didn't move. And didn't have to as Jem came into the hallway to join her. She heard Kacey say, "Hey, little man, let's get some of this yummy food in our bellies and leave those two sillies to settle for our leftovers."

Jem wasn't saying anything. He didn't look angry, or even disappointed. If anything, he looked...like he had a hell of a lot more compassion than she deserved.

"I feel like a ten-year-old playing dress-up on Halloween."

"You look...great."

Her heart sank. "I do?"

"Of course you do. You and Kacey, you're both gorgeous. A guy would have to be blind not to notice."

"How did you know?" She asked the most pertinent question. "Kace even took off her nail polish. I did her hair. She's wearing my jewelry and even borrowed my underthings."

He pulled her up against him, rubbing his groin against her pelvis. He moved closer until their lips were almost touching and stared into her eyes.

"I've already told you, Lacey. It's all in your eyes."

She wanted so badly to believe him. To know that, at least with one person, the only one who was probably going to matter from there on out, she came first.

"You looked into Kacey's eyes when she walked into the kitchen?"

"I always look for the eyes when you two are around. Especially since you've been leaving your hair down more and wearing her dresses. It'd be damned embarrassing if I grabbed the wrong woman, now, wouldn't it?"

She felt like an idiot. On several levels. "I'll make sure I don't ever dress like her again," she told him, grinning, but completely serious, too. "It's up to me to protect you from ever making such a blunder."

"You could both be naked and I'd know," he said. And then shook his head. "Please," he said, looking her straight in the eye. "Do not ever test me on that one. I don't think I could survive it," he said softly.

And then took a small nip of the lobe of her ear. "I'm still recovering... How about you?"

"I've been starving all day."

"Too bad all we get to eat tonight is dinner..."

She kissed him then, long and hard. A reminder of what they'd shared, what they could be starting. An invitation for more meals to come. If all went well...

JEM GAVE LEVI his bath.

While Levi landed a plastic airplane in the bubbles with his good arm, his casted arm wrapped in plastic resting on the side of the tub, Jem stood in the hallway just outside the open door and returned Tressa's call from half an hour ago. She'd had a great weekend, but didn't want to go to work the next day. She planned to quit her job and really wanted Jem's approval before she did so.

She wasn't threatening, or crying, or screaming. She just didn't feel comfortable at the bank anymore. Her outburst had embarrassed her, and she didn't feel like the people who answered to her respected her anymore.

Because she was probably right, he reluctantly gave his agreement, but told her that she was going to have to find another job. Immediately.

She agreed.

He also told her she was not coming to work for him. His gut was knotted while he waited for her response. Tantrum or no, he couldn't let her force him into something that he knew was not right. But if she went off again, so soon after the last time, if Lacey found out...

"I know, Jem. It would be like going backward, huh? I'd go crazy seeing where you are every minute of every day, wondering if your new client is cute, if she makes you laugh like I used to..."

So there *was* a God. He relaxed against the wall, keeping an eye on the arms he could see above the bubbles in the tub just beyond the door across from him.

"But...could you ask around for me?"

His first thought was of Mick, of the position she'd put him in.

"You know so many more people than I do," she told him. "You're so much more outgoing, and with your job, you deal with small businesses every day. I think that's where I need to be, Jem. Running the finances of a small business. Look what I did with yours. It's what I'm good at. Besides, then I don't have to work with so many people and there's less of a chance I'd piss anyone off or offend somebody."

This was the woman he'd known in the early years. The one who was rational and honest and thought of others. He knew this woman wouldn't be around to stay; he'd been through the upheavals enough times to know they'd always be back. But he'd also learned to be grateful for the good times.

"I'll ask around," he told her and then used their son in the tub as an excuse to end the conversation.

JEM DIDN'T TAKE Levi into bed to read stories. Or even out to sit on the couch and watch a video. He sat his son down in his booster seat at the kitchen table and poured milk in a sippy cup, pushing on the lid to make certain it was secure.

He wanted no chances of spilled-milk interruptions.

Grabbing himself a cup of coffee from the one-cup-at-a-time maker, he took his seat.

"We having a man-to-man talk, Dad?" Levi asked, his brow slightly furrowed.

He wanted to laugh. To get the moment on video.

"Yeah, we are," Jem said instead. They'd had them a time or two in the past, these man-to-mans—when Tressa had moved out, again when Levi had moved from the day care class to pre-school to discuss the new rules and expectations. And before he'd taken the boy to a work site without a trailer present. The trip had been unavoidable and Tressa had been in the city.

"What's the trouble?" Levi asked, his rounded *r*'s making him sound so adorable Jem wanted to haul him up and hug him. Levi's good arm was crossed with his casted one on the table in front of him.

God, how he loved that kid and saw how careful he had to be, too. He'd noticed Levi mimicking him more and more lately. How many times had he asked his son "What's the trouble?" in just that tone over the years? Pretty much every time he'd come to him crying.

It was what his own father used to say to him...

He took a sip of coffee. Motioned toward Levi's cup with the back of his hand and waited while his son sipped.

"You know about man-to-mans," he said, bringing his head down enough that he could meet Levi's gaze almost head-on.

Levi nodded.

"We talk about hard things and we might not like them and we always tell the..."

"Truth." Levi emphasized the word with a nod of his head.

"Right."

He didn't feel good about this. Would have given up his savings account if he could have bought a way out of the conversation.

But Lacey wasn't going to let Levi go back to Tressa's without making Sydney aware of the incident she'd witnessed. She hadn't said so. But, like he'd been telling her, he knew her.

Knew her conscience. Knew how seriously she took her work and how much she cared. Even after all of his introspection over the past days he remained fairly certain Lacey was wrong to worry about Levi, too. There was no way on earth Tressa would hurt Levi, or that the boy wouldn't tell him if she had.

If the hospital hadn't called—due to red tape

because of the number of hospital visits, he remained certain of that, too—there'd be no one even looking into their lives.

"Am I in trouble?"

Four-year-olds didn't have much of an attention span. Or patience, either.

"Of course not."

He was off on the wrong foot already. No way could he get through Levi's defenses if he thought he'd done something wrong. And he had to get through to him.

To assure himself once and for all that Lacey Hamilton was wrong and no one was hurting Levi.

Because she'd managed to instill that one bit of doubt.

"I want to talk to you about your mom." One parent should not berate another in front of the children. He knew the rule.

"Did *she* get in trouble?" Levi sounded mildly curious. And nothing more.

"I don't know." He took the opening. "Do you think she should be?"

He shrugged and Jem's stomach knotted into physical pain. Not mere discomfort, like that caused by Tressa's shenanigans, but bend-over physical pain.

"What about Kacey?" he asked, the words coming to him slowly. "Should she be in trouble?

"'Course not!" Levi said. "Kacey's fun."

The knot tightened another notch.

"How about Lacey?"

"No…" The word was accompanied by a vigorous shake of the head. "She's nice, Dad, huh?"

"Yes, she is. I like her a lot."

"I like her, too." He took another sip of milk. Jem sipped his coffee.

"So how come you don't know about Mommy?"

Levi shrugged again.

Jem's certainty dissipated.

CHAPTER TWENTY-SEVEN

HE WAS IN over his head. Had no training in dealing with possible victims of abuse. But he knew how to be a dad.

"Son, remember, this is a man-to-man. Rules are you have to talk," he said. He didn't want to be like Tressa and create drama where there wasn't any. Didn't want his son overreacting like his mother every time something didn't go exactly as he wanted it to.

But Lacey's reaction to Tressa's outburst the other night... She hadn't said a lot, but it had been enough to tell Jem that she'd found the behavior outside the bounds of acceptable.

He'd found it pretty tame.

The disparity in their reactions to the same situation had prompted this conversation. If he was wrong...if Tressa was abusing their son in any way...

"Why do you think Mommy should be in trouble?"

"I don't," Levi said, his chin to his chest.

"Levi, look at me."

The boy did.

"This is really important, son. More important than anything that has ever happened before in your whole life."

How was that for scaling down the drama? He hated hearing the words coming out of his mouth.

Levi's eyes were wide, his mouth open as he nodded.

And Jem's gaze fell to the cast his son had been lugging around for weeks.

"Tell me about that cast," he said, zoning in, as though guided by an instinct he hadn't known he'd had.

"I fell."

No mention of Tressa.

If you don't, Jem, I'll...

He heard her voice.

"Do you remember having a bad dream the last time you spent the night at your mom's house?"

Levi nodded. And then, as though remembering he had to speak, he said, "Yes."

"Can you tell me what it was about?"

He shook his head.

"Levi?" He put enough warning in his voice to let the little boy know he was serious.

"I don't remember it all." The boy was looking right at him.

From the odd place of calm he'd sunk into, Jem asked, "What do you remember about that bad dream?"

"I can't tell you."

He barely stopped himself from flying out of his chair. To pace the room. Breathe. But he couldn't leave the moment.

His boy needed him.

"This is a man-to-man, Levi. You have to tell me. It's the law."

Tears sprang to his eyes. "Then I have to go away?" His voice rose and wobbled.

"What? No, son. You aren't going away. Ever. At least, not until you're all big like me, and then only if you want to."

So Tressa was the one who'd had it right? All of this...uncertainty...stemmed from Lacey's first visit?

But Levi had said she was nice. So... "Who told you that?"

"I can't..." Levi looked at him. Covering his son's hand with his own, wanting instead to pull the little guy onto his lap and shield him from every bogeyman ever, Jem took a sip of his coffee.

And then, keeping a hold on the fingers sticking out of the little cast, he nodded toward Levi, who took a sip of milk.

Okay. Normality.

"Tell me what you remember about the night of the dream, buddy."

"Do I have to?"

"Yes." He held on to those fingers. Not coddling. But loving. And doing everything he could to let Levi know that while he had to man up, his dad had his back.

"I waked up with Mommy shaking me. She was mad."

He held on to those fingers. Maybe for himself now.

"Why was she mad?"

"I hit her in the face." Levi started to cry again. "I'm bad and now do I gotta go away?"

What the hell?

"You hit your mother?"

He shrugged.

"Levi."

"She said so."

Everything in him stilled. "You don't remember hitting her?"

"I remember sleeping."

He was getting the picture, more clearly than ever. And felt bile in the back of his throat.

Tressa had called because Levi was having a nightmare and she couldn't wake him. He'd been flailing his cast in the air and she'd said that she was afraid he was going to hurt himself.

That grain of truth. The goddamn grain of truth that led one down the wrong path. She wasn't afraid he was going to hurt himself. At least not at that point. She'd been afraid because he'd hit her and she'd overreacted.

"You aren't in trouble," he said softly, floundering as he tried to corral his thoughts, determine how bad things were and figure out what to do. But one thing was a given: taking care of the little boy that he loved more than life. "You aren't bad. What happened wasn't your fault because you were asleep, and we can't help what happens when we're asleep, can we?"

Levi shook his head, his little cheeks still wet with tears.

"So do you remember anything else about the dream night?"

"I threw up."

Lacey had had that one right, which didn't surprise him as much as it should have.

"And that's all?"

Levi nodded, but he didn't meet his gaze.

Jem racked his brain for more words. What came next? Where did he go with this?

"The swimming," he said aloud. "You told Lacey and Kacey a story about you learning to swim," he continued, hoping to hell his voice was filled with loving interest—not accusation.

Levi nodded and then said, "Yes."

"Did Mommy get mad then, too?"

He nodded, eyes wide again.

"How come?"

"She told me do this…" He moved his arms in a crawling motion. "But I jumped under and drownded."

He'd scared the shit out of Tressa. He'd had that part of the story already, almost to a T.

"Then what happened?"

"She held me." He put his hands on his sides at his rib cage. "And made me stay under and bringed me up."

"How many times?"

"A hundreds." Levi's word for more than he could count.

"What happened next?"

"I sneezed a lot."

He'd had water up his nose.

"Then Mommy buyed the basketball and we played and it was fun."

All's well that ends well.

Except that, if Lacey's source was correct, his son had worn bruises all over his torso as an aftermath to that event. Tressa gripping him out of anger, not fear? Or both?

Which led him to another question. Who'd called Lacey? Because she'd known about those bruises.

And Tressa hadn't had any reason to take Levi to the hospital. Nor had he had a doctor's appointment during the time Jem had been gone. Even if Tressa hadn't told him about a visit, he'd have seen it come through on his insurance...

He leaned down. "Man-to-man, son, why didn't you tell me these things?"

Levi's head dropped.

"You have my word you are not going to have to go away," he said.

If you do, Jem, I'll...

"Did your mom tell you that you'd have to go away if you told me what had happened?" To save her own ass. At the expense of her son's.

The little boy's eyes filled with tears again as he nodded.

And Jem wanted to wring that little bitch's neck.

CHAPTER TWENTY-EIGHT

LACEY WASN'T SURPRISED when she got a call from Jem later Sunday night. She was in her room, sitting in bed trying to read, but had really just been reliving delicious moments from the night before. Over and over again.

And so, when she saw his contact come up on her phone, she answered with "I've been lying here thinking about you."

"Hold that thought." He didn't sound sexy at all. "Seriously. I want it. Just..."

"What's wrong? Is it Levi? Is he okay?"

"He's fine. Probably better than he's been in a while. He's in bed, sleeping soundly."

"Is it Tressa? Did she call you again?" She'd been expecting the other woman to be a problem. Just hadn't known how soon.

Her territory had been threatened. And she thought Jem had had only one date. When Levi visited her again and mentioned Kacey and Lacey, all hell was going to break loose.

But Sydney would know before it happened. She'd have a measure in place...

"She did, but she's not on a rampage, if that's what you mean," he told her. "She was actually better than I've heard her in a long time—rational, kind, thinking of others."

Lacey felt a twinge of jealousy and turned away from it. She wasn't going back down the road of self-doubt. It was unhealthy—for her and for those she cared about.

Jem wasn't hers.

And even if they were officially together, if he suddenly decided he wanted his ex-wife, Lacey wanted him to say so and go. Because if he truly felt the need to be with her, then that was where he was meant to be. Right?

Her thoughts were all over the place.

She hated it.

"You were right, Lacey…" Jem sounded beaten. The self-doubt came clearly over the line and scared her.

"Right about what?" She clutched the sheet up to her chin.

"About Tressa. And Levi. I don't think it's actionable," he said. "I've got a pretty clear picture now. I only wish I'd seen it sooner. He's been suffering through this all alone and…"

"No." Relief made her giddy. Such relief. Levi was going to be safe. *Safe*. And Jem? "He wasn't suffering alone, Jem. He had you all the time. Your constant love and attention give him security. And we caught it in time."

"But..."

"Look at how well he took to Kacey and me and going off alone with either one of us. That's the sign of a secure kid."

"He cried when I left him at his mother's house."

"Understandable."

"But I didn't understand. I just thought he was upset because he couldn't come to work with me. Or work on the boat. Or..."

"Be with the dad who made him feel safe," Lacey finished for him.

"Anyway, I need to know where we go from here."

"What did you mean when you said there was nothing actionable?"

"I've been doing some reading. Tressa's got control issues. She overreacts. When she's sad, she bursts into tears. When she's happy, she's like a little kid. When she's angry..."

"She lashes out?"

"Not physically," he said. "At least, not like I've been reading about. She doesn't hit him. At all. I asked him over and over. He swears his mother has never so much as slapped him on the bottom."

"And you believe him." She could only be a friend. After having slept with Jem, she was the furthest thing from impartial when it came to his ex-wife.

"I do."

Problem was, she didn't completely trust his judgment on the subject, either. Most particularly after the way he'd made excuses for the other woman after her despicable behavior the previous week.

He told her about Levi flailing around in his sleep and hitting Tressa in the face with his cast when she was trying to wake him up from his nightmare. About her losing it and shaking him. About him almost drowning and then her forcing him to learn how to hold his breath underwater.

"What about the broken arm?" she asked.

"Levi wasn't really climbing up the bookcase. His mother had him up on the counter trying to wipe his nose and he wasn't letting her. She grabbed his arm, meaning to haul him toward her and get him in a clamp-hold, but she pulled too roughly and he fell off the counter."

"You've spoken to her, then?"

"Not yet. I had to talk to you first."

The ice around her heart softened. But she knew she couldn't advise him.

"Levi told me his version of things. Putting it together with what she's said and what I know about her, I think I've figured out what happened."

She wasn't sure he had. But thought he could have. Still...

He hadn't mentioned anything about himself, about Tressa's misuse of him. To the contrary, he was still justifying her behavior.

Lacey wasn't jealous about that. At least not much. She was concerned.

Jem was never going to be free of the woman's manipulation unless he could see that what she was doing to him was wrong. Unless he could break away from her hold over him.

And she was the last person who could have that conversation with him.

"So what do we do?" he asked.

The "we" brought tears to her eyes.

"You need to call Sydney first thing in the morning, Jem. Tell her everything you just told me. She'll work with you from there."

"What do you think she'll do?"

"I can only speak as your...person." She'd tried to say *friend*, but couldn't minimize what he'd become in her life. Right or wrong, she was laying claim.

And giving him to Sydney, too.

"You consider yourself my...person?"

For the first time since she'd answered the phone, that certain tone was in his voice. Her body reacted immediately.

And she wondered what that said about her.

"I do." For now.

"Good. Because I consider myself your... person, too."

She felt kind of stupid sitting there alone, grinning through tears.

"So...as my...person, can you give me a bit

of practical insight as to what I might be in for when I make my call in the morning? Should I take Levi to school first?"

"Definitely take him to school, and leave strict instructions that he isn't to be released to his mother's care."

"Can I do that without a court order?"

"Yes, because you're the primary custodial parent. She can challenge it, but then they'll either call social services or the police, and either one will protect Levi."

"Okay, then what?"

"Then Sydney will probably want to meet with you. And maybe you and Tressa together. She'll assess how bad Tressa's situation is and go from there."

"Can you give me some parameters as to what the 'go from there' could look like?"

He was already thinking of ways to help minimize the damage for Tressa. To prevent a tornado from disrupting their lives. She didn't have to see inside his head to know it. She'd seen it enough times to recognize it. Even just as a...person.

"She could be required to go through some kind of anger management course before she's allowed to see him again. More likely she'll be required to be assessed by a court-appointed psychiatrist. And will be allowed only supervised visits until the court determines that Levi is safe alone with her."

"So they won't arrest her or anything?"

"Not if she cooperates..." Lacey broke off, knowing she'd made a mistake. She'd just told an abused husband how to fall prey to his ex-wife's manipulation. Jem was going to contact Tressa before Sydney had a chance to. She knew it as well as she knew she'd take her next breath.

Jem was a victim. She'd known that before she slept with him. Before she'd started to fall in love with him.

She just wasn't sure how anyone could help him to see it if he was incapable of looking. He hadn't been able to recognize that his own son was being victimized...

And if he didn't see it, he was never going to be free to be in any kind of a committed, one-on-one relationship with anyone. It would always be about appeasing Tressa—hiding things from her, placating her, doing what he had to do to keep the storm at bay.

It didn't matter what Jem wanted, what he promised Lacey or how much he might care about her. As long as Tressa had a hold of him, he wasn't a free man, no matter how much he loved or needed someone else.

Her heart shriveled in her chest. She didn't cry out. Or shed any tears at all. Not then. She just... knew.

"One other thing..." Jem broke into the silence that had fallen.

"What's that?"

"Can you confirm who called in the first place, if I guess it right?"

"Of course not."

"I figured it out."

"That's nice." She was at work, having a conversation with a stranger. Not a woman lying in a sexy nightie talking to her new lover.

"I just… I want them to know how much I appreciate what they did," he said. "I have to be able to thank them, Lacey. Or at least to stress that they did the right thing. So they'll do it again. Anytime. Every time. For every child. If not for them, I still wouldn't know, and Levi could have been paying for my ignorance for the rest of his life."

She'd been about to tell him that his son would likely have told him eventually, when he got old enough that his anger outgrew his need for security. But, thinking of Jem, of the abuse he'd taken at his sister's hands, and the fact that she was the only one in the world he'd ever told about that, she kept her mouth shut.

Levi was a lot like Jem.

At least she'd been able to help one of them in time.

NO CHARGES WERE being filed against Tressa. Jem was so relieved he wanted to call Lacey immediately and let her know the good news.

He accepted Tressa's hug instead, holding her tight because he knew she needed it. He could feel how badly she was shaking. Knew how hard the hearing had been for her. And knew, too, that she was determined to be a mother who was safe for her son.

Their son.

It had been three days since he'd first called Sydney. As Lacey had predicted, the social worker had met with him first, at her office. And then she'd met with Tressa. He'd asked if he could be present, and when he'd been told that he could be, he'd called Tressa to let her know they were on their way to her place.

He'd told her that Levi had had some problems, and the truth had come out. There were no accusations because he knew she hadn't meant to do any of the things she'd done.

He'd had an entire night to calm down between his talk with his son and his conversation with Sydney. Even more time before he'd spoken with his ex-wife. Time to assimilate. To get on top of the situation with his son's best interests forefront in his mind.

He'd reassured Tressa that everything was going to be fine. As long as she cooperated. He'd told her that he'd be there with her every step of the way. That they'd get through it together. And that he didn't hate her.

But he had. For a few hours.

Until he'd realized that hating her for something she couldn't help wasn't good for anyone. Least of all him. If he allowed that kind of anger and hate to rule his life, he'd turn into his sister, and he wasn't about to do that.

No, the way out of this was to get help for Tressa. Sydney had taken statements from both of them. She'd helped Jem file for a court hearing, to amend their custody rights—leaving Tressa with only court supervised visits for now. And finally, three days after the ordeal had begun, it was done.

"Can I come over tonight?" Tressa asked as she climbed into his truck so he could take her home.

She'd asked him if he'd drive her to court, and because he thought it in all of their best interests that she be as calm and stable as possible, he'd agreed to do so.

He probably would have, anyway. It was the decent thing to do, given the circumstances.

"You know my rule regarding you at my place," he said, hating to be firm, but he couldn't go back to having her unexpectedly popping up in his life. And most certainly not now that Lacey was a part of it.

He hadn't seen Lacey since Sunday. He'd wanted the cement floor to cure for a week before he started framing her room. And he'd been focused on the mess with Tressa. But he'd talked to her every night, lying in his bed while she lay in hers. Her voice had been the last thing he'd heard before sleep. Four nights in a row now.

He figured that was long enough to form an addiction...

"But I want to see him, Jem," Tressa said now, her voice getting wobbly. "You've already said you're working this weekend and I can't have him at my place without making prior plans so someone from social services can be there. And Sydney said Thursday's too late to make those plans, at least this week, because the Santa Raquel office is so small and everyone is busy..."

He could feel the storm brewing. It was only noon. Levi's doctor's appointment for cast removal was at 1:00 p.m. If all went well, they'd be done by 2:00 p.m. Which gave him three hours before his date with Lacey.

Kacey was leaving on Saturday and had been asking for more Levi time before she left. She had a cast off party all planned for him.

"How about if I bring him by your place as soon as he gets his cast off?" Jem improvised. He wasn't going to have Tressa in episodic mode ruining the evening he had planned. "You can be the first to celebrate with him."

Maybe they could turn the broken-arm moment with Levi's mother into something healthy. "It would be a good chance for you to apologize to him." Sydney had stressed that Tressa had some damage to undo with her son. Starting with acknowledging that she'd been the one who'd been bad, not him, and assuring him that no one was ever going to do anything to take him away from his father.

"Okay." Tressa sat back, her head against the seat, watching the traffic in front of them. "I don't deserve you, Jem."

She didn't have him, either. Not anymore.

"But I'm thankful for you. I want you to know that. You really had my back this week."

"I know how hard you try to be a good mother to our son."

"I do, you know." She turned to look at him. "I love him more than life."

He nodded, understanding completely.

"You know what bothered me the most?" she mused, looking out the window again.

"What?" He was mildly curious. Mostly he just wanted to drop her off so he could call Lacey.

"The thought that our son would grow up and know that his mother had been thrown in jail for hurting him. I know how that feels, Jem, what it does to a person. You spend your whole life fearing that you're going to be just like them, because, after all, you have their genes."

Both of her parents had been arrested for abuse. Against each other. On different occasions. Several years apart. They'd each spent a night in jail while the other was at home with the kids. And then been released when the other refused to press charges. They'd never lost custody of their kids.

"I'm going to do all of the counseling, and then some, Jem. I'm going to get this right." Tressa sat up and turned to face him. "I will not let my mom and dad win this one."

It was one of the sanest things he'd heard her say in a long time.

And he breathed a sigh of relief.

It had taken the week from hell, the threat of losing her son and possibly going to jail, but Tressa had finally seen the truth. They'd turned the corner.

Maybe, months down the road, after counseling, he'd be able to introduce her to Lacey and they could all be friends.

Today was proof that miracles did happen.

CHAPTER TWENTY-NINE

IT HAD BEEN one of the hardest weeks of Lacey's life. To finally find someone who really valued her above anyone, and then have him be in the trance of someone else... It was too cruel even for her paranoia to conjure up.

But her most acute pain wasn't even for herself. It was for Jem. A man in a million. A giver. A truly gentle man who had more strength, physically as well as emotionally, than anyone she'd ever met. And the power of abuse was taking advantage of everything good about him.

Some days she didn't ever want him to come face-to-face with the truth. Afraid of how it could change him when he saw how his willingness to do the right thing by Tressa had put him in a position to be manipulated without him even seeing it.

Other days, she prayed for his release. Not for herself, but because he deserved to be honored and respected, not abused. To be loved and cared for, not...used up.

Thank God for Kacey. Her sister had spent the night in Lacey's bed with her one night, sitting up and watching old movies until Lacey had finally fallen asleep. Every night after work, she'd dragged Lacey around to choose furniture for her new room. To dinner at the new Mexican place by the water.

They walked on the beach and stopped at an outdoor pub to have drinks and talk about the good old days. Lacey had been surprised to find out how many of them there really had been. That had been the previous night. They'd stayed to listen to the first set played by the band that had shown up at nine, too. And still, Jem had just been finishing with Tressa when he'd called and found Lacey already in bed.

They'd been preparing for the emergency custodial court hearing that had been set for that morning.

It was after noon and she still hadn't heard how it had gone. It was way too early for anything to be on public record. The judge wouldn't even have had time to give his minutes to the court recorder for filing.

And knowing that she and Sydney couldn't discuss the case, knowing, too, that Sydney knew now that Lacey's personal involvement was more than just casual, she'd steered clear of her colleague by taking herself out of the office to make well-check visits.

She was almost back to the office, planning on having the salad Kacey had packed her for lunch before an afternoon hearing, when her car's speaker bleeped announcing an incoming call. Glancing at her radio dash, she saw Jem's number on the screen and pushed the button on her steering wheel to answer.

"Thank God you answered." She could hear the adrenaline in his voice. "I was afraid I was going to have to settle for voice mail."

"I've been watching the clock," she said. "Waiting to hear." She hoped to God she didn't sound peevish. She didn't feel it; she just…missed him.

"I've got full custody." He told her the most important fact first.

"I knew you would, but what a relief to hear that it's done," she told him, only then realizing that she'd been holding her emotional breath on that one. Regardless of how the world was changing, courts still oftentimes tended to rule in favor of the mother, and Lacey knew how likable and convincing Tressa could be. Hell, she'd found herself thinking she and the woman could almost be friends the first time they'd met.

"Tressa was ordered into anger management if she wants a chance to earn back her rights. And she was granted supervised visits."

"No charges were filed against her for child abuse?"

"It was like you said—there wasn't enough

there to prove anything. Because, really, in each incident, an accident was involved."

And he was justifying. Holding your child underwater to force him to hold his breath, leaving bruises on his torso as you did so, was definitely actionable.

But Jem was right. It would be Tressa's word against that of a four-year-old. One who remembers having a great time playing basketball with his mother in the pool after he learned to swim. And who also remembered misbehaving, almost drowning and having his mother save him.

"So...we're still good for tonight?"

It wasn't until he asked the question that she admitted to herself she'd been half expecting him to cancel. Because Tressa would surely need him, after the trauma of the day's events.

It fit her MO. Unless, maybe Amelia would be around. The real estate attorney had been in LA all week, arguing a case for a brokerage company.

"Of course we're still good," Lacey told him, and had to add, "I've missed you. A lot." Because it was so true.

"I've missed you, too, babe. You have no idea how much."

She had an inkling. Evidence pointed to the fact that she wasn't the only one who'd fallen hard here. She wanted to believe that.

She just wasn't sure how she fought the demon

that was threatening to keep them from ever sharing a true partnership.

JEM DID SOME double takes over the next couple of weeks, finding it hard to believe that life had finally become what he'd always believed it could be. Kacey was back in Beverly Hills, back at work, but she came to Santa Raquel both weekends. They'd all have dinner together as a family on the Friday nights—both times at Uncle Bob's at Levi's request.

And Saturday nights Kacey spent with Levi— "getting her baby on," as she put it. She wanted a home and family, and caring for Levi was like Alcoholics Anonymous to her, reminding her that the life of nightly partying that she'd led, no matter how easy and convenient to fill lonely hours, was not the life she wanted.

Saturday nights were for Jem and Lacey. All night long. They'd spent the night at Jem's one night. At Lacey's the other.

Levi thought slumber parties with Kacey were better than going to Grandma's. Not that Jem passed on that little tidbit to his parents.

Tressa was doing well with her anger management counseling. She was attending extra meetings and classes in addition to those required and reading everything she could get her hands on.

Jem had helped her land a job with a window supplier in a neighboring town. While she didn't love the fifteen-minute highway drive, she did love the job and seemed to be settling in well.

She'd had four visits with Levi. Three of them had been supervised by social services, and one had been at her house supervised by Jem, so the boy could swim. Because he had said he wanted to play with his basketball hoop.

And now this, the fifth visit, was under Jem's supervision, as well. It was the Fourth of July. Lacey was in San Diego with Kacey and their parents, spending the weekend at her folks' beach cottage.

He and Levi had been invited to go, but Amelia was visiting her folks in Wisconsin, and when Tressa had told him everyone else had plans, too, he knew he couldn't ask her to give up her visit with Levi.

She'd want to know where they were going, which would have involved more lies than he wanted to tell at this fragile stage of the game. Or risk setting Tressa off before she'd had a chance to get a firm hold on the new, calmer life she was making for herself.

He couldn't risk everything because he had a selfish need to be someplace else.

They were at the park in town, getting ready to watch the fireworks. Tressa had packed a picnic, and while Jem was uncomfortable sitting on the blanket with them, eating sandwiches his ex-wife had prepared, as though they were a happy family holidaying together rather than on a supervised custodial visit, he was also content to know that his son was getting the time with his mother that he needed.

"I wanna slide!" The boy was jumping up and down on the blanket. The bowl of coleslaw Tressa had sitting on a paper plate almost capsized. Jem grabbed the boy just as she grabbed the salad.

"The slide's too crowded," Tressa told him, her tone sounding irritated but softening by the last word. Jem was impressed. Those classes were really working. "Too many big kids. Someone could go down behind you, ram into you and..."

"Tressa." Jem said only the one word. She looked at him.

"I'll go over with him. Make sure that no one goes down after him until he's on the ground," he said.

"The metal will be hot. He could get burned, and then how would I explain that? It could look like I did it, or at the very least, that I should have known better and been able to prevent it."

He saw the fear in her eyes and understood completely. She felt hunted. She was going to lose everything by simply being herself.

"Give it time, Tress," he said, feeling real compassion for the sweet, loving person trapped inside damaged emotions.

She nodded.

"I'll check the slide. If the metal's hot, he won't go down."

She nodded again.

"Yeah! Slide!" Levi cried out. He took Jem's hand. And then stopped, turning back to hold out his other. "Let's go, Mom!"

Jem saw Tressa wipe away a tear as she got up to join them.

LEVI SLID AGAIN and again, climbing the stairs, yelling for his parents to watch him and then putting his hands in the air as he made the quick trip down.

It was great fun. Until he tried to get fancy and lift his legs up in the air like he'd seen another kid do.

That kid, who was easily twice Levi's age, had lain back, his head on the slide, as he'd gone down.

Levi failed to put his head down and hit it on the end of the slide when he reached the bottom.

Jem had moved in as soon as he'd seen what was happening, but hadn't been in time to prevent the head bump.

Levi took it like a man. He rubbed his head. Stood up. And turned to Jem. "Did you see that, Dad? That was cool!"

Ready to tell his son to keep his feet on the slide if he wanted to go down again, Jem didn't get the chance as Tressa rushed up. "Are you okay?" she asked, feeling the back of the boy's head. "Oh, God, Jem, he has a bump. He has a bump on the back of his head."

He'd already felt the head himself. There was a tiny welt where Levi's head had hit the metal, but it would be gone in an hour or so. There was no real swelling and no broken skin.

"He's got a bump!" Tressa said, pulling Levi away from the other people. "Feel it!"

Levi's lower lip started to tremble as he looked up at his father. Jem knew he had to defuse the situation immediately.

"He's fine, Tress."

"I don't even hurt, Mommy," Levi said, taking Jem's tone.

"He could be concussed," Tressa hissed. "Oh, God. On my watch. They're going to hang this on me. I just know it…"

The day was going nowhere fast.

"I'll watch him like a hawk," Jem said. "He's not concussed. He didn't hit his head hard enough to even raise a decent bruise. But even if he was, they'd just have us keep him awake for the next few hours, to watch his behavior."

"We have to take him in, Jem. My life will be over if something comes of this and we didn't take him in. I'm going to lose my chance to see him at all if one more thing happens with me. If he's hurt one more time. You heard the judge, Jem. That's what he said. But I can't risk Levi's life because I'm afraid of getting in trouble. That's what I already did. You heard it, Jem, you know."

The storm was brewing. He saw it coming. He couldn't let Levi get caught in it. Never again. He'd made a promise to his son, to himself.

And though she didn't know it, to Lacey, too.

"I know of an Urgent Care in Santa Barbara," Jem said, herding them back to collect their blanket. "They'll take one look at him, tell you he's fine, and we can be done with this," he said, coming up with the plan as he went.

It didn't dissipate the sick feeling in his gut.

"An Urgent Care?"

"In Santa Barbara. They'll see two overconcerned parents and one very unhurt little boy. They won't have anything to report. Probably won't even put our name in the system. But if they do, it won't be connected to the hospital here."

"So no one will know we've been!" Tressa was throwing things in the basket as quick as she could, but stopped to look up at him. She was grinning through her tears. "Thank you, Jem. I knew you'd know what to do to save me. You always do."

"Aren't we going to watch the firecrackers?" Levi, who'd caught on to the fact that they were leaving, cried out. "I wanna watch the firecrackers."

Jem wanted to go home, sit at his fish pond and drink a beer.

Maybe call Lacey later. And listen to Levi's even breathing coming over his nursery monitor as he slept.

"If we hurry, we'll make it back in plenty of time to watch the fireworks," he said, infusing his voice with a joy he didn't feel. "They can't do them until dark, and it's a long time until then." An hour and a half. At least. If he was lucky.

Feeling duplicitous, running off to the next town to hide a doctor visit, Jem nonetheless prayed that traffic was light. That the Urgent Care wasn't filled with patients who actually needed to be seen. And that someday he'd be free from Tressa-induced stress.

CHAPTER THIRTY

LACEY LOVED JEM. She hadn't come right out and told him so, but she'd admitted the truth when Kacey had asked, and again when Kacey told their parents about the man in Lacey's life.

Kacey thought Lacey was sabotaging herself again—borrowing trouble where there might not be any in her concern over Tressa's hold over Jem. But Kacey had spent the past ten years working in a world of pretense, not dealing with victims of domestic violence as Lacey had.

She knew the signs. Impartial or not, she could run through a checklist. Jem had every sign of being a victim other than physical bruises.

Being without him on the Fourth intensified her worry. Not out of jealousy—she knew by now that he did not enjoy his ex-wife's company—but because he hadn't been able to tell Tressa that he wanted to take Levi away for the holiday.

He'd explained it all to her. How Tressa was all alone. How holidays—times when everyone else went off to be with family—were hardest for her.

How she was doing so well and he couldn't risk setting her back. For Levi's sake.

She'd read between the lines, too. But had been unable to tell Jem what she really thought. He'd only deny the truth.

Because if he could see it, he'd be doing something about it.

Trouble was, he thought he saw it clearly. And he thought he was the only one who truly knew Tressa, truly understood her. The only one who could help her get through this.

But he thought that way because she'd made him do so. To keep him on her hook. He didn't see that part.

By the end of July, Lacey was almost willing to pretend she didn't see the truth, either. They'd had an idyllic few weeks since her return from San Diego. She and Jem and Levi had dinner together every single night. She'd even spent a couple of nights at his place during the week.

He'd picked her up in his truck and driven her home in the morning. She didn't like that aspect of it so much, fearing that he was placating Tressa by making sure there were no unfamiliar cars in front of his house or in his driveway all night. But, as Kacey continued to tell her, she could just be borrowing trouble.

They'd had a near-miss when Levi had mentioned Lacey during one of his supervised visits with Tressa. Sydney had been there and told Jem, who told Lacey about it. Tressa knew that Levi was to receive counseling anytime he appeared to be struggling. She'd just assumed that Lacey was his counselor, since she'd been his initial case-worker. Sydney hadn't disabused her of the idea.

The level of Jem's relief had given Lacey serious pause in the midst of a seriously happy day at the beach. She'd paused again when he'd mentioned that Tressa and Amelia were in San Francisco for the weekend, visiting Amelia's brother. She'd been thrilled when, with Kacey in LA for a movie premiere she had to attend that weekend, he'd suggested a day at the beach for the three of them—him, Lacey and Levi—thinking he was finally ready to quit coddling Tressa by hiding upsetting things from her, that he was moving toward the idea of he and Lacey and Levi becoming a family publicly as well as at home.

She'd been wrong.

Just as he was wrong in his apparent assessment that anger management meant someone else managing anything that could cause anger.

She didn't pause, however, when, that night, after Levi was bathed and in bed asleep, Jem reached for her hand and pulled her down the hall to his room. Their love life was unyieldingly happy. She couldn't get enough of him.

And couldn't get enough of how much he wanted her.

"The room should be finished this week," he

told her as he shut the bedroom door behind them. Levi's monitor, on the bedside table, would alert them if he was disturbed. "I'll begin mudding and sanding tomorrow."

He'd taken that day, Saturday, to go to the beach and would be spending Sunday at her house working while she and Levi went grocery shopping and made dinner.

He'd spent the previous weekend running electric, putting in outlet boxes and hanging drywall—among other, more private things, anytime Levi had been otherwise occupied. The little boy had been watching a lot of television. But only on weekends, and only in spurts, after playing at the park, building puzzles or teaching Lacey how to piece together track for his unending car collection.

"So...I was thinking..." He held her to him with a hand on her backside, rubbing the front of his shorts against the front of hers. "Maybe we ought to start thinking about, you know, moving some things around."

She'd purchased new furniture. He knew that, since he'd told her when to have it delivered. "What things?"

"Like, maybe a toothbrush here and a toothbrush there..."

They already had toothbrushes at each other's houses. She'd bought one for Levi, too. Just like the one he had at Jem's house.

She stared at Jem, not breathing as easily as she had been. Was he asking her to marry him?

She'd expected him to wait until Tressa had improved before they took their relationship to the next level. And marriage...that was a long way off.

"I was just thinking that maybe we should bring some of your clothes here, and some of mine to your house. And...Levi's, too. Once I'm done working, I won't need to be over there every day, and I don't want to get out of the habit of spending our weekends together."

He wasn't proposing. Okay. Feeling disappointed was natural. But she hadn't been expecting to talk about marriage. Wasn't sure she was ready to do so. Not until he could be honest with Tressa.

"You aren't saying anything," he said.

"I'm not sure what to say. I didn't think we were spending all of our free time together because you were working on my house. I thought we were doing it because we're on the way to joining our lives in some kind of permanent fashion..."

Oh, God. Had *she* just mentioned marriage? She hadn't meant it that way.

Now he wasn't saying anything. And wasn't rubbing himself against her anymore, either. Probably trying to figure out how to tend to her feelings and keep her away from Tressa at the same time.

She'd tried to talk to him about telling Tressa the truth. Once. He'd told her he wanted nothing more and would do so as soon as he could.

"Anyway, I was just taking for granted that we'd continue to spend our free time together." She tried to salvage the conversation. She wasn't rushing him.

Didn't want him to feel pressured by her. He had enough pressure in his life.

She also didn't want to marry him until he was ready, and had to face the fact that he might never be. No matter what Kacey said...

"Did you hear that?" Jem stepped away from her, toward the closed bedroom door.

She hadn't heard anything.

"It sounded like a car door."

Tressa was in San Francisco. She hated that his ex-wife was her first thought. His anxiety was rubbing off on her.

It wasn't healthy. Or right.

"Probably just a neighbor."

She was talking to his back. And slowed her step behind him when she heard the doorbell ring.

She wanted to go out there. To stand next to him as he greeted whoever was dropping by after ten o'clock on a Saturday night. If someone needed help...

But she didn't. She cowered in the hallway instead. Because she figured that was what he'd have asked her to do.

Just in case.

"You're screwing someone!" She heard the words even before she heard the door open. Which meant Tressa was screaming at him through the door. "Amelia told me, so don't you dare stand there and try to deny it, Jem Bridges. All this time, you and me and Levi, us being a family again, you having my back, and all the time going around behind my back and..."

Lacey started to shake and closed Levi's bedroom door, glad that the little boy could sleep through a drive home and being put back to bed. He'd probably make it through this, too, if they were lucky.

What was she thinking? He'd probably learned to sleep soundly because the first couple of years of his life had been spent living with episodes like the one going on out front.

Odd, though, that the last time Tressa had shown up, wanting to see Levi, Jem had put his ex-wife off with the excuse that if she went in Levi's room, he'd wake up. As if Tressa didn't know how soundly her son slept?

"Damn you!" Something slammed against the storm door Jem had yet to open. Glass shattered.

"Where's Amelia?"

Lacey's mouth fell open. That was all Jem had to say? Glass had just shattered and he asked after Tressa's friend?

"I left her in San Francisco. She actually took

me there to propose to me." Tressa was screaming loudly enough for the neighbors to hear.

Would it be wrong to pray that one of them called the police?

"I'm sorry that wasn't what you wanted, Tress."

It was like being backstage for the filming of one of Kacey's episodes. Only, you knew that was fake…and therefore safe.

"I mean, if a girl's going to be proposed to, she at least needs some warning that the relationship is moving to an entirely different level."

"I'm sure she thought she was doing something nice…"

"She *knows* me," Tressa said. "She knows that I need to be wooed into anything new. And then when I told her that I couldn't think about getting hooked up with someone else while you and I were… Well, she knows that you're first for me. I'd told her that from the very beginning. But she acts all hurt and then tells me the truth. That she's seen you around town with some blonde. And saw Levi at the beach with her, too…"

Another slam. Something against metal. "How could you, Jem? You let some whore take my son to the beach? Where other people could see them out together? I'm going to sue your ass. Both of your asses."

"Calm down, Tress." Jem's tone was…normal sounding. "I'm sorry you found out about Lacey like that, but…"

"Lacey? As in Levi's *caseworker*? You're seeing our son's caseworker? I'm going to sue her, Jem. Oh, is she mine. She'll be out of a job before I'm done with her..."

Wanting to find a bathroom, afraid she might throw up, Lacey stood rooted to the wall, trembling. She hadn't done anything wrong. But she *had* started out as a caseworker to this family.

The investigation was closed when she ran into Jem and Levi again at the beach, and she hadn't been anywhere near it since she'd been seeing Jem socially.

But the woman could make things look bad for her. Really bad. She could have a mark on her reputation. And...

She had to trust Jem. He'd take care of this. He'd see what Tressa was doing to her...

"Let's talk about this, Tress. You know you don't want to do any of those things."

"Are you really seeing her, Jem?"

"It's not what you think."

"What?"

"Amelia didn't see Levi at the beach with Lacey. She saw him at the beach with her twin sister."

"There's two of them?"

He was siccing Tressa on Kacey, too?

"Are you screwing them both?"

"You don't want to do this, Tress. Think of your classes. Of Levi."

Think of her classes? Of Levi? She needed to be thinking about what she was going to tell the police as soon as they were called.

"I thought we were going to be a family again."

"We'll always be family." *What?* "You're Levi's mother."

Lacey's heart fell, hard, even as she recognized what he was doing.

"I broke your glass."

"You were going for the door handle and missed. Is your hand okay?" He was doing what any man would do when danger appeared at his front door, defusing the situation in the only way he knew how, in order to protect his family.

Problem was, Jem's way only enabled Tressa. Giving her more power, not taking it away.

There'd been a pause. And then "Yeah. The cut's not that deep."

"Let me take a look at it." Another pause. "You're right. You got lucky."

"I'm sorry." She sounded it. She was calmer, too, because Jem was giving her what she needed.

"Don't worry about it. I'll have a new piece in there by morning." That was it? *Don't worry about breaking the glass in my front door with your hand when you came barging in after ten o'clock at night, uninvited, at a house you've been told to stay away from? Don't worry about it?*

"So…this woman…Lacey… You're not…like…"

"I told you, Amelia misunderstood."

He was lying because it was the only way he knew how to get rid of her. Once she was gone, they'd call the police. And then, finally, this whole nightmare would end.

CHAPTER THIRTY-ONE

JEM CLEANED UP the glass as soon as Tressa's car pulled slowly away down the street.

He'd have to deal with her in the morning, like he'd promised. But for now, the storm was averted.

He'd managed to put out another fire.

And was damned tired of the life he'd been dealt.

"What are you doing?" Lacey had appeared at the end of the hall. He'd hoped that she'd stayed in the bedroom. Maybe even had jumped in the shower, where she wouldn't have heard a word of what had been said.

Her face looked calm. She had to at least have missed the part about Tressa suing her. So there *was* a God.

He'd had the thought before.

Maybe it would serve him well to remember it more often.

"Just cleaning up. Tressa reached for the door handle and put her hand through the glass."

"She pounded the glass, Jem." Her words

were calm. No emotion, or accusation. Yet they stopped him cold.

"You don't know how Tressa gets when she's caught up in her drama. She's clumsy. Believe me, I've seen it before. She just missed the door handle."

Lacey's mouth fell open. "You really believe that, don't you?"

"Of course I believe it! I know it. I've been living with this kind of thing all my life."

"Right. First JoAnne and then Tressa."

But not Lacey. Thank God again. If ever there was a time that a woman would be pushed into losing control, it would be now. And she was standing there watching him. Not screaming.

"You need to leave that as it is," she said, coming closer and taking the broom and dustpan from him. "It's evidence."

"Evidence? Of what?" Hadn't she heard a thing he'd said? This was Tressa at her worst. When she was upset, she was careless. "Don't you get it?" He looked at her. "She found out we're seeing each other, and now she's over it. I have to tell you, it went a lot better than I'd feared it might."

Her jaw dropped again. "You thought this went well?"

"Are you kidding? She was out of here in five. I've had nights it took hours to talk her down. I have to tell you, those classes are really making a difference."

He wanted to believe they were. And wanted her to believe it, too. He wanted her to quit looking at him like that.

To get over the past few minutes and get on to what really mattered. Her. Him. Together.

They'd just crossed a major hurdle to making their lives together official. Give Tressa a few months to get used to the idea, and maybe accept Amelia's proposal—he'd suspected for a long time now that they were lovers—and they'd be home free.

"You have to call the police, Jem," Lacey said. "If not for yourself, for me. Because if you think she's going to leave this alone, you're wrong. If it was just you, then yes, I would believe it. Because she has you where she wants you and she has to give you your way where she can to keep you there. But me... I'm a threat to it all. She has to get rid of me. Period. Or have her whole world come tumbling down."

"It's just talk, Lace. I swear. You need to trust me on this."

"You've asked her repeatedly not to come to this house. Yet she continues to show up."

"Only when she's beside herself upset..."

"And isn't it for just that reason that you don't want her here? So that you don't have to live under the constant threat of dealing with her drama?"

Into each life a little rain must fall. He remembered the quotation from his childhood. His grandmother Lillie said it every time anything upset any of them.

He was tired. Needed to lie down. Hold Lacey and sleep it off. "Please, Lace. I took care of it. She's gone. Just let it go?"

"You led her to believe that there's nothing between us…"

He was sorry as hell she'd heard that. "She knows I didn't deny that there was. I'm just giving her time to adjust to the idea. It's the way things work with her."

"You seriously aren't going to call the police?"

"Of course not. That would just set everything back. Way back."

"You need to get a restraining order, Jem. You'd be granted one immediately just for what happened here tonight."

"I'm telling you she didn't mean to break the window. And even if she did, she'd say she was going for the door handle, and how are you going to prove she wasn't?" He'd been through this so many times it was old hat to him. But he had to slow down and understand that it was all new to Lacey.

Tressa could be…alarming…at first.

"I'm not talking about the window. You've told her repeatedly to stay away from your house. She didn't. That's grounds for a restraining order."

One thing he knew was how to be patient. "She wouldn't abide by it, Lacey. The best way to deal with Tressa is to handle her exactly as I'm doing. You'll see. She'll get used to the idea of me and you just like she got used to the idea of the divorce. And Levi living with me."

"You went through this each time?"

Now she was getting it. He almost smiled. "Yes."

"And you never even called the police?"

"Of course not."

"Well, this is the last time, Jem. Or I'm out of your life."

He wasn't sure he'd heard her right. Lacey? Threatening him? She hadn't even raised her voice.

"You are a victim of domestic abuse, Jem. I've been waiting for you to see that, just like you finally did with Levi, but you don't get it. The woman comes here, puts her fist through your door, screams loud enough for the entire neighborhood to hear, threatens to sue you and then to ruin my career—which she can do, you know, just by spouting her trash in the right places, or at least put doubt on my spotlessly clean record—and you plan to stand there and let her get away with it?"

"You don't understand..." The words just kept repeating themselves in his mind, overriding anything she might have to say. "You don't understand..."

"I'm not asking you to crucify her, Jem. I'm

asking you to think of yourself. Of Levi. Of our future. You need to call the police. Even if you don't want to file a restraining order, at least there's evidence of what happened here tonight, of her threats, so that if she does try something, we've got protection."

"But…"

"I need this, Jem," she said. That look of hers… it sank into him. As deep as he went. "I need you to call the police. For me. That way if she does try to threaten my career, I'll have the means to protect myself."

"She could go to jail…"

"If she does, it would only be for one night."

And that one night would unleash a hurricane…

"You don't understand, Lacey."

"I do understand, Jem. And I'm telling you. This isn't negotiable. I need you to call the police, or I have to end my association with you."

"You're threatening me." Tressa was a master at it.

"No, I'm telling you you've put me in a position where I have to make a choice. If you can't stand behind me, protect me, then I have to go."

One thing he'd learned, well, at the hands of his sister and Tressa, was that the minute he gave in to a threat, he gave up himself. He pulled his keys out of his pocket.

"Take my truck. I'll be by for it in the morning."

He expected her to pretend to go. Even to collect

her purse and head out the door. When his truck started, he gave her marks for trying.

It wasn't until his truck had been gone for more than an hour that he realized the truth. She wasn't coming back.

LACEY HAD THREE weeks of vacation coming to her. On Sunday, when she was already on her way to Beverly Hills, she made an emergency call to arrange to have the next week off. She'd had to get out of town and home to Kacey. Had to have some distance from the worst night of her life. To figure out where to find the rest of her life.

She knew she was running and admitted it fully. To herself. To Kacey.

Her sister, for once, didn't tell Lacey to look on the bright side. Her words "He actually chose to put her first over you?" still rang in Lacey's mind.

She wasn't overreacting, or feeling sorry for herself. Living in the past, or being paranoid. She was facing the truth.

Jem had put Tressa's needs over hers. And his own.

"I know why," she told Kacey later that night as the sisters sat on Kacey's balcony with a bottle of wine on the table between them. "It's because I don't make waves. I get mad, but I get over it. And everyone who knows me knows that."

Kacey's silence didn't hit her at first. Until it hung there, between them, for more than five minutes. She glanced over to see tears sliding slowly down her twin's face.

"What? Oh, my gosh, Kacey, are you in pain? What's going on?"

Shaking her head, Kacey looked over at her. "You're right."

"What? That you're hurt?" Ready to call an ambulance, she knelt at Kacey's feet. She couldn't lose her. Kacey was her rock. Her foundation. Her...other self.

"Don't you dare kneel at my feet," Kacey said, pulling Lacey up and directing her back to her chair. She knelt then, at Lacey's feet. "You're right that you're easy to disappoint, Lacey. To take advantage of. Because your mad is so...not ugly. You get quiet. That's it. And then you get over it and life goes on. That's why you got passed over and I got chosen, don't you see? Even with Mom and Dad. Because I made a stink. I made noise. I made it hard for people to pass me up."

"So what are you saying? That I should make more of a stink?"

"No! I think you're perfect." Kacey ran a hand along Lacey's cheek and Lacey turned her head, placing her lips in her sister's palm. "Don't ever change," Kacey said. "The world needs more yous. More kindness. Understanding. More selflessness. And the rest of us...we need to protect you from our own selfishness."

She was talking nonsense, of course. And

yet…her words struck a chord. Hadn't she had a similar thought about Jem? About Tressa taking advantage of his goodness?

Tressa the noisemaker, the one who would create hell if she didn't get her way. While Lacey… she'd understand. Be steadfast in her kindness. Get quiet. And get over it.

Except that she hadn't.

She'd gotten out. For the first time in her life.

She walked out on the one person who truly loved her above all others. Forever. When he'd needed her most.

JEM DIDN'T CALL Tressa Sunday morning. He called Lacey. And when she didn't answer, he went by her house. His truck was out front right where he'd told her to leave it. He'd told her he'd bring a second set of keys when he came to pick it up.

He pretended that all was well. With Levi by his side, he mudded Lacey's birthday-gift room. She'd be back. She was as steadfast as the sun that set each night. And when she showed up, he'd be there.

He had a key to her home, just like she had a key to his.

He cooked dinner from the leftovers in her fridge and put his son into her bed. And sometime after midnight, he joined him there.

Tressa had left sixteen voice-mail messages

and sent him eighty-two texts. He didn't respond to any of them.

On Monday morning, after dropping Levi at day care, but before going to work, he called Kacey. And almost dropped the phone in relief when she answered. She was still talking to him.

Boy, was she talking to him.

She told him, in no uncertain terms, that he didn't deserve her sister. And that Lacey had taken a week's vacation. He was told to leave her alone.

He knew, in Lacey's world, exactly what that meant. Leave her alone. Do not call her. Do not attempt to see her. Or to contact her in any way.

To do otherwise could mean a restraining order.

On Monday, Tressa left fourteen voice mails. And sent ninety texts. He spent Monday night in Lacey's bed again. Levi slept in Kacey's room.

On Tuesday, Jem dropped Levi off at preschool and went to see Sydney. They talked for a long time. When he left her office, he had a name: Brett Ackerman, the founder of a local shelter for abused women. A man who'd been a victim of domestic violence himself.

He and Levi had dinner with Brett and his wife, Ella, while their infant child slept in a bassinet nearby. In a few short hours his life changed forever.

He saw himself, a young self, in some of the

childhood feelings Brett described. He heard Lacey in Ella's words.

He spent Tuesday night in Lacey's bed, with Levi right there beside him.

On Wednesday, right after he dropped Levi at day care—with a request to Mara, who'd always had a special affinity with Levi, to keep his son close to her that day—Jem called the police. He called victim witness—a public service that provided support for victims of domestic violence who needed to obtain restraining orders. And he went to court.

By Wednesday night, he had a restraining order against Tressa Bridges, with Levi as a named victim. He spent Wednesday night at home in his own bed.

He woke Sunday morning to banging on his front door. Gut instantly tight, he flew out of bed.

It took him a second to realize that it couldn't be his ex-wife. She'd had a visit from the police the day before, telling her she'd go to jail if she came within twenty-five feet of either Jem or Levi, their home or any of their property. The one thing Tressa feared, more than anything else, was going to jail.

Hoping to God it was Lacey, breaking out of her shell and that eager to see him—maybe having heard from Sydney that he'd finally seen the light and done the right thing—he raced down the hall in his cotton pajama bottoms.

Sometime in the few seconds it had taken him to get from hall to front door, he'd realized that if Lacey was pounding on his door, the news wouldn't be good.

More likely it was the cops....

The banging was still happening as he yanked the door open.

"Jem, let me in! Quick!" Tressa stood there, sweaty and disheveled, talking in a hushed tone.

But banging loudly on the door?

He looked for her car, but didn't see it.

"What's wrong? Where's your car? Were you in an accident?" Their history didn't matter. If she was in danger, he had to help her.

"No! Let me in!"

"Tell me what's wrong."

"I just needed to see you. And Levi. Amelia's at church, and I only have a little bit of time. She's going to leave me if I contact you, but this is you and me. Nothing and no one keeps us apart, right?"

What the hell was she talking about? After all of this?

"No, Tressa. You aren't right. Do you get that? You are legally banned from seeing your own son."

"You bastard! How dare you say such a thing to me?"

"Because it's true. And you know it's true. You also know that up until now I understood you enough to let it all go. But no more, Tressa. Get this very clearly. No. More."

He didn't raise his voice. Didn't need to.

He just calmly closed the door, found his cell phone and dialed 9-1-1.

THE POLICE DISPATCHER took his call, holding him on the line until a cruiser made it to his residence. When they pulled up in two cars, one right after the other, Tressa, damn her, was still out there, alternating between begging him and cursing him. Demanding to be let in. Interspersed with threats of how she was going to make him pay.

An hour later, the police called back to let him know that she was going to be held in custody, at least overnight. By that time he and Levi were showered and dressed.

The officer wanted to know if he wanted to press charges. He didn't want to, but he did so. He trusted that with time, and the counseling Brett had recommended, his guilt over that would ease.

By lunchtime that same day, the day Lacey, hopefully, would be returning home, the day before she was due back at work, Jem put the finishing touches on her dream room. With his son's hand in his, he took a last look around, put a couple of toothbrushes in his tool bag, left a key on the table and walked out, locking the door behind him.

CHAPTER THIRTY-TWO

SHE'D THOUGHT LEAVING Kacey was going to be the hard part. It wasn't. Pulling up in front of her house, seeing Jem's truck gone, was horrible. But Lacey got past the moment. She pulled into her garage. Grabbed her suitcase and went into the house.

She was going to have to find someone to finish her dream room. Kacey had already told her she'd be home that next weekend and they'd find someone together. Her sister thought she was going to pay the second contractor, too, but she wasn't. Lacey had enough in savings to build a whole new house if she wanted to. And she was going to stand firm on this one.

No more lying down in the middle of the road for her.

She didn't kid herself into thinking she was suddenly going to be bright and bold and bitchy, or even anything close. She was who she was. She got mad and she got over it. But she was going to learn how to speak up for herself. To demand what she needed.

In a kind way, of course, because it wasn't fair to those who cared about her if she didn't. Kacey's pain, her sister's guilt, had been a real eye-opener to her. She'd set Kacey up for failure by not expressing her feelings until the one night they'd spilled over and ruined her sister's world.

They were past that now. Had been over and over and over it all over and over and over again during their week together.

Avoiding the unfinished dream room, she passed through the kitchen and grabbed the key off the kitchen table, shoving it in the first drawer she came to, blinking back tears.

She'd made her ultimatum. He'd made his choice.

Neither one of them could take either back.

She'd been unfair to him. He'd been unfair to her, too. Neither of them could help who they were.

And if they couldn't stand up for each other, they weren't good for each other, either.

Promising herself that if she got through the night, the morning would be easier, she rolled her suitcase down the hall. She and Kacey had already talked everything through. She was going to unpack. Take a hot bath. Go to bed. Get up in the morning and go to work.

If she couldn't get to sleep, she was going to call Kacey.

And on Friday, Kacey would be there, filling her home. Just as she'd filled Kacey's the past week.

She flipped on the bedroom light.

Something wasn't right.

Heart pounding, she froze, looking around. The room had been disturbed.

She didn't have a gun. Her cell phone was still in her purse on the kitchen counter.

Had her bed been slept in?

Nothing else was out of place. Just the stripes on the comforter weren't lined up along the edge of the mattress. And the pillows were wrong. Cases went on the bottom, shams on the top.

There were wrinkles, too. As though someone had climbed around after the bed was made.

She stepped farther into the room and peeked into the adjoining bathroom. A cartoon caricature bandage wrapper was in the trash.

A washcloth had been used, and there was a glob of toothpaste in the sink. She definitely did not leave globs behind.

But Levi did.

Curious now, shaking, she moved through the house.

The bed in Kacey's room was made. But equally disturbed. The spare bathroom didn't look as though it had been touched. Except for the raised toilet seat.

The pillows on the living room couch were there, but not how she arranged them. The remote was on the left side of the table, not the right.

There were used glasses in the dishwasher that she hadn't used. And paper plates in the trash.

Had Jem and Levi stayed at her house while she'd been gone? She supposed she should be mad about the intrusion. She wasn't.

But she wanted to know why.

Attempting not to glance around the corner and down the hall from the kitchen toward the wall that was going to have an archway into her dream room, Lacey failed. She did a double take. There was an archway where an outside wall had been when she'd left.

It was rounded, drywalled, textured and painted. Feeling like a zombie, she walked down the hall to the archway. Stood and stared.

The room was finished. The porcelain tile she'd picked out for the floor was laid and grouted exactly as she'd pictured it, only better. Her furniture had been delivered. It wasn't arranged exactly as she'd planned, but it looked good. Inviting.

For what she noticed. Because she couldn't really focus on flooring or furniture. She couldn't take her eyes off the far wall. It was supposed to have been painted a sand color. It was windows instead, looking out over a newly planted garden with a rock waterfall. She could see it all, in spite of the darkness outside, because of the landscape lighting that had been installed.

But even that didn't hold her attention. She

couldn't stop staring at the portion of the wall above the windows.

It was a mural of an exquisite sunset. And in the rays of the setting sun there were three cloud-like forms—a tall, broad one, another that was a little shorter and more slender and then a tiny one. The tiny one seemed to be reaching toward the slender one. She knew she was just imagining the figures in the clouds. But every time she looked back, there they were.

She'd been standing there five minutes or more before she saw the envelope on the table. She recognized Jem's business logo where the return address should be.

A final bill?

It was so like him to finish the job he'd agreed to do. To finish his business, leave the key and go silently on his way. He also wasn't one to make waves. Unless you counted the ones painted beneath her sunset...

She wasn't going to open the envelope. Didn't want to spoil the moment with an accounting of cost owed. But she'd also never been one to avoid hard tasks. She was who she was. So she picked up the envelope and pulled out the pages inside.

And fell down to the couch.

The stop sheet was official all the way. A restraining order. Against Tressa Bridges. Protected persons were Jeremiah and Levi Bridges.

The second sheet was official, too. A police

report delineating all threats against Lacey. As well as a timeline of how she'd come to be in the lives of Jem and Levi Bridges.

The third sheet… She could barely make it out through the tears blurring her vision.

It was a single piece of plain white paper, with childish scrawl in awkward, uneven letters. She made out the word *Levi*.

The fourth page was easier to read…if she could just quit crying long enough.

I am a victim of domestic violence. I have spent the past ten years being manipulated, attacked and humiliated by my ex-wife. I am not proud of that fact. I am told I will have residual effects of this circumstance. I am also told that recognition and acknowledgment is the biggest part of my battle. Apparently I managed to be a survivor before I knew I was a victim.

I credit my parents and my son, Levi, for that.

Recently I found the love of my life. I couldn't believe in my luck at first. I was truly happy for the first time in my adult life. I felt complete. Hopeful for the future. And weighted down by the albatross I carried around my neck.

The albatross has been captured. Restrained. And my love…it's overflowing, like the water over the rocks outside your window. I am the water. You are my rock.

If you have an interest in feeling my touch flowing across you for the rest of your life, please call. If not, know that I love you first. Last. Always.

Jem.

She was crying so hard she could hardly find her purse in the kitchen. Or find her phone in her purse. Stumbling back to her dream room, she tried to see enough to touch Jem's picture in her speed dial widget.

Blinking away tears, she sniffled, looked outside at the fountain…and blinked some more. She couldn't see his picture on her phone, but she could see him outside. Him and Levi, too, pressing against the window.

"Jem?" she yelled loudly and dropped her phone.

"Lacey's home!" Levi's voice was strong and sure. "She's back, Dad. Look!"

She was probably dreaming, but she ran for the new sliding glass door she'd never seen before that night and pulled on the handle.

It didn't budge.

"Flip the latch." Jem's muffled voice came through the door.

She couldn't find the latch, so she pushed

against the black metal frame, then pulled the door. She even pounded on it for a second.

Then her gaze met Jem's. She calmed. He stared at her, and a smile broke out all over his face. And hers, too. He pointed down, where she saw the thin piece of metal sticking out from the handle, and she pushed it down with one finger.

The door slid open and she fell forward. Jem's body broke her fall, his arms closing around her.

"We've been doing drive-bys all afternoon" were the first words he said. Followed immediately by "I love you and want to marry you." There might have been more. She wasn't sure about anything but the feel of her man's body against hers. Her man's arms around her.

And then a smaller, but equally dear, version of her man was wrapping his arms around her knees. They had her in their grasp. Making her their world. As they were hers.

First, last and always.

In the room that they'd built for her.

The room where all of her dreams had just come true.

* * * * *

LARGER-PRINT BOOKS!

GET 2 FREE
LARGER-PRINT NOVELS
PLUS 2 FREE
MYSTERY GIFTS

Love Inspired®

Larger-print novels are now available...

LARGER-PRINT BOOKS!

GET 2 FREE
LARGER-PRINT NOVELS
PLUS 2 FREE
MYSTERY GIFTS

Love Inspired.

SUSPENSE
RIVETING INSPIRATIONAL ROMANCE

Larger-print novels are now available...

LISLP15

READERSERVICE.COM

Manage your account online!

- Review your order history
- Manage your payments
- Update your address

> **We've designed the**
> **Reader Service website**
> **just for you.**

Enjoy all the features!

- Discover new series available to you, and read excerpts from any series.
- Respond to mailings and special monthly offers.
- Connect with favorite authors at the blog.
- Browse the Bonus Bucks catalog and online-only exculsives.
- Share your feedback.

Visit us at:
ReaderService.com

RS15